MORRIGAN'S BIDDING

BINDING WORDS BOOK 1

DANIEL SCHINHOFEN

Copyright © 2018 Daniel J. Schinhofen
No parts of this book may be reproduced in any form by an electronic or mechanical means – except in the case of brief quotations embodied in articles or reviews – without the written permission from the publisher.
The characters and events portrayed in this book are fictitious. Any similarities to real persons, living or dead, are purely coincidental and not intended by the author.
Copyright © 2018 Daniel J. Schinhofen
All rights reserved.

CHAPTER ONE

Rubbing at his face, Sean wondered what he was even doing in this bar. He wasn't a drinker, and when James had contacted him and suggested meeting up for some 9-ball, Sean had wavered on accepting. Eventually he'd caved to James' prodding, having no real reason to refuse his best friend.

My only friend, for that matter, Sean complained internally. *Not that James is any better. He hasn't hung out with anyone else, not since her death.* Looking around the dingy bar, Sean wondered why James had picked this place. It was one they'd been to before, but only once, because the clientele that hung out here was less than savory.

"You are at my table. Vacate it," a deep bass voice that rumbled like thunder announced from behind Sean.

Rolling his eyes, Sean turned his head to find the guy that was starting shit with him. His eyes came even with a massive belt buckle in the shape of a thundercloud. Looking up, he saw a bodybuilder with long blonde hair and full beard behind him. "Your name isn't on it, use one of the others," Sean snorted and turned back around.

"No one dares to ignore me," the man rumbled as his hand slammed down on Sean's shoulder.

Sean stood up, shrugging off the man's hand. Turning around, he found himself staring at the guy's pectorals. He looked up to meet the man's eyes. "Look, asshole, I'm waiting for my friend, and this is currently my table, so fuck off."

"You would challenge me?" A deep, chest rattling laugh came from the blonde giant. "Draw your blade, if you dare."

"Blade? What are you, an idiot?" Sean snapped as he took a step back, his hand resting on his Colt 1911. "Just fuck off, dude. I'm not going to fight you, but I'm sure as fuck not going to cave to a bullying asshole."

Lips twisting into a prodigious frown, the bodybuilder leaned forward so his eyes were level with Sean. "You call *me*, asshole? You dare to lump me with my brother? Take back your words, or a fight you shall have whether you will it or no."

"Your brother? Oh yeah, that guy. He was way nicer than you," Sean smirked at the guy.

The bodybuilder's eyes seemed to darken, the color deepening to that of thunderclouds, "You would dare?" With a snarl, the man's fists clenched. "I will take some of his debt out of you, then, since you claim his friendship."

Before Sean could react, a fist the size of a ham slammed into his chest and threw him backwards into the wall. Clutching his chest in pain, he blinked, as his attacker was now standing twenty feet away. *I was thrown twenty feet by that punch, what the fuck?*

The giant closed the distance like an avalanche intent on burying him. Not bothering to get to his feet, Sean drew his sidearm. "Stop! Don't come any closer, or I will defend myself!"

"Hey! No killing! Take the fight outside," the bartender yelled.

"Stop!" Sean yelled at the blonde man, who was still advancing and now only ten feet away.

"I will send you to meet my brother's daughter. Give her my regards," the giant blonde snarled as he stepped closer.

"Self-defense!" Sean shouted as he flicked the safety off and fired twice into the man's chest.

The bodybuilder stepped back two paces, looking down where the bullets had impacted and back up, his face splitting into a visage of death incarnate. "Now you die!"

Shocked that the bullets hadn't killed the man- or even wounded him- Sean emptied the other six rounds in his gun into the man as quickly as he could pull the trigger. Again, the bullets didn't seem to have any effect. As the slide locked back, Sean looked up at his attacker as a foot came down on his chest.

The pain of his breastbone shattering and the splinters cutting into his lungs and heart was mind numbing. Coughing once, his blood spattered across the boot and leg of the bodybuilder. "What... are... you?" Sean gasped out as he felt his consciousness start to fade.

"What the hell?! I said no fighting!" The bartender's voice echoed in Sean's ears as darkness began to claim him.

I shouldn't have agreed to come, was Sean's last thought as consciousness fled his body.

Opening his eyes, Sean blinked in surprise. He brought his hand to his chest, but there wasn't any pain. "A dream?" Sean mumbled as he sat up. He froze as he realized that he wasn't in his room or still at the bar. He looked around at a place he didn't recall ever seeing before.

"You have awoken. Good, we can discuss your death and what we may do to remedy that unfortunate incident," a powerful baritone voice resonated throughout the room.

Jerking to his feet, Sean looked around the room. An older man was sitting at a table, sipping from a drinking horn. Two ravens perched behind him. Mouth opening in shock, Sean shook his head, stunned to see the one-eyed man gesturing at the chair across from him.

"Odin?" Sean said, his shock obvious.

"Ah, good. You have heard of me, that will make this easier. Come, sit. We have things to discuss," Odin beckoned him to the table.

"Wait a minute... The blonde guy who attacked me..." Sean's voice trailed off as he made the connection.

"My son, Thor. He has been told not to visit your world, but recently a way has opened again for him, since so many of you know of him." Odin sighed, just like any father would when his child had gone against his wishes.

"Wait— You're saying Thor came to Earth and killed me in a bar fight?" Sean shook his head, wondering when this dream would fade.

"Unfortunate, but true. Due to his involvement, I was able to intercede and bring you here. I have an offer for you, but please, come and sit so we can talk as friends."

Slapping himself hard across the face, Sean winced, "Ow. Well, that didn't work." He ignored Odin's raised brow as he crossed the room and took the proffered seat. "Okay, let's talk."

"I am glad you have joined me. I am going to offer you a place in Valhalla. Does this interest you?" Odin asked as he sipped at his drink.

"Wait, what? I don't even believe in you or your son. Shouldn't I be headed off to some pearly gates for judgement, or something?"

"You may have that, if you wish. You would have gone straight there, but as my son was involved, I was able to exert a little influence and bring you here first. You showed no cowardice and fought to the best of your abilities. You died as a warrior, and have earned a place in Valhalla. It seemed only fitting that I offer you the chance to enjoy eternity drinking, fighting, and wenching."

Sean couldn't deny that sounded at least a bit better than lounging around on clouds in the sky or suffering in pits of eternal fire. Lips pursed, he studied the God seated across from him. Something felt off about the situation, and he wanted to buy some time to see if he could figure it out.

"It is an offer far beyond anything I ever expected to get," Sean replied. "You wished to speak as friends, though, Odin. Don't friends share drinks?"

Odin's lips thinned, but he nodded. "Indeed, that is true on many worlds. I should not have forgotten such hospitality." Snapping his fingers, Odin sat back with an air of waiting. A minute later, a tall goddess of a woman wearing chain and plate mail came through the door from Sean's left. Blonde hair flowed down her back in a wave of gold, and atop her head sat a silver cap embossed with wings. "Thank you, Valkyrie. Present the horn to our guest."

Sean blinked at the heavenly vision that held a drinking horn out to him. "Err... thanks," he finally stammered.

"It is my *pleasure* to serve a guest of the Allfather. Is it true that you have done battle with the Thunder God?" The Valkyrie's voice was honeyed silk, caressing Sean's spine.

"That is enough, Valkyrie, you may leave," Odin said sternly.

"As you order, Allfather," she bowed her head before turning to leave. Just before she walked away, she met Sean's gaze with piercing blue eyes. "I hope to see you again," the soft words breezed past him, before she seemed to straighten further, her voice picking up to normal. "May you enjoy the Allfather's hall." Not waiting for anything else, she strode from the room like a battle maiden should.

"Good gods," Sean murmured without realizing it.

"She is but one of many Valkyries in my hall. Does that help you come to a decision regarding my offer?" Odin asked, his single eye twinkling with humor.

Sean coughed, tearing his eyes from the retreating form of the Valkyrie, absently taking a drink from the horn she'd given him. The honeyed taste of the best crafted mead hit his tongue, sweet but not cloying, and gentle warmth spread through his chest. "That is smooth," Sean said, impressed with the drink.

"Only the best mead is served in my hall," Odin beamed. "Now, about my offer. Have you decided?"

Sean took a slow sip, buying a bit more time. "I admit, Allfather, your offer is more than any man of my world could hope for."

Sitting up straighter, Odin grinned. "That is very true, Sean Aragorn MacDougal. So, do you accept my offer?"

"I wonder why you're in a rush, Odin. Shouldn't friends converse with each other at leisure? Yet, since my eyes have opened you've tried to get me to accept this deal you offer. Are there other options I need to inquire about? Maybe I should ask someone to counsel me so I make the best choice," Sean asked, taking another drink. He wasn't normally a drinker, but this was exactly what he would have expected Ambrosia to taste like.

"You should indeed," a resonant voice, similar to a clear trumpet, came from the doorway.

Craning his head to see who was speaking, Sean blinked to behold an Angel striding towards the table. White robes only partially covered the armor the being wore, and the sword on its hip, even sheathed, radiated a bright light.

"Michael. I thought we agreed that I would be able to speak with my guest alone first," Odin said, his face set in a false mask of welcome.

"And you had that chance, Odin Falsefather. This one belongs to my Lord, and he deserves to know that he does indeed have the right to enter the Heavenly Gates if he wishes. He should know his options, beyond what your lying tongue tells him." Michael's self-righteousness was as blinding as the radiance from his sword.

"Wait, I have more options?" Sean asked, his mind reeling from the shock of the day's events.

"Indeed," another voice added, this one full of dry, dark humor backed by the rustling of scales sliding across flesh. The door was pushed fully open as a well-groomed gentleman with dark hair and a three-piece suit came sauntering into the room. "Your soul doesn't necessarily belong to either of them. I, too, have some small claim on your immortal being."

Eyes widening, Sean leaned away from the approaching newcomer as wisps of black smoke rose from the gentleman. The wisps drifted up, shaping themselves into scenes of past sins Sean had committed before dissipating. "Lucifer, huh?"

"Glad to see you know my name." Lucifer pulled a chair over and sat at the table, where Michael snarled openly at him. "Back down like a good little puppy, Michael. You know we have an Agreement of neutrality while we deal with this aberration."

"You are not the only ones with an offer for him," another being said from the door. "In his youth, he worshipped me for a time, which gives me a claim to his immortal being as well."

Sean's head whipped back to the door to find the newcomer entering the room. Striding across the room was a tall, striking woman, with bright red hair that seemed to glisten in the light. Her figure could only be described as modest, but she walked with a certain sway that caught the eye and held it. "Can you name me, Sean Aragorn MacDougal?"

"Morrigan, Goddess of Battle, Death, and Fate," Sean said, his eyes locking with the dark orbs where her eyes should have been. He swallowed hard, feeling the strings of fate binding him under her gaze. "I never thought—"

"I did, and long have I waited for this day, Sean Aragorn MacDougal," Morrigan said in a warm voice before turning her gaze to the others. "Now that we are *all* assembled, shall we present the full range of choices available to this mortal?"

"You believe a single month of worship gives you the right to sit with us?" Lucifer asked with disdain. "My claim extends back years, to all of his unrepentant sins, some of which are quite damning. Ah, but let's do as you suggest. After all, Hell isn't like this lot," he hooked a thumb at Michael, "wants everyone to believe."

"Scum," Michael snarled, his eyes not wavering from Lucifer, hand twitching toward the hilt of his blade. "The Host shall grind you under heel when the Lord commands."

Odin snapped, "You are all in my hall. If you cannot conduct yourselves civilly, I will banish you, as is my right."

Morrigan pulled up a chair to Sean's right, across from Lucifer. "I am perfectly willing to let my offer be heard."

Odin's gaze sharpened as he looked to Morrigan, "Have not your followers been trod under my warrior's boots for years? Are you sure that you wish to open a new reason for enmity to exist between us again?"

"This is neutral ground for the moment, Odin Allfather,"

Morrigan smiled darkly. "I could choose to take those words as a threat, and as such, you yourself would be ejected from these talks."

Odin snapped his mouth shut and snorted, turning his unhappy gaze back to Sean, "Well mortal, who do you choose?"

"Umm... you offer Valhalla, which is a mighty tempting choice, Allfather," Sean stammered, before firming up his voice. "God's Fist has offered me guaranteed entry into Heaven, something that I've been told all my life was one of the only two options." He bowed his head to Michael, then turned his gaze to Lucifer. "Lucifer has only said that Hell is not as it is portrayed by the clergy, but I have not yet heard his offer. Would you care to explain, Dawn Lord?"

Lucifer's smile sharpened, looking like a shark closing on an unsuspecting fish, "Gladly. Hell has many different sections, and I would let you pick your place in any of the levels of Hell. I know you abhor drug use, so the third level would not be to your liking. Nor are you so enamored of food that the fifth level would suit you for eternity. Perhaps the ninth level would be a choice? I can offer a few that look like her, if that would add extra enticement," he nodded toward Morrigan with his last statement.

Sean shifted uncomfortably in his seat, Lucifer's words conjuring images he'd never considered regarding the Goddess of Fate. Morrigan just smiled faintly, a dimple showing on her cheek.

"False copies, with no skills of their own, only what they've learned to parrot under torture is what you truly mean, Fallen. Maybe you should let him see the small print in your contracts," Morrigan's smile was sharp, like a spear about to pierce a heart.

Shaking his head, Sean coughed to clear his mind of the images Lucifer had conjured. "What's this about a contract?"

Lucifer frowned, but produced from the air a stack of papers that climbed to the limit of the vaulted fifty-foot ceiling. "This is the contract you would need to sign."

Looking at the pile, Sean shook his head, "That seems like the worst idea I've ever heard."

Smile flattening, Lucifer leaned forward, his voice pitched as if offering a deal that he normally wouldn't. "Sean— May I call you

Sean? Look— you're in a bad spot here. Odin will let you into the halls of Valhalla, but you'll only be shunned and ridiculed. You never landed a hit on Thor, because guns don't count to the Norse. Michael wants to glue a lamp on your head, staple wings to your back and chain you to a cloud where you'll sing the praises of *his Lord* for all time. Morrigan shouldn't even be here, and has almost no power to really offer you anything of note. I'll waive the paperwork and let you have free run of any level of Hell. I'll even elevate you to Prince status, giving you the right to command the beings on the level you choose however you see fit. All you would need to do is sign your name to a blank piece of paper. What do you say?"

Shuddering at the sleazy lawyer vibe Lucifer gave off, Sean sat as far back from the Fallen Angel as he could get. "I'll take it under consideration," Sean managed, mentally vowing to do no such thing.

"You must choose," Michael said from behind Sean, the Angel's hand landing on his shoulder.

Shrugging off the Archangel's hand, Sean got to his feet and spun on the Angel. "Don't fucking do that. Good gods, you're all like sharks circling in the water as the boat goes down."

"All?" Morrigan asked, her hand going to her chest as if hurt. "I have not pushed, nor have I made grandiose promises, and you would lump me with them?"

Sean paused, then shrugged, "Okay, maybe not all. But even you're trying to claim my soul, aren't you?"

"Yes and no," Morrigan smiled. "If you wish to hear my modest proposal, I will tell you, but that is your choice."

"Why the fuck not? I've listened to all of them. What do you offer, Morrigan?" Sean said, waiting for the next grandiose promise.

"The continuation of life, but on a different world," Morrigan said simply, lapsing back into silence.

"You cannot do that," Odin roared. "His soul is up for grabs, but his body was splintered by my son."

"I concur with the Falsefather. His body is gone, you can't give him his life back," Michael stated.

Lucifer stood up, bowing to Morrigan. "I see that I've been

outplayed. As he's obviously not going to take my offer, I'll be withdrawing and taking my leave. It looks as if God's right hand might be occupied for some time..." Lucifer let the sentence trail off and vanished in a puff of smoke.

Coughing at the sulphurous stench of brimstone, Sean waved the air clear. "Why do you offer what they say can't be done, Morrigan?"

"They don't understand everything. You see, we each have many worlds that we can act in. Odin's pantheon and my own were driven from Earth by Michael's Lord. Yet, there are many worlds in the multiverse, and there is a world that I think would suit you. I can place you there, in a body created by the Tri Dee Dana themselves."

Sean frowned, trying to recall who the Tri Dee Dana were. "Wait, the three gods of crafting?" His brows shot up, "You're saying I'd have a body made by the gods of craft?"

Bowing her head a fraction, Morrigan nodded. "Indeed. Your essence would be placed into a body crafted by them. Several of our number would gift you small blessings, then leave you to your own devices on a world to explore at your leisure."

"This goes against some of the Agreements," Odin growled.

"Indeed. The Lord will be most displeased if you do this, Morrigan," Michael warned.

Morrigan ignored them, her jet orbs locking onto Sean's hazel eyes. "We have spoken at length and are all willing to break those Agreements, if you will agree to my proposal, Sean Aragorn MacDougal."

"Why?" Sean asked, perplexed. "Why would your pantheon anger other deities to offer me this?"

Morrigan looked down, then met his gaze again. "For, long ago, we failed greatly. We seek to right a wrong, and we can, if you will let us. I cannot speak of it, but I promise you can find the answers you seek on that other world."

"This farce has gone on long enough," Michael finally snapped, his heavenly demeanor giving way to righteous anger. "Choose, Sean Aragorn MacDougal."

"Valhalla awaits," Odin added, his voice a deep growl underscored by thunder booming outside the chamber.

"It is your life, or afterlife, Sean," Morrigan said, her midnight gaze still locked with his. "Know that, unlike them, we will not hold your choice against you."

As Sean continued to stare into her eyes, he could see three futures before him. In one, he sat on a cloud with a blissful smile, gently strumming a harp and singing the Lord's praises. The next showed him in Valhalla, drinking, fighting, and wenching along with the other warriors, his face twisting into that of a brute, very much like Thor. The last was different; it showed him a vision of himself, standing on a bluff overlooking a green valley as a dragon flew overhead. Glancing back, he saw dozens of people smiling and cheering, waving weapons in the air as they proclaimed their support of him.

Sitting back as the visions fled, his heart was racing and cold sweat beaded on his forehead. "The fuck?"

"Vile bitch, you seek to cloud his mind with false visions," Odin roared.

"The vision of Heaven was not false. Does it not appeal to you, Sean Aragorn MacDougal?" Michael interjected, trying to impart how wonderful that vision was in truth.

"Call the Norns to show him then, Odin. They will only concur with me," Morrigan said simply. "He has the right to know what fate lies before him, depending on his choices," Morrigan shuddered, her body wavering and going smoky for a moment.

"What's happening to you?" Sean asked, his mind still reeling from the visions.

"I used more of my power than I should have," Morrigan gasped as she wavered in and out of focus. "The choice is yours, Sean. We will wait for you, if you choose us."

Odin shot to his feet, his single eye boring into Sean, "CHOOSE!" The word boomed with the power of thunder and shook the room.

"Choose!" Michael added in clarion tones, his hand landing on Sean's shoulder again.

"At least *she* has been direct and honest with me," Sean snapped.

"I accept your offer, Morrigan, and you two can go fuck yourselves or each other for all I care."

With those words, the room vanished and he found himself floating in darkness. As he tried to figure out what happened, Morrigan's voice wrapped around him. "You will not regret this, Sean Aragorn MacDougal, on my power. Now rest, while the Tri Dee Dana craft a new body for you."

CHAPTER TWO

Floating in darkness, Sean wondered what was going to happen next. "Sean Aragorn MacDougal, we need input from you on your new body," a voice washed around him.

"Who?" Sean asked.

"You may call me Goibniu," the voice replied.

"I am called Credne," another voice added.

"And I am Luchta," a third voice said.

"The Tri Dee Dana," Sean murmured. "What is it that the three gods of craft wish from me?"

"We are about to craft your body, but we wish to ken what you would prefer your body to look like. We can craft anything you imagine, so show us what it is you would wish for this body to be," Luchta said.

Frowning, a dozen different images of himself flashed through Sean's mind. "Can I be other than I was?"

"Of course," Credne replied, "you can be as tall or broad as you wish, and as wide or long as you wish." The last few words were pitched low, making Sean think less than innocent thoughts. "Exactly, we can do that."

A frown appeared on his face as Sean considered what they meant. "I can be totally different than I was, or exactly the same?"

"Aye," Goibniu said. "Just form the image in your mind and hold it for three beats of your heart."

Sean let the possibilities parade through his mind for a moment. He dismissed the idea of being built like Thor, thinking that too much muscle meant you lost too much agility. He didn't want to be a stick, either, so he compromised on something between the two extremes.

He held the image of a well-muscled gymnast in his mind. Good, solid muscles without being beefy, average of height, narrow of waist, and a decent set of shoulders. He left his hair the same brown it had always been, and kept the same hazel eyes. He firmed up his jawline just a touch, and narrowed his nose a shade. He adjusted the bits Credne had pointed out as well, but nothing too drastic.

Holding that image in his mind, he waited for his heart to beat, which it seemed to do, but slowly. Eventually, Luchta spoke again, "We will do this. Know that we are honored that you have agreed to undertake this task, MacDougal. It shames us to know that you will aid us in correcting a grievous error, deepening our debt to you."

"Wait, what are you talking about?" Sean asked.

"Go to work," Morrigan's voice, weaker than it had been, echoed in the darkness. "You have already said too much, Luchta."

"Morrigan, explain, please," Sean said.

"Not everything is as simple as I originally made it out to be," Morrigan said.

"Of *fucking* course. Never trust a God to be honest," Sean snapped.

"I was, and am honest, Sean," Morrigan's whisper dimmed even more. "I just left off our great shame. We will make no demands of you, but hope that you will do us a favor when you are on the world we are sending you to. Our people are beyond our help there. We are barred from the world, until the Queens have been dethroned. If you can accomplish that, we would be able to help our people and make things right for them once again. The full story can be found there, if you wish to find it, along with our shame. Possibly our redemption, as well."

Sean would have bit his lip if he had one, "What does this all mean? Tell me plainly, please."

"We cannot. That Agreement holds us silent regarding what awaits you. We've waited a long time to see this day come, and have been forced to wait for someone who would agree to help. Still, we will not threaten, cajole, or try to trick you into choosing any path," Morrigan's voice was nearly gone. "Follow your heart, Sean Aragorn MacDougal, for surely your line knew the truth when we were blind."

Before Sean could speak, the darkness around him shimmered, and he felt a sensation of falling. That's also exactly what it looked like, as small pinpoints of light flashed by him faster and faster. He approached a world, green and vibrant, with small bodies of water dotting the giant land mass. Two moons flew past him, one white and the other blue, as the world rushed up to meet him.

I wonder if it will be friends with me, Sean thought as he shot towards the ground. Just as he was about to become one with the planet, as a crater, his motion stopped and he dropped the last three feet as if he'd stepped off a small ledge. "Thanks for not making me a pancake," Sean muttered as he took in his surroundings.

He stood on a ledge overlooking a forest. A small village was visible a handful of miles distant. The wooden roofs spoke of simple folk, living in past centuries. That image made Sean take stock of his own clothing. Trousers and tunic made of a rough material, but the inside of the clothing was soft and slick to the touch. Pulling the tunic away from his neck, a look inside confirmed that it was silk-lined. His feet were clad in silk-lined, short leather boots. A plain leather belt encircled his waist, upon which a small pouch and blade were tied.

Drawing the large dagger, he frowned as he examined the forearm length, double-edged bronze blade. The craftsmanship was undeniable, but Sean couldn't figure out why the Tri Dee Dana would use such an easily dulled metal instead of something that could hold an edge like iron or steel. He realized the two buttons on his boots and the simple ring on his belt were also bronze. Taking a stance, Sean tried to recall his time in the fencing club in college and his year with the live steel group in the SCA.

After a few attacks and retreats, Sean let out a soft whistle. His reaction time was faster than it had ever been before. His strikes were faster and had more strength behind them than he was used to.

"So an improved body all around," Sean muttered as he looked at the coloration of his skin. Same Irish coloration he was used to from his old life, "Guess that isn't a surprise, considering who made this body."

"Better than I was before. Better... stronger... faster," Sean chuckled as he started down the path towards the village. "Guess I'll see what the people here are like."

As he walked, Sean wondered about the gifts that Morrigan had mentioned. As soon as the idea occurred, ethereal lettering appeared before him.

> **Metal Bones-** Your bones are not ordinary calcium, but Adamant and Iron. (Crafted by Goibniu.)
> **Viney Muscles-** Your musculature is built of Iron Vine, reinforced with traces of Adamant. (Crafted by Luchta.)
> **Mithril Blood-** Your blood is not the red watery stuff of normal people, but Mithril blended with Iron. (Crafted by Credne.)
> **Magic Bond-** Able to learn and wield the magic of the world. (Gift of Beag.)
> **Mending Body-** Your body will repair any damage with time and energy. (Gift of Dian Cecht.)
> **Death Ward-** Force death away if enough energy is present. (Gift of Aed.)
> **Linguist-** Know and speak every language. (Gift of Oghma.)
> **Hunter's Blood-** Master of woodcraft. (Gift of Cernunnos.)
> **Infinite Possibilities-** Blessed to be able to learn all Talents. (Gift of Dagda.)

A soft whistle escaped Sean, "Talk about blessed by the gods."

All I'm missing for this to be a proper game, he thought, *is a character screen.* As his thoughts touched upon the idea, the ethereal words morphed into a status screen. Blinking, with both brows shooting up, Sean shook his head as he looked over the new information.

Sean Aragorn MacDougal
Human
Age: 33

Gifts:
Metal Bones, Viney Muscles, Mithril Blood, Magic Bond, Mending Body, Death Ward, Linguist, Hunter's Blood, Infinite Possibilities

Spells:

Talents:

Bonded:

The soft breeze ruffled his short-cropped hair as he walked down the path. The weather was just touching on autumn, but Sean found himself warm despite the chill breeze. *Maybe because of the crafted body I have,* Sean mused internally as he strolled along, letting the late morning sun warm his skin.

A little under an hour later, Sean approached the outskirts of the village, his steps slowing. He was sure the village had been at least five miles, but he had just walked that in about an hour, while taking his time.

Shaking his head, Sean looked at the dozen homes that dotted either side of the dirt road. The houses were made of the same wood as the forest around them. Four women were chatting outside the largest house in the village. One of them went wide-eyed as she spotted a stranger walking through the village, pointing him out to the others. Four sets of wary eyes watched him as he approached.

"Excuse me, ladies. I happen to be a bit lost and am looking for some directions," Sean said.

"If you're here in our village, of course you're lost. This be the arse end of nowhere," the woman who had spotted him first said.

"Can one of you tell me the name of this place? Maybe that'll help me figure out where I am," Sean said, knowing it wouldn't help at all.

"This is Oakwood," one of the other women said, brushing auburn hair from her forehead.

Sean took in the sun roughened skin and the large number of freckles the quartet had, knowing them to be of the same descent as himself. "Sadly, that doesn't help much," Sean sighed. "Does the village elder have a map that might help me find my path?"

One of the women who hadn't spoken yet chimed in, "He's meditating at the moment. I can see if he would be willing to speak with an unnamed traveler."

"I apologize. I'm Sean MacDougal," his smile was polite as he introduced himself, hoping that would help ease the wariness they all exuded.

"You can stay right there, and I'll go tell him about you," the woman replied as she darted into the large house.

"Where did you come from to end up all the way out here?" the first woman asked him with narrowing eyes.

"I doubt you've heard of the small town I'm from. It's called Waterrock," Sean answered, keeping the same smile on his lips, though the name sounded odd as he said it. Waterrock was the literal meaning of the small desert town he had lived in, but not its name.

"Never heard of it," the last woman finally entered the conversation. "Which direction is it in?" The last question provoked intense stares from the trio of women.

"I'm not currently sure," Sean shrugged, "but I'm sure I'll have that figured out if I see a map."

The fourth woman exited the house, leaving the door open behind her, "He says he'll see you."

Sean didn't move. "Thank you, miss. If you will all excuse me."

Motioning to the side of the door, he tried to make it clear they were in the way.

Stepping aside, the quartet of women watched him as he entered the home, mutters starting up behind him as he shut the door. *Well I'm no fantasy story protagonist, obviously, or they would've all been throwing themselves at me*, Sean chuckled to himself.

CHAPTER THREE

The interior of the home was as plain as the exterior. The wooden floors and walls were barren of everything except for one small rug in the middle of the room, upon which sat the sole occupant.

The room he'd entered had two doorways leading off. Both doorways were open; in one room, Sean could make out a bed and in the other a fireplace, which hinted at a kitchen.

Sean examined the older man for a moment. His grey hair still had bits of red visible in it here and there, and his thick beard was bushy, but obviously kept from going completely wild. Wide shoulders that were just starting to hunch told of a powerful man who was reaching the end of a long life. Various scars marred the bare torso of the man, who sat with his eyes closed. Tattoos of intricate scrollwork in blue adorned his arms, still heavy with muscle, from shoulder to wrist.

"Excuse me, sir, I was hoping you might help me find my way," Sean said.

"Traveler, welcome to my home. Please take a seat," the older man said as his eyes opened to reveal white, sightless orbs.

Sean's steps faltered when he realized the man was blind, but he took the spot a few feet in front of the man, sitting down. "My name is Sean MacDougal, sir."

"My granddaughter told me. You may call me Darragh. What brings a wanderer to our humble village?"

"I'm lost," Sean stated simply.

"That is a given, we are the farthest village to the south of the Quadital," Darragh gave a tight smile. "Would you like some tea while we help you find your way?"

"Sure," Sean replied.

"Misa, tea for two," Darragh said.

At Darragh's words, the sound of rasping scales came from behind Sean, causing him to look around. In the doorway of the kitchen, a strange being stood balanced upon its tail. It had the body of a large serpent, a pair of arms sprouted at what would be its torso. The three-fingered hands were laced together at its front. The face was definitely that of a serpent, but the eyes glowed with intelligence. "Orange, massster?" The 's' was elongated nearly into a hiss.

"Will orange suffice, MacDougal?" Darragh asked Sean.

"Err... yeah, orange tea is fine," Sean stammered.

"I will make," Misa said, the words formal. Turning, the serpent slithered out of the doorway while maintaining its upright position.

"That was your first time seeing one of the Lesser Naga?"

"Uh, yeah," Sean said as he pulled his eyes back to the man across from him.

"They are rare as Bonded," a ghost of a smile flitted across Darragh's face. "She has made me very grateful to have agreed to our Bond. She makes my last few years easier."

"Bonded?" Sean asked without thinking.

A thoughtful look crossed Darragh's features. "Hmm, yes. Bonded. Could it be that..." Darragh trailed off, lost in thought.

Sean didn't want to press him for an explanation, realizing that he might be giving away his outsider status by his ignorance. The silence stretched for a couple minutes before Darragh shook his head.

Coming out of his reverie, Darragh smiled again, "I apologize for the silence, MacDougal. I do believe you are lost in ways I hadn't considered before. Tell me, who currently rules the Quadital?"

Licking his lips, Sean knew he'd outed himself as not being a native. "I don't know," he said after a pause.

"As I had thought," Darragh looked at the ceiling with his blind eyes. "Is it time after all? No, surely I'm mistaken," the words were muttered softly, with a clearly worried tone.

A piercing whistle sounded from the kitchen, and Sean barely refrained from jumping to his feet. A moment later, Misa came slowly slithering into the room as she balanced a tray in her hands. A copper kettle and two cups sat on the simple wooden tray. "The tea, massster," Misa said as she placed it before Darragh.

"Serve for me please, Misa," Darragh said as he brushed at his beard for a moment. "Misa, what would you tell a stranger of your race?"

Misa paused briefly in her task, before going back to pouring tea. "We are not to be trusssted. Naga, even lesssser sssuch asss me, are not to be trusssted at all, unlesss Bonded."

Sean took the cup Misa held out to him, "Thank you, Misa."

Misa's stared at him, pupils widening, before she bowed her head once. She placed the second cup into Darragh's hands and retreated back into the kitchen. Before she vanished into the other room, she cast a long look back at Sean, her tongue flickering in his direction.

"That was a very unusual thing to do," Darragh stated as he sipped his steaming cup. "Life Bonded are treated as things, normally. Favored pets at the best of times, and almost never acknowledged by guests."

Brows constricting as he considered the words, Sean's lips twisted. "How quaint."

Another brief smile flitted across Darragh's face. "Indeed, but such is the way of life under the Queens. You're obviously an Outsider, and will have issues with some things here. I can try and give you an idea of what life is like for those under the Queens. Will that help you find your way, MacDougal?"

Sean considered the old man across from him again. Darragh had obviously been a warrior before he'd gone blind. The many scars attested to that, but his demeanor was not what Sean would have expected from an old warrior.

"Darragh, I would be honored if you would help me find my way, but please call me Sean. I feel wrong calling you by your name while you're using my surname."

"I did not wish to impose on a guest, but I will do as you ask. Since you are obviously not a normal guest, and being new to our world, you seem to have a distaste for the way Bonded are treated. Would you object to having Misa join us?"

"I won't object," Sean quickly replied as he sipped the tea. The hint of orange helped cut the bitter flavor some, but it was still on the edge of his ability to drink without choking.

"Misa, come out," Darragh said, his voice warm as if addressing a longtime friend.

Slithering out of the kitchen, her tongue flicked rapidly in Sean's direction as she went to Darragh. "He tassstesss of metal," Misa whispered to Darragh. Sean caught the words, which had an odd accent to them.

"I used to work with metal every day," Sean said, making it known he had heard her.

Both Darragh and Misa froze for a second, before Darragh coughed once. "For someone who claims to have never seen a Naga, I am surprised you know her tongue."

Knowing he had made yet another mistake Sean sighed, "Yeah about that. I think I can understand and speak every language."

Misa's eyes narrowed as her tongue flickered at him again, "He'sss uncertain."

"Sean," Darragh said gently. "You have secrets you wish to keep, I do not doubt, but I will need a starting point to help you find your way. It is up to you to decide how far you will trust an old man in a village far removed from the Queens."

"Let's just say I was given a few gifts that I don't fully understand, and I found myself on the cliffside overlooking your village a few hours ago."

"Have you ever met one of the Queens or one of their nobles?" Darragh asked idly. Misa straightened up at the words.

"Nope," Sean said, watching the Naga. "Who are the Queens?"

A snorting chuckle came from Darragh. "Who indeed? The two Queens are the rulers of this land. The Winter Queen is coming into power over this region now."

"Wait," Sean blinked, a finger held out before him, "Winter Queen? You mean the Fey Queens?"

Darragh nodded his head. "Indeed. Winter and Summer, the Elvish Queens of All, The Twin Fey."

"Fuck," Sean said, rubbing at his eyes. "Humanity got here through some kind of bargain, didn't they?"

"Many have come here through Agreements with the Queens, or one of their nobles," Darragh replied. "Though it is not as common as it was in the past, according to the stories we have. The last great exodus to this world is said to have happened over a thousand years ago."

"Your ancestors were part of that?" Sean asked, already fearing the answer.

"Aye, those of the Green were brought over in the Agreement that the Queens arranged with our *Gods*," the last word was almost spat, as if the word tasted bad in his mouth.

"Those would include Dagda, Morrigan, Oghma..." Sean trailed off as he watched Darragh's face twist with each name.

"Those and more," Darragh said as Sean paused. "They are not remembered with kindness for leaving us to the Queens."

"I see," Sean said, taking a large swig of tea and wincing at the taste.

"Your road will be a hard one," Darragh said suddenly. "If you aren't the vassal of one of the Queens or their nobles, then you shouldn't be here. You've been tossed to the wolves, and I think I can guess who's done that."

"Can you ease that road by helping me understand the world a bit better?" Sean asked.

Darragh paused, before asking a question in return, "Will you swear that you will do no harm to me, or anyone in the village, unless your life is threatened by one of us?"

"I can agree to that," Sean said, nodding. The instant he agreed, he felt a weight settle over him. "What was that?"

"The law of the Queens," Darragh stated. "All deals are binding. That is your first lesson."

"Huh." Sean took a moment to think that over. "All deals?"

"Aye," Darragh said, "if the terms are stated clearly and accepted by both parties. It is the basic block that all power is based on here. Bonding works off that idea, but is much more invasive, and usually involves magic or Talents."

"If someone can use magic, then they can Bond, as Misa is with you?" Sean asked.

"Anyone can be Bonded. The most common reason is so the Bond Holder can gain access to the magic and Talents their Bonded possess. Misa is Life Bonded to me, which is not to be idly done, as it links the souls of the two together."

"I have a lot to learn," Sean sighed.

"Yessss," Misa hissed softly. "All newcomersss do."

"Darragh, what would you require in exchange for teaching me enough to not look like a fool when I encounter other people of this world?" Sean asked, starting to understand how the world worked.

"Having the other party start the Agreement can be a good thing," Darragh smiled slightly. "I would ask for you to toil with the others in the forest, by either hunting or logging during the day. During the evening, you will have a place here in my home, and I will teach you the beginnings of knowledge that you will need to survive."

"What if I wanted to be taught about magic as well?" Sean inquired.

Darragh's lips pursed as Misa leaned towards Sean, her tongue flicking out faster than it had before. "I tassste no energy in him," Misa said.

"I can use magic," Sean said firmly. "I would be surprised if the one who gifted me the ability to do so was wrong."

"I can try, but it is not something lightly taught. That would require more. We should table that discussion until you have proven your worth to the village."

"The deal is for me to work during the day as a villager, and in return I will be provided lodging here in your home, and be tutored by you in the ways of this world?" Sean repeated, wanting to be sure the terms were clear.

"If that is the deal you propose," Darragh said, his head tilting slightly.

"That deal, but either party can break it without penalty on any day that I have not yet worked for the village. Do we agree?"

"I will agree if you will agree to a simple addendum. Misa will be treated with respect," Darragh said simply.

"I accept and agree." As the words left Sean's mouth, another weight, this one slightly heavier, settled over him.

"We shall start your training when you return for the evening," Darragh said. "Misa, take Sean to Cian. He can help with the logging today."

"Asss you wisssh, massster," Misa said as she made for the door.

Sean gave Darragh a small bow before getting to his feet. "I look forward to learning from you, Darragh."

"We shall see how you feel tonight," Darragh chuckled.

CHAPTER FOUR

Misa ushered Sean out of the house, her speed increasing as the midday sun warmed her. Sean almost had to stop strolling to keep up. Misa glanced at him, her face betraying no emotion except for a single slow blink. When they entered the forest, Misa slowed, her head pivoting as she led him, tongue flicking at regular intervals.

"What lives in this forest?" Sean asked.

"Many thingsss," Misa hissed softly. "Nothing will bother usss while we get to the cuttersss."

"Why are they cutting inside the forest instead of at the edges?" Sean asked.

"Agreement," Misa stated.

Her abrupt answer left Sean to wonder who, or what, the village had come to an Agreement with. He didn't have long to wonder; it only took them a few minutes to reach the place where a handful of large men were trimming branches off a tree on the bank of the stream they were following.

"Cian, Darragh had me bring you thisss one, Sssean MacDougal. He isss to aid you today," Misa called out to the men.

One man, who sported glorious mutton chops instead of a beard, stood up as Misa and Sean entered the clearing where they worked. Two vivid green eyes looked from Misa to Sean, before he nodded once. "Fine. As Darragh declares, so shall it be. Grab one of the hand axes and join us, we need to get this one into the stream." Cian motioned to a pile of tools, then went back to work without waiting to see what Sean would do.

"Work well, Darragh hasss vouched for you," Misa hissed softly before slithering away.

Sean went to the small pile of tools, looking over the selection of large and small axes. He frowned as he examined them. Only one axe wasn't bronze, but a dark grey metal that seemed to drink in the sun. Shaking his head, he chose the sharper of the two bronze hand axes and joined the five men around the felled tree.

Each of the men working glanced at him, then back to their work. Shrugging off the seeming indifference of the others, Sean started at the opposite end and brought the axe down on a two-inch thick limb. A sharp snapping sound echoed as the limb was shorn from the tree.

Sean stood up, holding the branch in one hand and the axe in the other. The blade of the axe was deformed from the force of driving the bronze head through the limb with a single strike.

All five men looked at him with raised brows as they stood up. "What did you do?" Cian asked with a frown.

"Cut the limb. Just, not like I expected to," Sean said as he tossed the branch at the pile the others were building. Turning his attention to the axe, he could see it would need a lot of work to get it back into decent shape.

One of the others picked up the limb he'd tossed and examined it. "Cian, it's cut clean through," the man said, handing the limb to Cian.

Sean let the axe dangle at his side as he felt the growing tension. Cian looked the limb over, before tossing it back in the pile. "Do it again," Cian said, motioning to another, larger branch.

Sean held up the axe, "It's a bit broken."

Cian's lips twisted in anger. "It takes time to make the blades worthwhile. Use that blade and cut another limb."

Rolling his eyes at the man's tone, Sean bent and hacked another limb free. The limb came free, the blade deforming even more. He tossed the limb to Cian, "Your axe is about to be worthless."

Cian caught the limb and dropped it on the pile. "You're a detriment to our tools. Use the one real blade we have, it should survive you." Turning his gaze back to the others, he grunted, "Back to work. We need this tree in the stream before the sun drops too far, so we can get our own tree down."

Sean dropped the ruined axe back in the pile of tools and grabbed the dark bladed axe, weighing it in his hand. Holding it up, he eyed the double-bitted axe, the edges seeming to almost glow to his sight. Gently testing the edge, Sean winced as the blade cut him. Briefly examining the cut, which was bleeding a silvery-red fluid instead of the dark red he would have expected, Sean sucked at it. The blood tasted sweet to him, almost like cherry cordial. As he pulled his thumb back out of his mouth to look at it again, the cut was gone.

A bit surprised at healing so fast, Sean moved back to the tree. Careful with the extremely sharp axe, he began to trim the limbs off. Each careful swing sliced through the limb he aimed at, almost surgically removing them compared to the rough cuts the bronze had produced.

He removed all the branches from the bottom half of the tree while the others toiled along. "You want me to finish this up for you guys?" Sean asked with a smirk.

Cian stood up, stretching out his back and meeting Sean's gaze with a look of appraisal. "You're not tired? Your arms aren't numb?"

"Nope, I'm still good," Sean said as he propped the axe over his shoulder. "I think it will go faster if I finish, than if you guys continue, though."

"Cian, how is he still standing?" one of the others asked with wide eyes.

"Go ahead," Cian said, motioning the others back. "Let us know when you need to stop."

Shaking his head, Sean snorted as he went back to work. Shortly after he started, he was done, and his left hand had a faint tingle to it.

Flexing his fingers and shaking his hand, he turned back to see shocked expressions on the faces of the men. "What?"

"Only my grandfather has been able to wield this axe without tiring quickly," Cian said with a note of respect. "Even I would have had to rest before I could have finished half what you've done."

Cian's words finally completed the link for Sean. He looked like a younger version of Darragh. "I take it this weapon is special?"

Cian's lips pursed, but he nodded. "An understatement. Who are you?"

"Sean MacDougal, a traveler," Sean said, resting the axe across his shoulder again. "Though it looks like I'll be staying for a bit."

"Cian, we have to get the log to Oaklake," one of the others said as he glanced up.

Cian looked at the sun and nodded. "You are right. Who has to ride today?" He looked at the other four with a stoic expression.

A moment passed before one of them stepped forward, "Me."

"Just remember, Byrne—she gets one kiss, and you are not to come off the log," Cian told the younger man firmly. "She will try to tell you otherwise, but hold fast."

"I know, Cian. We all know, it's just difficult when she's there," Byrne said. "I'll be back tomorrow."

"Let's get it into the water," Cian said, leading the others to the log.

Sean put the axe down and felt the tingling in his hand stop. Glancing back at the blade, he frowned and went to help the others push the log into the stream. Cian told them to push on three, and they did.

What they hadn't expected was for the top section to go further than the rest of the tree. The log started ten feet from the river, and the top of the log splashed into the water while the bottom mostly just turned in place. All eyes went to Sean again, who was frowning as he looked at his own hands.

"Traveler, what are you?" Cian asked calmly as he fingered the dagger on his waist.

Sean took a step back, hands held up and palms out, "Human,

always have been."

Byrne shook his head, "Cian, if we don't get going, I won't make it by nightfall."

Cian frowned, but nodded. "I know." Turning back to Sean, Cian's frown deepened, "Sean MacDougal, will you please push the log into the river?"

"Okay," Sean said warily as he moved over to the group and gently nudged the tree. It rolled two feet, making even Sean pause for a moment. With a few more careful pushes, he got it to the edge of the water. Giving it a last tap, it fell in and began to bob on the current. He reached out and snagged one of the larger stumps from a limb that had been cut earlier.

Byrne stepped next to Sean with a wary look to his eyes, but he straddled the log with a pole in his hands. "Thank you."

Nodding, Sean let go and stepped back as the others moved up to the bank. "Come back safe, we'll see you on the morrow," Cian said.

"I'll be back," Byrne said as he used the pole to nudge himself out into the current.

Watching him ride the log down the waterway, Sean shook his head. After a minute, the others all turned to look at him. "So, what's next?" Sean asked casually.

"We cut down a tree for the village," Cian said as he picked up the dark axe. "Think you can do another?"

Rolling his shoulders, Sean nodded, "Easy. Want me to fell it for you?"

Cian's eyes turned dark for a second before his lips pulled up. "You think you can fell a tree so easily?"

"If you let me borrow that blade again, yeah," Sean said, holding a hand out.

The other three all seemed to hold their breaths as Cian brought the axe off his shoulder and bounced it in his hands. "Fine," Cian finally said, turning the haft to Sean, who took it from him. His eyes went to one of the three who began to breathe again, "Taavi, pick him a good one."

Taavi grinned as he pointed behind Sean, "That one will do, eh?"

Sean looked just past his left shoulder where a tree almost double the size of the last one stood. "You guys sure you can delimb it after I bring it down?" Sean asked, looking back at the grinning quartet.

That wiped the grins from their faces. "If you can even drop it," one of the others said.

"I understand hazing the new guy, it's as old as time," Sean chuckled. "How about a small wager? If I drop it, you all clear the limbs while I take a break. If I fail to drop it, you can tell Darragh that I was no help today."

Cian nodded, "Wager accepted."

Those words sent a chill tingling down Sean's spine. It wasn't the same as an Agreement being made, but he was still aware that he'd made a binding contract. "Game on, then," Sean chuckled as he marched over to the tree. Licking his lips, he recalled what he had been told by his dad regarding cutting down trees. "Upstrokes on the side you want it to fall to, down strokes on the opposite side," Sean muttered to himself as he got positioned, planning to drop the tree toward the stream.

Seeing how Sean was positioning himself, the quartet gathered their tools and moved out of the way. Lounging against trees, they watched as Sean seemed to be giving himself a pep talk. Taavi whispered, "I have tonight's bread on him failing."

Cian nodded sagely, but didn't reply until the others had accepted Taavi's wager. "I will match your wagers for the next three nights, if I lose, in the order you bet. But I get all three of yours tonight if he succeeds." The three men blinked at Cian, but agreed to his wager.

A few seconds after that, Sean took his first upstroke into the tree. The impact was clearly audible. Sean grumbled, bracing his foot against the tree to pull the axe free since the blade sank in to the midpoint. Shaking his head in annoyance, he took a less powerful swing to make sure he could pull the axe back cleanly. A chunk of wood came spinning free from the second swing. His next few swings were quick and efficient, making headway into the trunk at a remarkable pace. When Sean stepped away, a good third of the tree had been removed from the section he'd been working on.

"Cian..." Taavi said his eyes wide.

"I see it. I will be needing to talk with Darragh when we get back."

Sean moved around the tree and began to swing down on the other side. The angle of his cuts should drop the tree where he wanted, or at least close to it. Sweating as he worked, Sean could only smile. It had been years since he'd done this kind of pure manual labor and part of him reveled in the feeling. Faster than any of them would have thought possible, Sean made the last cut and the tree creaked as gravity took over.

"Timber!" Sean laughed as the tree fell almost perfectly, the very top of it gently splashing in the stream. Turning to the others, his grin was met with incredulous stares. "So I guess I get a break now, huh?"

The four men looked to each other in amazement before three of them scrambled for their hand axes. Cian walked to Sean with a slow, though steady, pace. "Sean MacDougal, we seem to have been wrong to judge you as we did. I apologize for our demeanor toward you when you first appeared. Truly you are a son of the Green, and we would welcome you as brother." Thrusting out a hand, Cian waited.

Sean went to grab the hand, but something made him grab Cian's forearm. "No hard feelings; the new guy always has to earn his spot." He handed the axe over and flexed his hand and left arm, which were both numb. "I do need a small break, but I'll join you after that."

"Take your time," Cian said with respect as he went to join the others.

Sean noticed that Cian had to pause and shake his arms after every branch he removed using his grandfather's axe, after the first minute. Halfway through Sean's break, Cian put down the axe in favor of one of the bronze hand axes. Sean's arm had stopped tingling during his break, and unable to sit still any longer, he went to join the others.

"Are you sure?" Cian asked as Sean picked up the double bitted axe again.

"If I need to, I'll take another break," Sean said as he moved to the top of the tree. Grabbing it, he yanked the tip out of the water, "I'll start down here."

CHAPTER FIVE

They were able to clear all the limbs off the felled tree much faster than normal thanks to Sean's help, though he did take another break when his arms started tingling again. His arms were just going numb yet again when he saw there were no more limbs to remove. The men started gathering the branches and sorting them into six piles while Cian gathered their axes.

"We thank you for your help," Cian said.

Sean took a seat on the trunk, watching them work as he waited for his arms to feel normal again. "Why didn't we separate them to begin with?"

"Normally the women separate them when they get here," one of the others said. "It's going to be a bit though before they get here and we can all go back, so why not make it quicker?"

Sean nodded, the logic clear, "Do we have anything to drink?"

"Just the stream," another of the men said. "Did you not see us all drinking from time to time?"

"Guess not. I was kind of focused," Sean said as he walked over to the stream, brushing the dirt off his ass as he went. Kneeling, he cupped his hand and brought some of the cold water up to his lips. It struck him suddenly that he had no idea what might be in the water and what it might do to him. He weighed the pros and cons as the water slipped through his fingers.

"It's pure," Cian grunted from near the tree. "They keep it that way, do not fear otherwise."

Cupping another handful of water, Sean risked dysentery and drank it. The pure, crisp taste of alpine water hit his tongue. He quickly took another two drinks before he stood, feeling more refreshed than he thought he should be from just a few sips of water.

"It's said that they also infuse the stream with energy, which might be why we can work as long as we do every day," Cian said as he stepped over to Sean. "How do your arms feel?"

Rotating his shoulders, Sean frowned slightly. The slight ache he'd felt a moment ago was entirely gone. "Good?"

"That is what I am talking about. Just enough to refresh the body some from its exertion. You can't live on it, but it helps with the hard labor. More so if you've been using grandfather's axe."

"So, what is the story with the axe? I notice it's the only one that's not bronze." Sean figured he knew why there were no iron tools, as in many stories, the Fey and iron were not compatible.

"It was something he got from one of the nobles when he was younger," Cian said. "He would have to tell you that tale."

"His eyes—he wasn't born blind?" Sean asked.

Face creasing into a thunderous frown, Cian grunted, "No, that is his Shame from the Summer Queen. Again, that is a story he will have to tell."

"Fair enough," Sean said, wondering how the leader of this village had upset one of the Queens.

Before he could say anything more, the sound of six ladies singing caught his attention. Turning his head to the trail he had followed Misa on, he smiled. The song was about a young lass taking a trip through the woods to find her beloved and bring him home.

"Did you hear something?" Cian asked as his hand fell to his dagger.

"Singing," Sean said, "I think the women are coming."

"I don't hear it," Cian said as he closed his eyes, trying to listen harder.

After another minute, Cian nodded. "I hear them now." Opening his eyes, he appraised Sean again, "You're a unique one in more than one way, it seems."

With a tight smile, he realized that he was doing things beyond the norm again. Sean nodded. "It does seem that way." He scratched at his chin, feeling the vaguest hint of stubble on it.

"Lads, they are coming," Cian said, turning back to the others.

"And we are done," one of them laughed. "Won't this surprise them?"

All eyes turned to where the path came out on the bank. The singers were now close enough for all of them to hear. The guys all took seats on the log and waited, while Sean leaned against a nearby tree, wondering what the meeting was going to be like.

The song came to an end as the women emerged from the forest. A man walked with them, arm in arm with one of the women. The newcomers stopped and stared at the men lounging around the clearing. "Now, doesn't that beat all? We've come to work and they are loafing about." The speaker looked to the other five women, raising her hands as if asking why.

"Now, Tamaya, maybe they have a reason for it, hmm?" one of the others said as they approached the men. "Maybe they were just enraptured by our song?"

"Enraptured with the idea of less work is more likely," Tamaya said as she came to a stop before Cian. "Tell me, husband, why are you not working?"

Sean looked at Tamaya, realizing she was the one who Darragh had called his granddaughter, realizing it was by marriage. She and three of the other women were the ones he'd encountered first, outside Darragh's home. He stayed where he was, as they were all ignoring him.

"Beautiful wife, one must wait when the work is all done and not enough time remains for more to be started. Byrne is well downstream, and this tree is ready for the village. We've just been waiting on you to get here," Cian said as he stood up, towering over his wife by more than a foot.

Tamaya paused, looking around the clearing. The other women had paired off with the men who Sean figured must be their husbands, except for one. Sean mentally paired her with Byrne, who was absent.

"Since when do you fell and clear two trees in a single day?" Tamaya asked with raised brows.

"We've had some assistance today," Cian said as his eyes went from Tamaya to Sean. "Darragh provided us with some unique help."

All eyes turned to Sean, who pushed off the tree to stand. "Pleasure to see you four again, and some new faces as well. I'm Sean MacDougal. I have an Arrangement with Darragh, so I'll be here for a bit."

Everyone eyed him for a few heartbeats longer than Sean was really comfortable with. "Well, since you will be part of our village, for a time at least, welcome MacDougal," Tamaya said before turning to the other women. "Come on ladies, we have to get the branches ready so we can head back."

"We've already done that," one of the men said.

"You've already done that, Walden?" the woman before him asked with a raised brow and pursed lips.

"We have indeed, Aoife," he replied before cupping her face for a quick kiss. "I believe we had an existing wager on what would happen if we managed what we did today, eh?"

Aoife blinked, "We do..." she ducked her head for a moment before nodding. "It will be upheld, tonight."

Walden slipped his arms around her briefly. "I'll be looking forward to it."

Tamaya coughed, "Later, you two. We have work now." Her eyes went to the tree that had been felled. "Are you lot sure you can get that back to the village? It's a bit bigger than you normally carry."

Cian looked to Sean, before turning his eyes to his wife. "I believe we can. If you will lead the way for us?" Cian motioned Sean over as the women went to the six piles of brush and began to drag them to the path. "Can you take the front end?"

Sean eyed the log and the other five guys, weighing his seemingly greater than average strength and nodded. "Shoulder carry?"

"Aye," Cian said. "You're the shortest, so we need you on one end or the other."

Sean nodded, as he couldn't deny they all topped him by a few inches. "Should be good."

"Let's not disappoint, then," Cian chuckled as the men all took up spots next to the log. Cian called out to the newcomer, "Eagon, no need to be that far forward. Sean can handle it."

The newcomer looked at Sean and then the tree, his doubt clear, but he shrugged and moved closer to the others by a few steps. "I hope so, as I fucking can't," were the lightly muttered words.

"On three, roll and lift," Cian said as he placed a hand on the tree, "Sean, temper your pull to match us please."

"Got it," Sean said as he waited for the count. Exerting less than half the strength he could, Sean still almost overdid the small roll and lift. Luckily, his roll was close enough in strength that the tree was soon settled on their shoulders.

"Time for home, lads," Cian called out as he began to sing.

Sean didn't join in, but soon found the rhythm of the song. The song helped them all stay in step with each other, and set the pace they walked at. Sean smiled at the lyrics—they spoke of a hard day that ended with a good meal and the company of a willing wife. As the song ended, Cian started it over again. This time, Sean joined in, singing the words in tune with the others, a little amazed that he could recall the lyrics so easily after hearing it once. As the song came to an end the second time, they'd made it back to the village and were directed to the home at the end of the village, where they dropped the log.

"Well done," Cian said, clapping each man on the shoulder. "Be seeing you for dinner," he added, the last to Sean as he clapped his shoulder, a small wince crossing his face as he shook his hand afterward. "You're a lot more solid than I had thought to begin with."

Shrugging, Sean replied, "Thanks, I think."

"Food is in Darragh's house just as the sun sets," Cian said. "We'll see you there."

"Sure thing," Sean replied as he watched the various couples split off towards different homes.

"Who are you, stranger?" a voice called out a moment later from the closest house.

Turning to the speaker, he found a redhead staring back at him, "Sean MacDougal. Who might you be?"

"Fiona," she said as she eyed him. "Where did you come from?"

"That is a very long story," Sean chuckled. "What of you? I didn't see you with the others."

"I'm different," Fiona replied, her lips turning down slightly. "Will you be here for a while?"

"In the village, probably. Darragh is going to be tutoring me," Sean said, wishing she would come out so he could see her better, as her face was only partially visible in the small window.

A soft whistle escaped her full lips, "Now that is a story I would like to hear; he isn't normally willing to teach others."

"I'd be willing to trade tales, but you won't be happy with what I'd share. It's not as exciting as you think," Sean told her.

Fiona pursed her lips in thought. "I think you might be worth the trouble. We have an hour before dinner. Would you like to come in and share some tea?"

"I would be delighted," Sean told her.

Fiona left the window and the door opened a moment later. "Do come inside, Sean."

Entering the home, he found it to be a single room of about fifteen feet square. Clearing the doorway he turned to Fiona, who closed the door behind him. As he opened his mouth to speak, he lost the words as he registered what he was seeing.

Fiona's left leg and arm were made of some silvery metal that had a faint green sheen. They transitioned seamlessly with her flesh as far as Sean could see. Sean couldn't help staring, he'd never encountered anything like it before, especially not in the form of a beautiful young woman. "I don't like being gawked at," Fiona said simply as she went past him to the small circular sitting table that stood about a foot off the floor, supported by four intricately carved legs.

"I apologize," Sean said as he tore his eyes off her. "I didn't expect to see artificial limbs."

Fiona frowned as she took a seat, "They aren't artificial. They're mine, just changed, for my Shame." Her smile was a bit strained as she poured the tea into two cups, "Please sit and speak with me."

Sean sat. His eyes kept wanting to drift back to her metallic arm, but he forced himself to meet her eyes. He blinked as he found her to be heterochromatic, one eye was a perfect leaf green, the other a pale sky blue. "You're one wonder after another," Sean said without thinking.

Blinking, Fiona's cheeks darkened slightly, "Thank you. I haven't heard a compliment in some time." She pushed a cup towards him. "I only have mint tea, and it is cold. I hope that is okay."

"That's fine," Sean said as he studied her features more.

Tracing her sharp cheekbones with his eyes, he watched as her dimples came out with her nervous smile as she brushed a strand of hair behind her ear. That drew his attention to her ears, which had the slightest of tapered points at the tops of them. Coughing, he grabbed the cup and pulled his eyes to the table, realizing he was being creepy. "Sorry about that, mint tea is fine," he took a sip and found the mint to be sharp.

"You really don't seem to mind being here," Fiona murmured softly, probably thinking too softly for him to hear, but he heard the words clearly. "I would like to hear your story about your Agreement with Darragh, if you don't mind. I will trade you a tale in its place."

"That's fine," Sean said, "but as I said, it's nothing special."

CHAPTER SIX

Sean told Fiona about his short and unimpressive first meeting with Darragh. Finishing his story and his tea at the same time, he met her eyes to find them watching him with interest. "So, umm, yeah. That's it."

"You accepted Misa? That easily?" Her eyes narrowed, searching his face for any sign of dishonesty.

"I have no reason not to. I didn't understand the concept of Bonded, or know that I should be wary because she's a Naga," Sean said, meeting her dual colored gaze. "Which, I've already been told, is unusual."

Fiona nodded, "I see."

"What story will you tell me about you?" Sean asked as she refilled his cup.

Fiona sat back as she considered what to say. Her hand idly rubbed the tip of her ear before brushing her hair back. "I have tales I could tell. Is there anything specific you would care to hear?"

Pulling his gaze away from her face as she shifted her eyes to him, Sean sipped at his tea. "How you came to be here, maybe?"

Fiona cocked her head to the side as she studied him again. She could see the faint reddening of his cheeks, which she hadn't seen a man do in years, not since... Shaking her head to stop that thought, she took a deep breath.

"That isn't much of a story either, but I will tell it," Fiona said, her eyes again going to Sean's face and catching him watching her before he looked away again. "I don't mind, just not my Shame, please," Fiona said softly. "Now for my tale."

At her words, he met her gaze and she began to talk. Sean felt himself drawn to her words almost as much as he was to her beauty. He marveled at how closely she resembled his idea of the perfect Celtic girl. Well, aside from the metal limbs, but those held an equal fascination for him. Pulling himself from his own thoughts, he focused on her story.

"It's been a little over two years since I met Darragh," Fiona said, refilling her own cup. "I was approached by him as he was adjusting to his new life. He wanted to speak to me about how to better adjust to being Shamed. Four months after our meeting, he was ordered by the Summer Queen to create a new village to extend the reach of the Courts, and she sent him this way."

Sean sipped his tea, watching her and listening to her soft voice. She wasn't looking at him, or anything, her eyes focused on the past as she told the story. He closed his eyes, trying to visualize her story as she told it.

"Knowing he had little time before he had to set out, he began the preparations to start a village, gathering those he could trust who would accept Misa being his eyes for him. He gave up all he was before to fund the beginning of this village, keeping only his axe as a memory."

Pausing, she took a drink and smiled at Sean, who kept his eyes closed. Watching his face, she continued, "It was during those preparations that he came to me and told me that he would be leaving, and why. He knew this place would have use for my talents and asked me, quite humbly, if I would accompany the clan he was assembling. I asked for time to consider it, and he acquiesced to my request."

"He seems the kind to listen to those he values," Sean said, opening his eyes.

"He wasn't always so easy to speak with, but that is not this tale," Fiona said with a smile, their eyes meeting again.

"I'm sorry for interrupting. Please, continue," Sean said, closing his eyes again and returning her smile.

"I waffled on whether to join him or not for nearly a month, as I had set aside my Talent when I was Shamed," her voice dropped, the sadness palpable to Sean. "I meditated on it, and on the night before he came for my answer, I felt a faint call in this direction, something I had not felt for years. When I woke, I began packing my belongings and arranged to accompany them on this journey. By the time Darragh came to ask for my answer, he found me readying myself for the journey and thanked me."

Pausing to sip her tea again, she wondered if he was enjoying the story as he sat there with his eyes closed. Shaking her head, she pushed on with the tale. "Meeting the others was... unpleasant. I will not go into details. My name and Shame were known well in the Quadital and all nearby cities and towns. Darragh even sent two couples away, as they made him choose between them and me. I don't know why he did that, I would have stepped aside from his group if he had wanted."

"Maybe he values you more than you think," Sean suggested.

"Possible, but he is Darragh Axehand. He rarely needed help before..." Fiona tapered off as she realized she was going to say more than she wanted.

"We digress. Please, go on with the story," Sean said, giving her an easy way back to her story.

"Of course, but it's almost over," Fiona said. "The trip took us some time. The mayor of Oaklake was welcoming enough, but when he saw me, he was just as glad when we left. Once we reached this spot, Darragh called a halt. Taking only Misa with him, he went into the forest. A day later, he came back and told us he had an Agreement in place with the local wild fey for us to build the village, and a list of rules relating to the Agreement. We have been here for the last season now."

Opening his eyes, Sean gave her a broad smile, "Thank you, Fiona."

Fiona seemed to steel herself before blurting out her next few words. "Do you *really* not know me?"

"I don't," Sean said.

"I used to be Fiona Treeshaper; now, they call me Fiona Silvershame," Fiona said and stared at him, obviously waiting for a reaction.

"I'll just call you Fiona, if that's okay?" Sean said as he set the empty cup on the table.

Brow furrowed, she shook her head, her eyes searching his face with disbelief, "You really have no idea."

"I don't," Sean said. "Maybe one day we can exchange more personal stories, but I think dinner is soon. Might I accompany you?"

Jaw dropping an inch, she looked at him like he had grown a second head. "You really don't mind being seen with me?"

"Fiona, I truly don't know anything about this world, but I would like to, including being able to call you a friend," Sean said as he stood and extended a hand to her.

Without thought, she took his hand and let him guide her to her feet. "You are truly odd, Sean."

"I've been told that by my friend for years. I hope that bastard is doing alright," Sean said, his smile faltering for a second as he wondered what James would think of where he was now, and how he had dealt with Sean's death.

Seeing the sudden shift in his mood, Fiona squeezed his hand before letting go of it. "Let me grab something, please wait for me outside."

"Alright," Sean said absently as he left the house, his mind still on James.

Fiona watched him go, then gathered what she needed. A few minutes later, she came out, closing the door behind her. Her short top and shorts had been replaced with a long-sleeved shirt and pants. "Thank you for waiting," she said.

Shaking off the thoughts of his old friend, who might very well have been jealous of Sean for being in a new world, he turned to Fiona. His brow furrowed as he took in the change of clothes. "I take it the others aren't comfortable with your metallic limbs?" As soon as the words left his mouth, he silently cursed himself as an idiot for asking the question.

"No one is," Fiona said simply as she started towards Darragh's house.

"I am," Sean said softly, hurrying to catch up to her.

Face turned away, her cheeks heated as her sharp hearing had caught his words. Biting her lip, she wondered if he was real, or if he had been sent by a noble of the courts to hurt her. Once her blush faded she glanced at him as they approached Darragh's house.

Catching each other trying to covertly look at the other, they chuckled. "The door is open," Sean said, trying to get past the moment of embarrassment for both of them.

"It always is when dinner is served," Fiona said as she paused outside the door. "I think it would be best if I went in a bit before you."

Studying her for a second, Sean shook his head. "No. I've never stepped away from a friend just to be viewed well by others. I won't start doing it now."

Fiona sighed but nodded, "Alright, but remember- I tried to spare you."

Just as they were about to step into the room, Sean picked up a fragment of the conversation from inside. "He is different, but I'll find out how and why during his st—" Darragh said.

The conversation cut off as the two stepped into the room. "We're not late, are we? Fiona was kind enough to keep me company and I lost track of the time," Sean said into the silence, as all eyes focused on him and Fiona. He noted the appraising looks at him and the small frowns that briefly crossed the faces of many as they looked at Fiona.

Six people he hadn't met were in the room, as well as everyone he had met, minus Byrne. One of the people new to him spoke up, "So, you're Sean MacDougal? I don't see what all the fuss is about." The resonant tenor of the speaker went with the broad chest of the heavily muscled man.

"I surprise people," Sean said with a shrug. "So, dinner hasn't been served yet? Good." Ignoring the fellow who'd spoken, Sean found a spot where he could sit with Fiona, "There's room here, Fiona, if you don't mind."

Fiona paused as she took in the feeling of the room, including the obvious hostility from the hunters. "I think it would be best if I sat over here, Sean, but thank you."

A micro-frown fluttered across Sean's lips for a moment, "Alright. We need to talk more later, though. I still have stories to tell."

Looking away from him she agreed, "Of course, but later."

"What stories could you possibly have?" the same guy spoke up, a sneer in his voice.

"Whelan," Darragh said calmly, "he is my guest."

The big man shut up instantly, "Of course. My apologies, Darragh."

"You've met most of the people here, but not all of them," Darragh said to Sean, then turned to the rest of the room. "If you have not yet met my guest, please introduce yourself."

The one lumberjack he had worked with, but didn't know the name of, spoke first. "I'm Ward. My wife," he put his hand on the shoulder of the woman seated next to him, "is Leena."

Sean greeted them, and the man who had accompanied the women to pick up the limbs spoke up. "I'm Eagon. This is my wife, Riana."

Greeting them in kind with a smile, he was about to turn his attention to the ones he hadn't met when a woman spoke up. "I'm Byrne's wife, Rylee," she said.

Taavi spoke up quickly when his wife nudged him, "Oh, ah, this is my wife, Enna."

Sean gave her a small wave and a chuckle. "Nice to meet you, Enna."

"These others are my hunters," Whelan said, his lip curling in a sneer. "Aiden, Duggan, Kalen, Zaire, and Myna."

Sean nodded to each as they were named. The hunters gave him flat, uninterested stares, except for Myna, who accorded him a short bob of her head.

"I can see we will all be fast friends," Sean said with a sardonic smile. It struck him as he looked around that Myna was the only person in the room wearing a hat.

"Food," Misa called from the kitchen as she brought a tray out and set it before Darragh. "Fiona, help?"

"Of course," Fiona told Misa as she went to assist the Naga.

"Both the freaks should stay together," Whelan muttered under his breath.

Sean frowned as he caught the words, even though no one else seemed to. He bit back a retort, but filed away Whelan's comment for later. He turned his attention to the seared meat on the platter before Darragh as his stomach rumbled loudly.

"Already wanting to live off our toil," Whelan snorted.

"He brought down that tree we carted in, and helped us with another," Cian said evenly. "He has earned his fill for today, and possibly even tomorrow. Who failed to bring us food yesterday?"

Whelan's nostrils flared, "What was that, Cian? Do you care to challenge me?"

"Enough," Darragh said softly, his words carrying a physical weight that pressed on everyone. "Not on the first day we have a guest. The next one who shames our new clan will be having words with me."

Cian bowed, "I'm sorry, grandfather."

"I apologize," Whelan said, still eyeing Cian with twisted lips.

"Good," Darragh said as Fiona and Misa came back into the room with more trays.

"One thing, Misa," Cian chuckled as Misa began handing out food, "I won a bet with my friends. I get their bread tonight."

Everyone seemed surprised. Sean just looked lost. "Truly?" Misa asked.

The trio of guys who'd lost the bet all agreed that it was true. "We didn't think he would fell the tree without a pause," Walden said with a shrug, getting an elbow from Aoife.

"Fine," Misa replied, shifting the bread from three of the plates onto the one she set before Cian.

Sean thanked her when she handed him his portion on a thin wooden plate—a few ounces of seared meat, two green plant husks, and a sliver of rye bread. Once everyone was served, Darragh spoke again. "We give thanks to the forest for providing for us."

"We give thanks," everyone said in unison, trailed by Sean, earning him another look of contempt from Whelan.

Conversation was nonexistent while they ate. The meat tasted of deer, but was tougher than he was used to. The husks brought to mind a cross of broccoli and asparagus; he choked it down, knowing he needed the calories, even though he hated the taste. The bread was rye, but it was crunchy, as if going stale.

Sean finished before the others, as the meal was smaller than he was used to. Sitting silently, he closed his eyes and relaxed, since no one was talking.

CHAPTER SEVEN

When everyone had finished eating, they started leaving. Whelan contrived to stumble against Sean as he made his way to the door, and was surprised when Sean didn't stagger aside from the contact. Sean had seen the hunter's intention, and was braced for it. With an annoyed grunt, Whelan kept walking, trailed by the other hunters.

Cian gave him an apologetic smile as the lumberjacks and their wives filed out. That left Darragh, Fiona, Misa, and Sean as the only four in the home.

Getting to her feet, Fiona curtsied to Darragh. "Thank you again for allowing me into your home."

"You will always be welcome here, and in the clan, despite what some think," Darragh replied.

"Sean, I will see you again at some point. Thank you for your company earlier," Fiona said as she again brushed her hair back behind her ears.

"It was my pleasure, Fiona. Maybe I'll be able to stop by again tomorrow," Sean said as he got to his feet.

"Are you not staying?" Fiona asked, confused.

"My father taught me to walk friends out," Sean said with a grin. "So, I'm obligated to do so for you."

"Ah. I accept, then," Fiona said as she walked past Sean on her way to the door, a small, but bright, smile on her lips.

Watching her walk down the road, Sean caught Whelan watching Fiona from the small window of one of the homes with a twisted expression. Pursing his lips, he re-entered the home and closed the door, coming to sit before Darragh.

"Whelan seems to really hate Fiona," Sean said.

"I still hope he will learn to overcome his prejudices, but so far he has not," Darragh replied. "But for now, we will try to educate you on the world, as per our Agreement. Were there any questions you had? We can start there."

"Shame. The word seems to carry a weight to it. What is the Shame Fiona has mentioned—not hers, specifically, but the overall meaning to the way she was saying it?"

"Shame is handed down by the Queens, in one of two ways," Darragh said, pausing as Misa brought a kettle and cups out of the kitchen. Once she'd poured the tea and handed it out, she went to wait behind Darragh. Darragh took a moment gathering his thoughts to make the explanation easier.

"Is Misa not going to join us?" Sean asked, disrupting the moment.

The two seemed a little taken aback at his question. "Misa, would you care to join us?" Darragh asked.

"It isss not for a Life Bonded to join her Holder when guessstsss are presssent," Misa hissed softly.

"I'm fairly certain Darragh considers you more than just a Life Bonded, and I would feel bad for disrupting your life by being here. Please don't let me stop you. If you would normally join him for tea, then please, join us now," Sean said.

"You are decidedly odd," Misa said before she went to the kitchen and returned with another cup. Sitting to Darragh's right, she poured herself a cup. "I will sssee how much you truly mean your wordsss."

"Sorry for the interruption, Darragh. Please, continue," Sean requested.

"If you did this with almost any other Life Bonded and Holder you would be asking for a lot of trouble, but you are correct that Misa and I are unusual in that regard." Darragh paused, his hand gently stroking Misa's tail before he withdrew it and continued with the explanation. "If a person breaks an Agreement, then the other party can level a Punishment on the one who broke it. The problem is that if the Punishment is too harsh, the Queens get involved. It is normal for a Punishment to be half as severe as one would think, to be sure they don't over Punish and draw the Queens' ire."

"Can you give me an example?" Sean asked.

"If we made an Agreement to deliver a log to the mill in the next town every two days, and we failed, the person who held the Agreement might demand the next five logs we cut in payment. That would be going too far and draw the Queens' ire, but if he asked for the next three, it wouldn't. It would also mean we would have to re-enter an Agreement with him, which would place us at a disadvantage in the negotiations, due to us having broken the last one."

"Okay, so if he asked for five, then what?" Sean asked, seeing that the idea of Punishment was nebulous, which could cause all sorts of issues.

"If the Punishment is too harsh, the Queens know. The Queen in power can call the offending party before her, then lay a Shame on them. Shames are severe," Darragh paused, one of his hands twitching as his sightless eyes blinked rapidly for a second. "To have a Shame is to be known as an outcast, for you have brought the Queens' ire upon you."

"So, Fiona's left side and your eyes are Shames, then?" Sean asked to make sure he understood.

Misa flared up, "How dare you!" With a hiss she opened her mouth, two fangs suddenly growing. "You would dare bring his Ssshame up ssso casssually, after he invitesss you into hisss home?"

"Misa!" Darragh snapped, though quietly. "He is learning, and doesn't understand the insult he is offering. That is why we are teaching him."

Misa settled down, her fangs vanishing as suddenly as they'd appeared. "Asss you wissshhh, massster," she said, but she stared at Sean with angry eyes.

Giving Darragh a bow from his seat, then one to Misa, Sean spoke up. "I apologize. Darragh is right, I don't know what's right or wrong to say. I have much to learn and am honored that you've agreed to teach me. Please forgive my blunders and help correct me—without fangs, preferably."

Darragh chuckled as he reached over and stroked Misa's tail again. "Fangs, Misa? You know better than to bare them at guests."

"I wasss defending your honor," Misa said as she lowered herself to the ground. "Sssorry."

"It's fine this time, but unless he threatens violence, no fangs. He is a guest and we have much to learn from each other," Darragh said, his hand sliding up to rub at her head. "Understood?"

"Yesss, massster," Misa said, her eyes closing slowly as she pushed her head into his hand.

Sean wondered at the dynamic between them; at times it seemed friendly, and at other times it seemed more like lovers. At the moment, Sean was reminded most of an owner with a beloved pet. Shaking his head, he realized that he'd gotten lost in thought and they were both looking at him. "Sorry, I got caught up in my thoughts."

"I apologized," Misa said simply.

"I accept, and hold you no ill will. You were defending Darragh's honor," Sean said, holding out his hand. "We good?"

Misa froze, her tongue darting out before she slowly took his hand. They shook once, then Misa leaned back and studied him even more intently than before. "Odd," was all she said.

"Do you understand the concept of Agreements, Punishments, and Shames now?" Darragh asked, his sightless eyes focused on Sean.

"I have the rough idea, but how do you know what is right, or too much, for a Punishment?"

"No one knows, which is why everyone tends towards the cautious side, as no one wants to be called before the Queens," Darragh said. "There is also the option to just hand the case to the Queens and they will level a lesser Shame on the one who broke the Agreement, but that also carries a risk. If the Queen deems the case minor, they will Shame the one who brought it before them."

"Arbitrary and convoluted. Got it," Sean said as he considered the implications. Any Punishment could be called before the Queens for any reason, it seemed, which made everyone fear being called and kept people as honest as he would expect, on the Punishment end of things at any rate. "Only they know what will call a case before them."

"That is correct," Darragh said. "Be wary of breaking an Agreement with a noble close to the Queens, for that will surely catch their attention."

Sean could see how that would be the case. Most people would never be called before either Queen, but if they came to their attention, it greatly increased the chance that they would be. "Has anyone ever objected to a Shame?"

Darragh nodded, "Not for years, but yes, people have. It is then brought before the other Queen. If she agrees that the Shame was just, then it is made worse. Only once, that I know of, has the other Queen disagreed. That Shame was erased, and the Shamed was given a Boon by the Queen who'd levied the Shame."

"Hmm," Sean mused, considering the risks and rewards of the appeal system.

"Did you have questions about any other subjects tonight?" Darragh asked.

"I was curious about your axe," Sean said. "Why does it cause my arms to go tingly, then numb? And what magic is it that Fiona does that makes her needed here?"

"We will answer those two tonight. Then we will sleep, as morning comes early," Darragh said as Misa refilled his cup.

"That's fair," Sean said, accepting a refill. "Thank you, Misa."

"You are welcome, odd one," Misa said, her face holding a hint of humor. Sean wondered how he knew that.

"My axe is known as Dark Cutter," Darragh said after taking a sip. "The metal it is crafted from, as well as the magic woven into it, allows it to cut deeper than other axes. It keeps its edge by taking energy from the person wielding it. Many people cannot use it for more than a short time before their energy is gone and the blade begins to sap their vitality. That is the tingle you felt. If you keep using it much beyond that point, you will not be able to drop the blade. Once your hands, arms, and chest go numb, you are almost gone. That is the last point where it is possible to stop. If you continue to press on, your perception will go fuzzy and eventually, you will die, as the axe makes you keep using it. I wielded this blade for many years."

"It's a cursed item?" Sean asked with a raised brow.

"All items of magic have their limits and their drawbacks," Darragh said, "otherwise everyone would have items of power."

"Fair point," Sean agreed.

"As for Fiona," Darragh paused, "she is a Shaper. They are not common, and can be quite powerful. It is she who crafts the planks for our homes. Did you not notice how smooth they are?"

"I was curious about that, as well as why we left the log next to her house," Sean said. "She said her old name was Treeshaper, before her Shame."

"Yes, she was well known for producing some of the best goods in her city," Darragh said. "She all but vanished shortly after her Shame was placed on her. I found her to get help with dealing with my own Shame."

"Massster," Misa hissed softly, "too far off the path."

"Of course, Misa," Darragh coughed. "She uses her magic to bend plant matter to her will. She was invaluable to us in forming our village."

"I see," Sean said as he considered the information. "Can her magic be taught?"

"It is tied to her blood, so I wouldn't think so. It is a Talent, not a spell, but the world is full of wonders," Darragh said. "You still believe you can use magic?"

"I'm pretty sure," Sean said.

"Tomorrow night then, instead of questions, maybe you would like to learn a simple spell from Misa?" Darragh inquired.

"That would be agreeable," Sean said quickly. "What kind of magic?"

Misa lifted the lid off the empty kettle and held her hand over the opening. After a moment, water began to pour from the air into the kettle. "Basssic water sssummoning magic. You mussst know the bassse to build off," Misa said.

"I'd never have to worry about needing water," Sean said with a grin. "I accept."

"Good," Darragh said as he got to his feet. "I will have Misa bring you bedding. Sleep well Sean, for tomorrow brings new things to learn. Will you go with the hunters or the lumberjacks for work tomorrow?"

"I'll go with Cian, at least for the next few days," Sean said.

"Very well. Pleasant slumber to you," Darragh turned and walked unerringly to his room, a fabric curtain dropping behind him and blocking off the room as he entered it.

"I'll be back," Misa said as she followed Darragh.

CHAPTER EIGHT

Sean woke once during the night, when Misa went from the kitchen to Darragh's room. It took him a bit to get back to sleep, as the noises that drifted out of that room shortly after she entered it were not conducive to his rest.

Stretching as he woke the second time, he felt alert and ready for the day. He was a touch stiff but, considering his dreams, that wasn't surprising. Standing, he began to twist and stretch to loosen up his muscles. He was in the middle of squats when Misa came out of Darragh's room.

"Morning," Sean said, fighting to keep a smirk off his face.

"I jussst woke Darragh," Misa said after a moment of hesitation. "Breakfassst will be sssoon," she added as she hurried past him to the kitchen.

Sean bit back a chuckle. It wasn't his place to comment on who was doing what with who, if it was consensual. He didn't see the attraction in a snake-woman, but then again, who knew what the real history was between her and Darragh? It might be love, instead of lust. *Hell, it probably is, asshole*, Sean thought to himself. *Darragh is probably thrilled someone still loves him after being Shamed by one of the Queens.*

Hearing Misa working in the kitchen, he wondered if he should offer to help. As he debated, he heard her faint words, "Flame, I call you forth. I require your warmth and blessssing for my tassssksss."

He looked around the frame of the door, catching a glimpse of an open flame above her palm as she pushed her hand into the fire place. A moment later, the kindling caught and began to burn. He looked away before she saw him.

Magic requires words, Sean thought, *but, she didn't say anything last night when she summoned water.* Shaking his head, he knew he would have to wait until tonight to really find out. He had an Agreement, and he didn't want to break it.

Darragh came out of his room a few minutes later. "Morning to you, Sean. Did you sleep well?"

"Not the best, but far from my worst night. I thank you for the bedding," Sean said. Though the pillow was soft, he'd been poked by the ends of feathers a few times, which had been an annoyance. "The fur, is it wolf skin?"

"Yes and no," Darragh said as he took a seat in his usual spot. "It came from a Canine Moonbound. It was the first beast I slew in my time as a..." Darragh let the sentence trail off, a deep sorrow resonating from him.

"My apologies," Sean said softly, "I didn't mean to bring up sad memories."

"It is fine. How could you have known?" Darragh laughed bitterly. "The clan will assemble for breakfast soon. Are you still going with Cian today?"

"I think it best. Whelan has an... aversion to my company. I would like to learn how they hunt, but maybe it would be better to wait a few days."

"Very well," Darragh nodded. His head came up shortly after Sean heard movement coming towards the house. "Ah, someone is early."

A knock on the door brought Misa from the kitchen. She ushered Fiona in, then went back to the kitchen. Fiona pushed the door wide and came to join the other two. "Darragh, your table is done. I'll finish the chairs tomorrow night."

Sean noted the dark circles under her eyes. "Pulled an all-nighter?" he asked curiously.

"I work best when I won't be interrupted," Fiona yawned. "It causes less issues for me."

"I was wondering—what would I have to do to be allowed to watch you work?"

Fiona's eyes snapped to him, narrowing. "Why?"

"I was told you can literally shape wood, and I am fascinated by the idea," Sean said, letting himself fall into her dual-colored eyes. "My old home didn't have anything of the like."

Fiona closed her eyes, her tongue darting out to wet her lips. "You are strange, Sean. I keep trying to understand you, but you say and ask for the oddest things." Taking a deep breath, she nodded as her eyes opened again. "I will allow it, but you must not distract me while I work."

"If you do that, you might have issues with keeping our Agreement," Darragh pointed out. His tone hinted that he was curious how Sean could manage to stay awake for over a day.

"From yesterday, I take it that two trees a day is normal for Cian and his crew, is that right?"

"Two trees could be seen as the average," Darragh said slowly.

"So, if we finish four trees today, would that cover me for missing tomorrow's work?"

Darragh tilted his head and considered Sean's words. Eventually, he nodded. "If you can bring down four acceptable trees, sending one to the town and three back here before nightfall, I will accept it as an addendum to our Agreement. If you fail those conditions though, you are not allowed to miss tomorrow."

"Done," Sean said easily. He turned his gaze back to Fiona, "I will be free of duties tomorrow, so tonight will work."

Fiona frowned, "They've never been able to drop three trees in a day, much less four, and have them all done before nightfall. I am not as sure that you are going to be as available as you seem to be."

"How about a wager then?" Sean asked, a smile on his lips. "If we do manage it, tonight you have to explain how your Talent works while I watch. If I fail, then not only will I not be free to watch you, I will never ask to watch again."

"No," Fiona said quickly. "I don't accept. I will say that if you fail, you must not ask for information about my Talent, but you can watch it when you are free."

"Agreed," Sean said, feeling the now familiar weight settle on him.

Fiona sighed, "I tried to stop you."

"Tried to stop him from what?" Whelan asked as he came through the open door, followed by the other hunters.

"Nothing that concerns you, Whelan," Sean said simply.

"Figures," Whelan scoffed. "Are you going to join the providers of the clan, or go back to attacking inanimate objects?"

"I'll be joining Cian and his men for the next few days, so I can understand everything I can about their task. After that, I was hoping to join your crew."

Whelan laughed. "I doubt you will be able to keep up with us, but when the time comes, I will have one of mine coddle you so you don't get killed by the beasts we hunt."

A tight smile stretched across Sean's lips, "Which of your people would you task with protecting me?"

"Myna, when he comes with us he is your responsibility. Understood?" Whelan barked at the woman with the hunters.

Myna nodded but kept silent, her lips turning down. Sean gave her a small bow of his head, "I will be most grateful, Myna. Before that day comes, I will ask you for a bit of your time so I can better understand the tasks you do. Hopefully, that will help me not be as big a burden."

Myna glanced to Whelan, who was laughing, before nodding once, "Agreed."

"You need Myna to teach you to hunt? Did your village know nothing of survival?" Whelan laughed.

"Is he causing issues already?" Cian asked as he and the rest of the lumberjacks came in.

"Cian, he is going with you. Hunting is too scary for him, it seems," Whelan laughed again.

Cian frowned, "I doubt that, Whelan. You will be surprised when he goes with you, I think."

"Cian," Darragh said softly, "your task today is the same as always. However, Sean has made a wager with myself and Fiona. He has claimed you will be able to drop four trees, send one to the town, and bring three back before nightfall."

The lumberjacks all went silent, their eyes turning to Sean. Whelan and his crew, minus Myna, laughed at their looks. "Trees, such fierce opponents," Whelan stated.

"Enough, Whelan," Darragh said.

"Of course, Darragh," Whelan said as he chuckled.

"You think you can handle four?" Cian asked Sean intently.

"If you allow me to do what I can, then yes."

"I would call you a fool if not for yesterday," Cian said as he looked to his crew. "Are you ready for a busy day?"

The group all nodded, with Eagon speaking up, "If he can do as you said last night, then we can."

"Breakfassst," Misa said as she brought a cauldron into the room, placing it before Darragh. As she retreated to the kitchen, Fiona went with her.

"Always helping the serpent," Whelan muttered under his breath with contempt.

Feeling his jaw clench, Sean bit back his words. He didn't want to antagonize the hunters, not before he had proved himself. Otherwise, his first trip might be even more eventful than it was already going to be.

Breakfast turned out to be some kind of porridge, with a bitter black tea. Once everyone was done, Whelan and his people quickly left the house. As Cian and the lumberjacks were saying goodbye to their wives, Fiona gave Sean a tired smile, before she left as well.

"Misa," Sean asked with a bit of embarrassment, "where is the bathroom?"

"We have no bathing room," Misa replied.

"The outhouse, privy, or chamber pot?" Sean quickly clarified.

"Behind the homesss on the other ssside of the road," Misa stated.

"I'll be right back," Sean told the others, his bowels reminding him of simple biological needs.

CHAPTER NINE

The walk out to the stream was quiet in the predawn gloom. No one was talking, and the men all seemed to be on guard. Once they made it to the bank, Cian let out a deep breath. "I thought today would be the day."

"Day for what?" Sean asked while Taavi marked out the four trees for the day.

"Darragh has an Agreement with the being that calls this section of forest theirs. It allows for its minions to ambush us once every tenday."

"That is news I hadn't heard before," Sean said. "Is there anything else I might want to know?"

"For us, no," Cian said. "For the hunters, if they target something and attack, then they are fair game for the rest of the day. Be careful when you go with them; Whelan seems to dislike you more than most."

"I got that impression," Sean said. "I don't like bullies either, so we're even on that score."

"I've got them picked out," Taavi told them.

"You good for dropping all of them?" Cian asked Sean.

"I'll need to rest between them, but I think I can do it," Sean replied. "Can you all trim them without me?"

Cian laughed, "If we don't have to drop them we can do it, though we'll be sending Ward downstream around noon."

"Let's not waste time, then," Sean said as he went to the first tree, Darragh's axe over his shoulder.

It didn't take him long to drop the first tree, but he started feeling pins and needles in his hands by the time it fell. Pausing, Sean leaned against the next tree while the others got to work trimming the first one. His hands stopped tingling, but he waited a handful of extra minutes before starting in on the second tree, which he dropped the other way so it would be clear of the first one. His arms had started to tingle and his hands were mostly numb by the time the second tree fell.

Moving off to the side, he took a seat and waited for his hands to unclench enough to set the axe aside. When he did, Cian came over and grabbed it. "Let me know when you're ready for it back. We're going to trade it off to speed things up with the trimming."

"Will do. It's going to be an hour before I'll want to tackle the next one," Sean said as he rested his back against a tree.

"We'll finish up the first one quick, so you can drop the third whenever you're ready."

"Got it," Sean said as he yawned. "I got enough sleep…"

Cian nodded, "Just recover for a bit. We already have two down and the sun is hardly above the horizon."

"Good idea," Sean said through another yawn.

Sean wasn't sure how long he'd nodded off for, but the woodsmen were working on the second tree when his eyes opened again. The dark axe was resting just in front of him, and the first denuded log had been moved down the bank.

"Time to get back to it," Sean muttered as he picked up the axe and got to his feet. "How you guys doing?"

"Maybe halfway through this one," Cian called back to Sean. "You about to drop the third one?"

"That's the plan," Sean replied as he walked over to his next target.

It took him longer for the third tree and his arms were going numb by the time it fell. Wincing, he took a seat again and waited to drop the axe. "Fucking thing is persistent."

"Aye, it wants to be used until you fall over," Cian said as Sean was finally able to set the axe aside. "We finished the second and can start on the third, but Ward will be going downstream before we finish trimming it."

"Understood," Sean murmured as he tried to relax and waited for his hands to return to normal. "The last tree is going to be harder than I thought."

"If need be, we can all take a few swings to spread around the energy drain," Cian said as he went to the third tree. "Just rest until we send Ward off, at least."

"That's a good plan," Sean replied as he closed his eyes, letting the muted sounds of the forest wash over him. He smiled as he listened in on the conversations, small talk between friends. It reminded him of James, and again he wondered how his only real friend was doing.

"Sean, we're sending Ward off," Taavi called out from the streambank. "Help us get it into the water?"

"Coming," Sean said, stretching as he got to his feet. Pausing for a drink from the stream, he felt more refreshed. "I've got it, if all of you will be ready to steady it for him."

A minute later, Ward was on the log, being reminded to be careful by Cian. With a wave, Ward said his goodbyes and started poling the log downstream.

"What lives down there that you guys have to kiss?" Sean asked.

"A Naiad. They control the lake and the stream down a bit from here," Cian said. "The Agreement is that we can have safe passage, but we must kiss one of them each time. The problem is that to kiss one is to want to kiss them more. That is why we trade off, so we all have days between kisses. Even with that, the temptation is strong."

"What do they get out of it?" Sean asked.

"A small bit of our vitality, and if one of them can lure us into the water, she can take us under and drown us. The bottom of the lake is littered with bones from their many victims."

"Fun times," Sean muttered.

"Ward will get to the town just before sundown. The sawmill will put him up for the night and he will walk back tomorrow. Byrne will be back at the village an hour before the women come for the branches. He will walk out here with them."

"Why the singing?" Sean asked as he looked at the fourth tree to be felled.

"Some things that live in the woods have a craving for women, but they will leave them alone if there is song. So they sing on their way out to us, and we sing on the way back."

"Interesting," Sean muttered as he picked the axe back up. "I'm going to get started on number four."

"It's just past noon, so don't rush it," Cian told him. "We've already doubled our normal productivity for a day."

"Wait, what? Darragh said the average was two trees a day," Sean said.

"If you take our best days as the average, then yes, two is the average," Cian chuckled. "I take it the crafty bastard angled you into four."

"I erred when I asked if two was the average," Sean sighed. "Right. No more volunteering information."

The men all chuckled at his obvious discomfort over being had. "Darragh knows the game of the Fey the best," Eagon said. "Don't feel too bad for being on the bad end of a deal with him. Besides, we might do this after all."

"Fair enough, Eagon," Sean said, getting ready to make his first cut on the fourth tree. "Here we go."

Sean stopped after he got the undercuts done, his arms starting to tingle again. "I'm not recovering fast enough," he told Cian after the others had finished the third tree.

"We can drop it," Cian said with a look of hesitation.

"If you do, we'll have issues getting it trimmed in time," Sean said as he flexed his hands. "After we get this one trimmed, we still need to carry the trunks back before the women come out."

"Oh, right," Cian said, not having considered that before. "We'll wait for you, then."

Everyone settled in to rest while Sean waited for his hands to stop tingling. "You've done more than we could have," Walden said. "None of us can use it for as long as you have, and cutting trees down with the bronze takes forever."

"I bet," Sean chuckled. "Too bad you only have bronze and not some of the harder metals."

"It is a crime to own iron, or anything that contains any large amount of it" Cian said. "We can use mithril or adamantine, but those cost more than we have. Like this axe," Cian continued, touching the haft of the blade. "It's the only reason we can get a log for the village every other day on average."

"So, we've already accomplished two days' worth of work?" Sean asked.

"Aye," Cian chuckled.

"I need to watch myself when making Agreements in the future," Sean said as he got to his feet. "Taking it down, then it's all on you guys."

"We'll handle it," Eagon said, quickly backed up by the others.

A few down cuts in, Sean's hands started to go tingly. Growling, he kept up the attack on the tree, chunks flying off it as his arms started to tingle and his hands went numb. "Motherfucker," he hissed as he pushed on. A few more cuts and the tree creaked, close to falling as his arms went numb and his chest began to tingle. Stopping, Sean took a few steps back and eyed the tree.

"We'll finish it," Cian said as the others all grabbed the bronze axes.

"No, I got it," Sean said, a touch of anger to his voice. "Just clear the area, it might not fall clean."

They all got out of the way as Sean took two steps forward and planted his foot just above his cuts. With a loud snap, the tree tumbled, twisting a little as it fell. With a savage grin, Sean called out, "Timber!"

Shaking their heads, the guys all moved over and patted him on the back, congratulating him. Smiling, Sean sat down and waited to be able to release the axe. "Thanks. I'll be over to help with a regular axe once I can."

"Just recover," Cian laughed. "No one is going to believe this until they see it."

Glancing at the sky, Sean gauged they had a little over three hours before the women came out to gather the branches. It would take them most of that time to clear the fourth tree. Hanging his head, Sean closed his eyes and took deep breaths as he felt his hands start to relax a little. After another minute, he was able to release the axe.

"I'll take it," Cian said. "We're going to pass it around to get this done faster, then we'll carry the first one to the village. I want to get all three trees in so we can help the women with the branches."

"Works," Sean said as he laid back on the ground. "I'll come join you guys in a minute."

"Sure," Cian chuckled and walked away.

"Sean, we're ready," Cian called out, what seemed like just a moment later.

"Huh?" Sitting up, he wiped the drool from the corner of his mouth. Blinking, Sean saw the sun dipping towards the horizon. "Shit, I fell asleep again?"

"Or, you were speaking in tongues," Taavi laughed.

"And snoring, great," Sean snorted as he got to his feet. "Okay. I'm lead again?"

"We think you can handle it," Cian said. "We should be able to grab Byrne when we drop this one off, which will make the other two easier."

"Got it," Sean yawned as he got to his spot.

The first log back to the village was easy. As they dropped it off, Fiona looked out her window with a raised brow. "So soon?" she asked.

"We have to make another trip or two," Sean grinned at her. "I look forward to speaking with you tonight."

Fiona's eyes got wide, then narrowed. "You're having me on."

"Not before the first date," Sean laughed. "See you later, Fiona."

Byrne came over, puzzled that they were back already. "Not waiting for the women?"

"Well, there's a story about that," Cian laughed. "Come on, we have to make another trip."

Cian explained to Byrne as they walked. Byrne looked at Sean with wide eyes, "You're human, right?"

"Last I checked," Sean answered with a chuckle. "You're going to be on your own tomorrow. I think you'll be good with just the one for the town."

Everyone chuckled, but Sean noticed the glances the others were giving each other. "We'll see what we can do," Cian said after a moment. "We won't try for four, or even three, but it will look bad if we don't get two tomorrow."

"Sorry," Sean winced. "I didn't mean to raise the bar."

"It's good. Something to strive for is good," Cian replied, patting Sean on the back. "Besides, you're still the lead carrier for the next two logs."

"Sure thing," Sean laughed with the others.

As they dropped the second log off in town, Tamaya spotted them. "Two logs for us? You sent one to town, right?"

"Yes, wife," Cian said as he grabbed her and kissed her. "We'll be back in a bit to walk with you to the bank, so don't leave without us."

"Wait, what?" Tamaya stood there staring, joined by Fiona who looked out her window again. "Cian, get back here and explain," she called after the men.

"Busy, be back soon," Cian laughed.

"You're going to pay for that," Byrne chuckled.

"Sure, but it will be worth it to see her face when we drop the third one," Cian laughed.

In high spirits, the woodsmen made good time back to the stream. Getting the log up, they marched along without singing, staying in step even without the song. When they made it back to the village, all the women were waiting by Fiona's house, and she was standing outside by her window.

"Three, with one sent downstream, for a total of four," Cian said simply. "I think you've lost a bet, Fiona."

Fiona looked at Sean, who wore a small smile on his face. "It seems I underestimated you, Sean MacDougal. I will not do that again."

"I look forward to our talk later tonight, Fiona Treeshaper," Sean said, deliberately using her previous name.

Fiona took in a sharp breath, turning and rushing into her house. The rest of the women scowled as they looked at Sean.

"I might have just fucked up," Sean sighed loudly.

"Yes you did, you idiotic moron," Tamaya snapped. "Come on ladies, we have branches to gather." With that, the women moved towards the forest, their song loud. This was a new one, detailing the many shortcomings of men.

The men gathered around Sean with looks of exasperation. "Well, you've landed all of us in the kennel," Cian said as he nudged Sean. "Come on, maybe we can grovel enough that they will forgive us. You, though, Sean, you are going to have a much harder time tonight."

Staying where he was as the woodsmen followed their wives, Sean shook his head. "I meant it as a compliment. Fuck me, I need to learn things faster." He turned and trudged after the others. He didn't notice the shutter open a crack, nor the single blue eye that followed his steps. A single tear fell from it before the shutter was gently closed.

CHAPTER TEN

They made it back to the village just as the sun was sinking below the horizon. A dozen people each dragged a pile of branches behind them. Sean's pile was the largest of them all. Fiona's window was still closed when they got back. Sean looked away from it, angry with himself for hurting her. Dropping the limbs near the garden behind the houses, Sean stretched as everyone else went towards their homes.

Finding himself all alone, he debated whether to go to Darragh's or try to apologize to Fiona. *Best to apologize without the hunters around*, Sean thought. Walking to Fiona's house, he felt a twist in his gut as anxiety kicked in. He'd never been good with women, always managing to say the wrong thing at the wrong time. *Just like today*, Sean chastised himself.

Taking a deep breath to steady his nerves, he knocked once and waited. He heard someone moving inside, so he kept waiting. No response came, so after a minute he knocked again. "Fiona, might I please talk with you? I wish to apologize."

A few seconds later, the door cracked open. Fiona looked around the edge at him, her face mostly obscured by her hair, her blue eye barely visible behind the curtain of red. "Speak," she told him, but the word was soft.

Closing his eyes briefly to center his thoughts, he spoke, "I am sorry, Fiona. I didn't mean to upset you earlier. I meant no disrespect or harm, I used that name as I truly think it fits you. I'm ignorant of the customs and ways of this world, though I am trying to fix that. If I angered you, I ask that you let me make amends for it. Whatever you think is fitting, I will abide by."

"Fool," the words were almost inaudible. "That is a blank slate, begging to be used against you." The door opened a fraction more, "We will speak of what you can do to alleviate the pain you caused. Enter, if that is truly what you want." Stepping back, she opened the door to him.

As he entered, he heard a mocking voice behind him. "Going hat in hand to a Shamed, you truly are pathetic," Whelan laughed.

Hands clenching, Sean felt his blood begin to boil. He paused in the doorway, torn between ignoring the taunt and having it out with Whelan, damn the consequences.

"Enter, or leave and talk to me no more," Fiona said from behind the door.

That made up his mind for him. His hands relaxed as he entered, and the door closed behind him. "I'm sorry to keep you waiting. There was a buzzing fly that annoyed me."

A faint smile came to Fiona's lips, "He will always buzz, that is what makes him feel special. The best thing is to ignore him. But you aren't here to speak of Whelan. Please sit, and I will pour tea for us."

Sean took the same seat as before. Fiona came over with two cups of mint tea, placing one before him as she sat. As he thanked her, he noticed that her eyes were puffy and red rimmed, and a sharp spike of pain hit him. "I apologize again, Fiona," the words were soft.

"As you should, Sean. Calling me by that name brought back everything I can no longer do. You dug up things I had buried and made me look at them again." She held out a hand to forestall his protests. "I know you didn't do it out of malice, as many others would, but it still stung me deeply. We are here to talk about moving past the blunder you already made."

Sean bowed his head, his sense of self-loathing high as he listened to her words. "I stand by my statement on your doorstep."

"Which is the most foolish thing you've done today, including calling me... Treeshaper..." She stumbled over the name, her face twisting in pain and anger. Shaking her head, she met his eyes. "Do you understand why?"

"Because here, words have more power than they ever did where I came from," Sean said. "I don't think I spoke wrongly to you though, Fiona. I trust what you would deem fair punishment for my words."

Her eyes searched his face, not finding any hints of malice or antagonism. "My price to rebalance the scales is simple. Tell me the truth about where you came from, and why you're here."

A weight heavier than any he had felt before settled on him. "That's a long story, and it might be hard to fully explain," Sean said, feeling the weight press down on him. "Can I hold off on the telling until tonight while I watch you work?"

Fiona licked her lips before nodding. "Agreed, but if you fail to do so, I will level a Punishment as severe as I can."

"Agreed. I won't disappoint you again today," Sean said.

Lips twitching, Fiona fought the smile from her face. "You really brought down four trees today?"

"I brought them down, but they had to trim them all," Sean said.

"I wouldn't think bronze axes would survive four trees in a single day," Fiona chuckled.

"They wouldn't, which is why I didn't use them," Sean replied as he sipped the astringent tea.

"Wait, you used Dark Cutter all day?" Fiona sat up straight, brushing the hair away from her face, eyes wide as she stared at him.

"I had to rest between the trees, even napped twice, but yes. Darragh is a better man than me, if he can wield that beast without issues," Sean said.

"He can wield it without issue because it's linked to his soul,"

Fiona said. Shaking her head, she looked at him with wonder, "All four trees?"

"Yeah. I'm sure Cian will be telling the story before dinner," Sean said. "Is it that odd?"

"Unheard of," Fiona said simply. "To use the Soul Linked item of another for so long in one day..." Shaking her head, she tried to find the words and failed, "It just doesn't happen."

"As I'll explain tonight, I'm not a normal person anymore either," Sean said. "Can I ask you to keep what I tell you to yourself?"

Fiona's head tilted slightly as she ran her tongue over her teeth, "As long as it won't harm the village, then yes."

"Thank you," Sean said as he downed his tea. "Let's head over to Darragh's. He might want to speak with me before dinner."

"Please, go on ahead," Fiona told him. "I want to get a few things together first, as I'm not used to company during the evening."

Sean paused halfway to his feet, before quickly standing. "Err... yeah, sure, no problem. See you later." He left quickly, his cheeks heating as his mind nose-dived at her words.

As he fled the house, Fiona watched him go, a smile coming to her and a soft giggle escaping her lips. "I didn't mean it that way, but it was interesting to see him blush so easily. It's been so long..." she let the murmured words fade away as her Shame came to mind again.

Making it to Darragh's house, Sean found all of the lumberjacks and their wives already there. Cian was chuckling as he explained Sean's snoring. He grinned at Sean as he walked in. "There he is, the mighty sleeper."

Arching a brow, Sean sighed, "That's what I get tagged as, after all that hard work today?"

"Tell me about it. My arms are sore from all that trimming," Eagon said.

"Yeah, it would have been nice to have the time for a couple of naps," Walden laughed.

"Assholes," Sean said, making a face at them. "Next time, you can chop down all four trees."

"No, no, that wouldn't be fair. After all, that seems to be your niche," Cian managed with a straight face.

"You're the worst," Sean said as he took a seat.

"You managed to wield it for all of the trees, alone?" Darragh asked.

"Yeah, but the last one was going badly so I had to kick it over," Sean replied.

"'Kick,' he says," Taavi laughed. "He would have been hard pressed to get more oomph with a maul."

"Is that so?" Darragh said, his sightless eyes staring at Sean. "We'll have to talk later, so I can hear it from you."

"I'm going to be watching Fiona work tonight," Sean reminded Darragh.

"That would be pointless," Whelan snorted as he came in, followed by the other hunters. "Ever watch grass grow? It's about as interesting and almost as useful."

"So still better than talking to you. Got it," Sean shot back before thinking.

Nostrils flaring, Whelan stopped. "What was that, Shame lover?"

"Enough," Darragh stated. "You will be civil in my home, or you will leave."

With a soft growl, Whelan took a seat, his friends all sitting with him. Sean realized now that the seating was following the same pattern as the night before, with the lumberjacks and wives on one side, the hunters on the other. Darragh and Fiona had been between the two groups and while Darragh was the cog between them, Fiona had seemed like a forgotten wheel, wanted by neither side. Sean sat in the same place tonight as well, a shade closer to Cian's side, without thinking about it.

"Sorry for the delay," Fiona said as she entered the room. The place went silent as all eyes turned to her. "I hope I haven't caused an issue for Misa."

Sean, not understanding the silence, craned his neck around. His mouth dropped open as he saw Fiona. Her normal attire had been replaced by a gown of dark green that left both her arms and legs bared to the night. Unable to stop himself, Sean dragged his gaze up her body, trying to file the image away. He eventually met her uncertain gaze and a smile bloomed.

"Beautiful," the word slipped from Sean's mouth with barely any sound at all.

Fiona's cheeks heated as her gaze dropped away from Sean's. "I heard that the lumberjacks accomplished a feat, and thought maybe it would be cause for a celebration."

"Indeed," Darragh said, pulling all eyes to him. "Today, they have done what they never have before. Four trees were felled, three for us and one for the town."

Whelan and most of his group seemed to silently scoff at the idea of that being a feat worthy of mention. Myna alone bowed her head to the others. She sat a little back from the rest of the hunters, so they didn't see her acknowledge the lumberjacks. "Is that really something to praise? It's not like the trees fight back, like our quarry. If they ever drop four of the Red-eyes in a single day, then I will have to concede praise to them."

Cian frowned, "Four? Interesting. I thought your best was two, and no trees ever."

"Why would I waste my time with wood? If our Shaper was any good, you wouldn't even have to chop them down," Whelan spat, his eyes full of venom.

"Enough," Darragh snapped, which shut everyone up. "I warned you already tonight, Whelan Spearbearer. If I have to repeat myself one more time, you will not be invited back into this home for a tenday. Do you hear my words?"

Whelan's jaw snapped shut and the grinding of his teeth was audible. He bowed his head to Darragh, "Yes, chief, I have heeded your words."

"That goes for the rest of you as well. One more uncivil word will not be tolerated," Darragh stated the words calmly, but an almost physical force radiated off them.

"We understand, chief," the others murmured, Sean a step behind them.

"Good," Darragh said. "Misa, is dinner ready?"

"Yesss," Misa said from the doorway. "Fiona, help pleassse."

"Of course, Misa," Fiona said as she hurried to help Misa.

Sean watched her go, quickly suppressing his thoughts when he realized the back of the dress had a cutout at the shoulder blades and she wasn't wearing a bra. It caused his mind to recall the firm, high handful she proudly sported. Rubbing his face, he looked around to find Cian grinning at him and Whelan sneering.

Dinner was a simple affair, identical to yesterday except the bread was fresh. The rye bread still had a trace of warmth from the oven. He dug into the food with a passion, realizing suddenly how ravenous he was. Finishing well before the others, he took a silent breath and fought the urge to ask for more.

"Misa," Darragh said as Sean sat there with an empty plate. "Bring Sean another helping of meat."

"Yesss, massster," Misa said, setting aside her own plate and retrieving a smaller platter with three more strips of meat on it. "Your food, MacDougal."

Sean took the offered plate, "My thanks, Misa and Darragh."

"Wielding a Soul Linked item for as long as you did would have drained your body of all easy energy," Darragh said as the hunters all muttered under their breaths. "No one here, besides maybe myself, could even attempt such a feat."

"What feat?" Whelan asked, his lips set in a snarl as he eyed the plate Sean was eating from.

"Could you wield my axe from sunup to sundown?" Darragh asked Whelan.

"Of course not," Whelan said.

"Sean did just that today," Darragh stated simply. "His body needs the extra meat to replace what was taken from him, because of that."

Fixing Sean with a dark look, Whelan said tightly, "I see."

"What did you bring in today?" Cian asked Whelan conversationally.

"There was no prey close by," Whelan replied, a hint of anger coloring his words. "As we are all done, we will retire. We have a busy day before us tomorrow. Darragh, clan," Whelan said as he got to his feet, leaving in a huff with his followers trailing after him.

"He's going to challenge Sean soon, Darragh," Cian said once the hunters were gone.

"All who are insecure in themselves challenge those they think are threats," Darragh shrugged. "Sean, when you do engage with him, do not kill him unless he aims to do the same to you. For all of his anger, he is still the best hunter we could hope to have."

"I'll do my best, Darragh," Sean said as he set the second, smaller plate aside.

"Fiona, before he joins you, I wish to converse with him privately for a moment," Darragh told her.

"As you wish, chief," Fiona said as the others filed out. "I will wait for him at my home. I will see you soon, Sean." With that, she rose gracefully to her feet and walked out.

Sean watched her go, his mind again pointing out how fit and beautiful Fiona was. A cough brought his attention back to Darragh. "I ask that you don't hurt my people. She is like a drowning swimmer, and you are the log that is within her grasp. Don't let her grab you, only to be too weak to keep you both above water."

Leaning back at the blunt statement, Sean blinked. "I wasn't planning on seducing her."

"You might not, but it has been years since she last had a man pay her attention," Darragh said before suddenly asking an unrelated question. "How old do you think she is?"

"Late twenties?" Sean guessed.

"Try forty-three," Darragh stated. "Just as I'm ninety-three."

"Huh, what? How?"

"Anyone who can wield magic finds their life span increased. The more powerful they are, the longer they can live. For Fiona, that is also augmented by other reasons, reasons which are her own to disclose. I would just point out she is acting like a young maiden again, and not the more mature woman she normally is, when she is near you. Do not hurt my friend and ally."

"Ssshe isss my friend asss well," Misa hissed from behind Sean. "I would be mossst dissspleasssed."

Closing his eyes against the anger he felt at being dictated to, he also understood their reasons. *I'm an outsider, who just showed up. I could be some kind of axe murderer...* Sean let the thought trail off as his lips tweaked into a smile at the choice of words.

"I understand, Darragh, Misa. I will not lead her on or do anything she doesn't ask for. As you stated though, she is an adult and if she presses me, I won't turn away. She is beautiful and talented. That combination intrigues me and I want to learn more."

"Agreed," Darragh sighed. "I wonder if accepting you into my village might have been a mistake? It is what it is. Did you wish to learn from me before you go learn from Fiona?"

"I would love to learn the water magic, but I think speaking with Fiona is a more pressing need, as I won't get many chances to watch her work."

"Yesss," Misa said. "I will leave the cover and pillow for you. Tomorrow, I will teach."

Sean stood and bowed to Misa, "Thank you, Misa. Thank you, Darragh. If you will both excuse me, I shouldn't keep her waiting."

Exiting the house, he heard Misa speak softly, "Ssshe wore a dresssss. Maybe ssshe isss going to try putting her passst behind her?"

Wondering about Misa's words, Sean headed to Fiona's home to learn more about her and her talents.

CHAPTER ELEVEN

Fiona was seated outside her home, next to the logs. The chair she was sitting in was simple, but obviously well made. "I would like to hear your story before I explain my magic," Fiona spoke softly as she looked at Sean. "I will be working while you speak. You may sit here, as I need to touch the wood." Standing, she moved to the first log, "Begin when you are ready."

Taking the offered seat, Sean arranged his thoughts, briefly wondering how she would react to his story. "It started with my friend calling me to play some billiards with him," Sean began.

"What are billiards?" Fiona asked.

"A game where the players use long dowels to push a white ball into colored balls on a table with pockets. The object is to sink your balls into the pockets before your opponent does."

"Interesting," Fiona muttered as she knelt on her metallic leg next to the log.

"My friend James called and asked me to meet him at a bar we had only gone to once before. It turned out to be a mistake. Or maybe fate."

"Wait, you said he called you. If he called, why did you meet him at the bar, instead of going together?"

"My old world had devices for long distance communication," Sean explained.

"Ahh. Scrying crystals, those are expensive," Fiona said, using her right hand to gently stroke the log. As her hand passed over the wood, the bark vanished, leaving unblemished wood behind.

"Close enough," Sean said, pushing on with the tale. "While I waited for him to show, another person accosted me. He claimed I was at his table and that I needed to move, which was odd as the bar was basically empty. Anyway, I objected as I dislike bullies, and he took further offense. He grabbed my shoulder and told me to move again."

"Sounds like Whelan," Fiona chuckled.

"Very much like Whelan," Sean agreed. "When I confronted the guy and told him to stop or I would fight back, he hit me. That punch all but broke my sternum and threw me against the wall, a couple dozen feet away."

Fiona paused to look at Sean before nodding, "He must have been infused with magic."

"Little did I know at the time," Sean said. "I used my, um, weapon to shoot him multiple times, but it did no good. It did nothing to him."

"Infused with magic and a shield, he would be a formidable opponent," Fiona said as her hand went back to smoothing the log.

"He was," Sean said with a frown at how easily she was accepting his story. "When he got to me, he caved in my chest with his boot, which killed me."

"Hmph." Fiona pursed her lips and frowned, obviously wondering how he could be here, if he was dead. Sean didn't leave her waiting for an answer.

"When I woke, I was in a majestic hall, with an old one-eyed man waiting for me."

"None of the nobles appear old, or would even be willing to take that form," Fiona muttered as she slid her fingers around the log and a three-foot section separated from it.

"Holy fuck," Sean breathed as he watched her.

"Continue, please," Fiona said as she set the section upright and began to run her hand over it again.

"The person waiting for me was Odin, an elder deity of the Norse pantheon," Sean said, and Fiona's breath caught. "You've heard of him."

"Yes. Many Gods have bargained with the Queens, and had people pulled to this world for various reasons, though not many appear anymore."

"Well, he had a deal to offer me, since his son Thor was the one who killed me," Sean went on, "but he wasn't the only one. In my youth, I followed a few paths, and each of those deities came to offer me a deal. The Christian God sent one of his angels, and Lucifer came as himself."

"I've not heard of them," Fiona said as the part she was working on started to lose mass.

"The last one to show up was Morrigan," Sean paused when he said the name, as he expected Fiona to react to it.

"The Morrigan? Battle, death, and fate, the Morrigan of the Tuatha Dé Danann?" Fiona's face was pale, her dual-colored eyes wide as she stared at him.

"Yes," Sean nodded. "Morrigan also offered me a deal."

"All of the Tuatha Dé Danann are liars and fools," Fiona spat, her eyes full of hatred. "They are the ones that trapped our ancestors on this world, with their Agreement with the Queens."

"Morrigan did say something along those lines," Sean nodded. "I took her offer, and because of that here I am."

Letting out an angry breath, Fiona stroked the section of wood she was working on and a leg, similar to the ones on the chair he sat in, appeared. "You're their puppet then?"

"No," Sean said firmly. "I have no Agreement with them, in that regard. The Agreement was for me to be given a new body and placed here to live out the rest of my new life."

"Would you swear that on your soul?" Fiona asked, turning hooded eyes to him.

"If that's what it will take to have you treat me as you did earlier, yes," Sean said, feeling the anger and distrust that radiated off Fiona. "I swear on my soul that I have no Agreement that makes me beholden to the Tuatha Dé Danann." A shiver ran through him, as if someone had plucked his soul like a harp string. "Gah, that was eerie as fuck."

Fiona let out a held breath, steadying herself against the log that she was crafting. "You so readily do things that could kill you," she muttered under her breath. "I'm sorry for accusing you, Sean. None of the Tuatha Dé Danann are thought of with kindness by those of us who descended from the ones they let the Queens take to this world."

"I'll make sure to not tell people, then," Sean replied. "That is my story. I appeared on a bluff a few miles away, and upon seeing the village I came this way, hoping to get help and information."

"I would urge you not to tell others that story," Fiona told him. "You would be viewed even worse than those of us who are Shamed."

"Considering the two Shamed I've met have been honorable and friendly people, I'm not sure that's a bad thing."

Shaking her head, Fiona glared at him. "Be serious."

"I am, Fiona. Both you and Darragh have been friendly, and willing to help a person with no knowledge, learn things to help him survive. For which I am entirely grateful."

"Fool," Fiona sighed. "Just don't tell others, or you will be outcast from the rest of society, even possibly hunted down and killed."

"I'll follow your advice, as that's what friends do," Sean said. "Now, about the magic you're doing?"

A snort of laughter came from Fiona, "Fine. You have upheld your Agreement with me, and I forgive you."

"Thank you," he bowed to her from his seat.

"What I am doing is called Shaping. It isn't magic, it's a Talent, and whatever affinities a person has dictates what they can Shape, if they have it. Wood, or any plant matter, is my affinity, due to part of my heritage."

"Hmm. So I couldn't learn to do it?" Sean asked as he watched Fiona Shape a second leg into existence from the log.

"If you are human, then most likely not. It is difficult to master

Shaping without a touch of Fey blood relating to the medium you are trying to Shape."

"If, and it's a big if, I wanted to try, how would I?"

Glancing at him as her hand smoothed over the next section of wood, Fiona pursed her lips. "You really wish to attempt this?"

"Why not?" Sean asked as he slid off the chair to kneel beside her.

"Shaping is not a warrior's Talent, and is viewed with disdain by any warrior." As she said the words, her eyes went briefly to one of the houses.

"People like Whelan?"

"And others. Darragh didn't always think highly of Shapers," Fiona said softly.

"Well, fuck'em. I would love to try."

"Place your hand on mine," Fiona instructed him.

Putting his hand over hers, he felt warmth and a faint vibration. "That's odd."

"That is my Talent at work. I can channel it through my normal hand to smooth the wood and Shape it. If I focus, I can cut through the wood with it—like when I pulled this section from the log."

The odd vibration started to spread from her hand to his. "It feels like my hand is vibrating in time with yours," he told her.

Fiona focused on their hands, her eyes widening, "How are you doing that so easily?"

"I'm not doing anything," Sean said as he felt the vibration increasing. "What is happening?"

"Your energy is syncing with mine," Fiona whispered as she slipped her hand out from under his, then put it on top of his. "Let me guide you," she said quickly. "Just think of the wood moulding at your touch." She edged over, pressing into his side as she began to guide his hand.

Doing his best to ignore Fiona's body pressed against his, he focused on his hand and what she wanted him to do. Barely touching the wood, he focused on it slimming beneath his touch. Eyes widening, he watched as the wood began to form as Fiona guided him down the section she had been working on. "Holy fuck," he whispered, warmth seeping from the log into his hand.

"Amazing," Fiona breathed in his ear as she watched their hands. "You can't be human, not with this amount of Talent at shaping wood."

The vibration spread from Sean's hand down his arm. "Fiona... it's spreading," his voice held a concerned note.

"Really?" Fiona's voice became excited as her metallic hand rested on his back. "Just focus on the soon to be chair for a moment, everything will be fine."

Swallowing hard, Sean tried to shape the section of log into a chair leg to match the other ones he'd seen. As he worked under Fiona's guidance, the vibration spread across his shoulders and into his chest, the warmth suffusing throughout his body. "So warm. It's like the wood wants to be Shaped," Sean murmured as his eyes closed, the image of a chair forming in his mind.

Fiona kept her hands on him, her breath catching in her throat as Sean began to lead the magic. Leaning forward, and subsequently into him, she watched fascinated as he worked. A tear formed in her green eye as she watched him. "So beautiful, how can you do it so easily?" The question was asked in awe as Sean's hand slipped from hers and his other hand came up to start on the fourth leg.

Blinking his eyes, Sean found a fully formed chair before him. His mouth was dry and a warm body pressed against his back. "What happened?"

"You Shaped the chair," Fiona whispered from behind him. She leaned back, removing her body from his. "I used to Shape that easily, before..."

"But how...?" Sean asked, his confusion clear to her.

"I don't know," Fiona said as she wrapped her arms around her legs. "It shouldn't be possible. Like you using Dark Cutter for so long. It breaks everything I know about my Talent, gifted from my family's bloodline."

"I don't have any..." Sean began, before recalling his gifts from the gods and the quasi-character screen from earlier. He focused on it, willing it to appear so he could see it.

Sean Aragorn MacDougal
Human
Age: 33

Gifts:
Metal Bones, Viney Muscles, Mithril Blood, Magic Bond, Mending Body, Death Ward, Linguist, Hunter's Blood, Infinite Possibilities

Spells:

Talents:
Shaping (Able to shape material you share a connection with.)

Bonded:

"Only those with a deep connection to plant life should be able to do this," Fiona went on.

"If..." Sean paused, then spoke very softly, "if my body wasn't exactly normal. If my muscles, for instance, were made of a special vine, would that account for it?"

Sean thought he had seen her shocked before, but he had been wrong. Eyes opening to almost the size of saucers, Fiona's jaw dropped and she reached out her hand to touch Sean's neck. Her fingers pressed gently into his neck. "They gave you a body of plant and metal?" The question was asked just as softly as his had been.

"Yeah," Sean said as he gulped, her hand still resting on his neck. "Umm... Fiona... your hand."

Snatching her hand away as if his skin had erupted in lava, Fiona leaned away from him. "I..." she broke off, clearly at a loss.

"You still have work to do, right?" Sean asked as he looked around for some water to ease his parched throat. "Can we work on the projects together?"

Remaining frozen for a moment, Fiona stared at him. She stood up suddenly and went to the door of her house, not saying anything. Sighing, Sean watched her go with a growing fear. *Fuck, I scared her off*, Sean grumbled internally.

Fiona returned a moment later, with a pitcher and two cups. "You should be thirsty," she said as she poured him a cup and held it out.

He felt his fear vanish, replaced by happiness. "Thank you, Fiona," he said, taking the cup. It was the same mint tea as before, and he eagerly gulped it. Finishing his drink, he found himself feeling refreshed.

"I would like to Shape beside you," Fiona said, licking her lips. "Can I rest my hand," her metallic hand flexed as she said the word, "on your back as we work? I thought I could feel it respond to your talent. I've been missing its use for Shaping for so long…"

"I would be fine with that," Sean said, taking her hand. "I don't mind at all."

With a beautiful smile, she pulled him over to the logs. "Let's get started then, shall we?"

CHAPTER TWELVE

The night passed by in a blur for Sean. He could recall snippets of conversation about what they were crafting from the logs. The thing he could recall most was Fiona, and her light, clear, laughter at some of the inane jokes he'd made. Sitting in one of the chairs that they had made, Sean looked over the chairs and wooden cots that were illuminated by the blue moonlight.

"We did good work," Sean said as he looked at Fiona, who seemed wide awake.

"We did indeed. I never would have thought we could finish all three logs tonight." Eyes going to him, then to the objects around them, her smile bloomed a little more. "I had incentive to strive again, for the first time in years, and I realize now that I'm not as crippled as I thought I was. If anything, I might be better able to do my Shaping. I hadn't considered letting my energy flow through my mithril limb. I tried it once, shortly after my Shame, and I couldn't get the energy to flow."

"Maybe you just needed to adjust to it," Sean suggested as he stood up. "I'm surprised I'm so used to this body as it is."

Fiona got to her feet, biting her lower lip. "Would you like to see one more thing Shapers can do?"

"Of course," Sean said eagerly. "If you are the teacher, then I'm sure it will be amazing."

Grabbing the thick staff that she had set aside during their work, she avoided his eyes. "Shaping is not viewed as a warrior's Talent. But if you know how, and practice, it can be something most warriors would kill for."

Stepping away from the furniture, she made sure she had a good fifteen feet of room. Taking a deep breath, she bowed her head and her feet slid apart into a broad stance. With no warning, she began a series of attacks with the staff. Sean watched her with interest as she flowed through the motions, her dress not hindering her movements at all. Moving as if she was dancing with invisible opponents, she stepped lightly as the staff flashed in attacks and defensive blocks.

His breath was caught in his throat as he watched the mesmerizing performance. His eyes widened as the staff changed between one step and the next. It was no longer a staff, but a sword that she continued to use in the routine, adapting her moves to the new weapon seamlessly.

"Amazing," Sean whispered as he considered the idea of being able to shape items while engaged in combat.

As her dance began to go faster, the sword changed again, becoming two smaller blades. Shaking his head at her grace and ability to fight while using her Talent, he couldn't help but feel she was beautiful in more ways than he had previously thought.

With a sudden flourish, the twin blades came together and the staff returned for one last flurry of attacks. She ended with the staff aimed at Sean, and a small secretive smile on her lips. "It can be a warrior's Talent, as you have seen," her voice was a bit fast from the exertion.

"Can the sword and daggers hold up to metal?" Sean asked as he stepped around the staff to her side.

"You use the extra wood to harden the edge. It isn't as sharp as a metallic blade, but it can still take a hit or two. As you go to strike, you focus on the edge and thin it down; if you have the Talent, you can form a cutting edge for a few moments."

"Amazing," Sean said as one hand lightly touched the staff and his other hand touched her mithril shoulder. "Thank you for tonight, Fiona. You have shown me so much. I should repay you in some way."

Shaking her head, her hair cascaded to cover her face. "No, we are even. We should move the chairs over to Darragh's home." Quickly moving away from him, she set the staff aside and grabbed one of the chairs.

"If that is your command," Sean murmured as he snagged a chair in each hand and followed her.

Fiona got everything arranged as she wanted, the two pausing to finish off the tea that she had retrieved from her house. "I'm going to sleep good today," Sean said, his eyes beginning to droop.

"Sean," Fiona said his name, then paused for a moment. "Darragh is busy with the wives stopping in." Pausing again, the next few words were a bit fast, "You can sleep on my floor instead, if you'd like."

Images of Fiona and him in the same room consumed his mind for a moment before he was able to push them aside. "Are you sure you want that?" Sean asked as he looked at the village. "I wouldn't want your reputation to suffer just so I can sleep."

Her soft hand took his, "It's just sleep, and my reputation with them can't get much worse than it already is. Yours might, though, so it is up to you."

Glancing at her, but only seeing her hair blocking her face, Sean squeezed her hand. "I will take my teacher up on her offer of a place to lay my head."

Her hand spasmed on his as he answered her, his choice of words invoking their own thoughts in her mind. "Yes. Yes, that is fine. I even have a cover and pillow of my own that I can share."

One of the doors in the village opened and Myna came out. She looked at the pair, who quickly stopped holding hands. Myna turned to approach them, but stopped as she saw a wooden cot before her. Lifting her eyes to Sean and Fiona, she bowed before picking it up and taking it back into her home.

"Why did we pick her to give the bed to?" Sean asked. "I mean, we are five short."

"She is the only one who hasn't given me grief the way the others do," Fiona said. "Besides, I think she will actually try to help you learn. This might give her a little more incentive for that."

"Whelan is going to be pissed when he finds out," Sean added.

"That too," Fiona giggled. "Let's go have some breakfast and get the furniture inside for Darragh, now that the others are waking."

Misa greeted them as they came in, rather taken aback when they brought the long table in. Fiona was having a little difficulty taking the one end by herself, so Misa helped once they made it inside. Placing the table in the middle of the room, it took up the majority of the space.

"Chairsss?" Misa asked.

"We'll get them," Fiona told her. "You focus on food."

"Yesss," Misa replied as she went into the kitchen.

Darragh came out of his room just as the last chair was brought in. "Darragh," Sean called out, "wait a second. Fiona brought over the table and chairs."

"I thought something had changed," Darragh said. "You were able to finish all of the chairs?"

"I had some help," Fiona said. "Sean is adept at Shaping, at least with plant life."

"Intriguing," Darragh said, his brows raised. "What will you be working on next?"

"Once they bring me more logs, I need to finish the cots," Fiona said as she turned to the kitchen. "I'm going to help Misa."

"That is fine," Darragh said as his hand found the chair before him. Sitting, his sightless gaze turned to Sean with eerie accuracy. "You finished all three logs?"

"Yeah," Sean said as he looked at the table. "Are there going to be specific seats for people?"

"Whelan will be on my right, Cian on my left, those are the only two that are spoken for. Fiona should sit at the end of the table," Darragh said.

Sean took the spot to the right of where Fiona would sit. "I'm exhausted now," Sean yawned loudly.

"I do not doubt it," Darragh said. "You used my axe all day, then Shaped all night. I'm amazed you can even speak coherently."

"Some think that even when I'm not tired," Sean laughed as Whelan entered the room.

"Morning," Whelan said tersely, taking the seat to Darragh's right as if it were his due.

"Morning," Sean replied, with Darragh just nodding.

The other hunters all filed in after Whelan, except for Myna. They all sat in a row with Whelan. Sean thought that was a bad idea, but kept silent.

"I see that she was able to finish the table, at least," Whelan said, his voice tinged with scorn.

"And cots for some of us," Cian said as he entered the house, followed by the other woodsmen. "I'm sure she'll finish the others when she gets more wood."

"She made you a cot, but I don't have one?" Whelan hissed.

"Gave all of us cots," Eagon said with a grin. "I'm sure you'll be next."

"She gave cots to all of you, while none of my hunters have one?" Whelan's voice rose. "Is she losing what little is left of her mind? Why would you be a priority over us, when we supply the meat for the table?"

"Without us bringing her logs, she wouldn't be able to make anything," Cian pointed out as the lumberjacks all took seats along the other side of the table.

"She will do as she needs to, Whelan," Darragh said. "I trust her to do what must be done. You will get yours in due time."

"Of course, chief," Whelan said with a grimace.

Myna came into the room a moment later, taking a seat at the end of the hunters group. "You're late," Whelan snapped at her.

"I was delayed, my apologies," Myna said, her voice soft as she bowed her head to Whelan. "I will not be late again."

"Damn well better not," Whelan growled.

Sean blinked tiredly at Myna, wondering again why she always wore a leather cap that came down the sides of her head, when none of the others wore any head covering at all. Shaking his head while rubbing his eyes, he wondered if he would be able to stay awake through the meal.

"Breakfassst," Misa announced a moment later, carrying out a tray. Fiona followed her with another.

Placing food before Darragh first, followed by Cian and Whelan, the two women served ten people before returning to the kitchen to bring more food out. Fiona took the seat Sean nudged out for her and gave him a smile as she sat. Misa took her bowl and curled up behind Darragh's chair to eat.

The meal was silent, something Sean was becoming used to, with everyone lost in their own thoughts. Sean found the grainy porridge a little bland, but filling, so he was content. The orange tea was bitter, but it helped give the meal some flavor. Whelan and the others left without comment as soon as everyone finished their meal.

"Maybe he is bitter at not providing meat last night," Cian snickered. "Sean," he said, turning his eyes to the almost sleeping man, "get some rest. We'll have you with us tomorrow, right?"

"That's the plan," Sean yawned. "Don't overdo it."

"Never," Cian laughed and led the others out.

"I ssshall bring the sssleeping ssstuff for you," Misa said as she finished gathering bowls.

"Don't," Sean yawned again. "I'll be sacking out on Fiona's floor. I don't want to get underfoot here."

Darragh's brows both shot up, "Fiona's?"

"I thought it best. My floor is as good as yours, after all," Fiona said evenly, her cheeks taking on a soft pink hue. "He won't be in the way when the wives stop by to speak with you, either."

"I see," Darragh said evenly. "I will not counter your wisdom Fiona, but are you sure this is a good idea?"

Brow furrowed, Fiona nodded, "Why wouldn't it be?"

"Sean," Darragh said, "would you mind excusing us for a minute or two?"

Shrugging and yawning again, Sean got up. "I'll be outside."

Minutes later, Fiona came out with a pensive look on her face. Stopping next to Sean, her face was turned away from him. "You still wish to sleep on my floor? Realizing it is just for sleep and that is all, right?"

"Yes, and yes," Sean said as he struggled to keep his eyes open. "If you're uncomfortable with the idea, I can sleep here instead. I would rather you be comfortable and happy than have me in your home."

Nodding, she turned to meet his sleepy gaze with a smile. "I just needed to verify, is all. Follow me and we'll have you asleep soon."

"Thanks," Sean yawned as he trailed after Fiona.

CHAPTER THIRTEEN

Sean dreamed of the Tri Dee Dana toasting each other over the freshly made body he now wore. He had just sat up on the slab they'd made him on, and was able to see the collection of Gods celebrating the completion of his body. Before he could ask a question, loud echoing footsteps made him look to the right, where Morrigan was striding towards him.

"Thank you for Agreeing, Sean Aragorn MacDougal," Morrigan said, bowing her head to him. "We will not ask you for any favors, nor impose any tasks on you. If you deem it a worthy task to topple the Queens from their perch, we would be grateful for the chance to return to our people. I have looked at the strands again and your future is far from set. You shall be a nexus of change, and no one who meets you will be bound to the path they were before. All will be given the chance to shake off whatever constrained them, and to grow as they see fit."

A deep, gravelly bass boomed out, "We have all come to see you off, and those who could gifted you some of their power." Sean's head turned to find the speaker, an old man with white hair and a wild beard. "Even I've given you a gift." The speaker's face and body changed, becoming that of a young man in his prime, the voice changing to match his appearance, "We should've listened before, but we didn't. Now it is your wisdom that will decide the future." Again, the voice changed to match a new face on the same being, a man with deep, fresh wounds marking his face. "From us, we wish you joy and a long life." The speaker bowed to Sean, followed by the others.

"If Dagda is done," a thin reed of a man said from the side, his hands moving in a weird pattern, "I have the portal ready."

"Hopefully we will meet again, in time," Morrigan added as Sean felt the slab tilt towards the thin man. "May your feet be always swift, and your vision sharp."

"Wait," Sean managed just as a white opening swallowed him whole and he began falling past the stars towards a planet below him. "Oh, fuck."

∽

Snorting, Sean jerked upright as real footsteps pulled him out of the dream. "Is it time to wake?"

Fiona sat at her table in one of the chairs they had made the night before. "I did not mean to wake you," she apologized. "You can return to sleep if you need."

Sean shrugged and got up. "It's fine. I need to be able to sleep again tonight, after all." Rubbing the gunk from his eyes, he took the open chair at the table, "What time is it?"

"High sun," Fiona replied as she poured him some tea. "You snore loudly," she said with a faint smile.

"Cian said the same thing yesterday," Sean chuckled with a smile. "I'll need to see about fixing that eventually."

"Did you sleep well?"

"Better than you, as I don't recall you snoring," Sean said as he sipped the mint tea. "I wonder, is this the routine that the village will continue with? Trees, Shaping, and hunting?"

"For years, probably," Fiona nodded. "It will be rather difficult to attract more people to something so far removed from the Quadital."

"What is the Quadital?"

"They are the four capital cities the Queens rotate amongst," Fiona replied. "They are separated by a lot of land, mostly farmland, though there are a number of cities and towns. Outside of the Quadital, cities and towns of various sizes extend for five hundred miles, and at the farthest reaches, you find places like this. Past that are the Wilds, where those who seek adventure or to escape civilization go."

"The Queens change capitals?" Sean asked, intrigued.

"Yes, they change with the seasons," Fiona replied between sips. "Always directly opposite the other as they circle the land, bringing Summer and Winter with them."

"Do the Queens cause the change, or do they simply follow the change?"

"The change follows them, or at least, the histories say that is the case. It is said that, long ago, the Winter Queen refused to follow the pattern. In doing so, she brought a terrible winter over the land and Summer ended up along her edge. The nobles of each court started fighting along the boundary of the divide. Summer proved to be more powerful in the end. Winter fled to where she belonged, and her grasp was broken. It took decades for the land that had been held by the long touch of winter to finally overcome the strain and begin to flower and grow again."

"Do the two Queens never meet face-to-face?"

"Once every hundred years, they meet at the center of the Quadital, barring emergencies that demand they meet right away. The city of Accord lies in the middle of the Quadital. It is the biggest of the cities, as it lies at the heart of the Queens' power. The buildings are fashioned from living trees or from the very earth, carved by the most powerful of Shapers. No single structure in the city was built—all were Shaped over the long years the city has been there. The Queens meet for a full year in Accord to renew the Agreements between them, and to start new ones. During that time, Accord is the most dangerous place to be, as agents of both Queens work in the background to weaken the other. When they leave the city, it grows peaceful again, becoming a beacon for anyone who wishes to grow. It is said that all the most powerful beings have spent long years in Accord soaking in the leftover energy the Queens expend during the meeting."

"Something to see, eventually," Sean said. "When is the next meeting between the Queens?"

"I believe it is in another thirty-three years," Fiona said, "but I could be off by a year or two. Why, are you planning on leaving soon?"

"Not soon, but I think seeing it without the Queens there would be for the best," he chuckled.

"The safest, at the very least," Fiona chuckled with him.

"Do you just wait for the logs before dinner?"

"Mostly. Sometimes, I lay out my fortune with the cards, or I read one of my few books again. There is not much else for me to do. I might have worked a little more, but we used all the logs last night."

"So we did," Sean smiled. His smile faded as an idea struck him. "Fiona, do you have anything made of metal that I might try an experiment on? Something you don't care much for?"

"I have a hair pin I never use, would that work?" Fiona asked as she retrieved the bronze stick engraved with butterflies. "What are you wanting to try?"

"You'll know soon enough if it works," Sean said as he accepted the bronze piece.

Fiona arched a brow at him in silence, waiting to see what he was going to do. Sean focused on the metal in his hands and tried to call forth the same feeling he'd had last night when he Shaped the wood. Staring at the bronze, he tried to feel a connection to it like he had with the log when Fiona had shown him. After a moment, a faint bass hum seemed to start in his fingers, the feeling growing as it rapidly spread through his body. Smile forming, he watched as the bronze hair pin began to shrink and widen. Fiona gasped sharply.

"You can't be serious. Plant *and* metal?" Fiona whispered, watching the stick in Sean's hands Shape itself to his will as his fingers glided over it. "Dual Shapers are as rare as hen's teeth," Fiona said, her eyes wide.

"Give me your hand," Sean said softly as he held the bronze on his palm, no longer Shaping it, but letting the energy stay strong.

"You can't mean—" Fiona stared in disbelief, then reached across the table to cup her hand under his. "My blood has no affinity for metal. I can't..." she trailed off as she felt a faint hum start to vibrate in her hand.

"Use your other hand," Sean urged her. "Focus on the similarity between your hand and the bronze."

Fiona changed hands, then took a deep breath as the hum started again, much stronger than before. "Do the Tuatha Dé Danann really care?" Her question was whispered, almost inaudible. "I would never have thought about trying this."

"The Shame the Queens gave you might have been an unintentional gift," Sean said as he dropped the bronze into her mithril hand. "Shape it, Fiona."

Focused solely on the squat piece of bronze, she began to pull and thin it. She pulled the metal into a long, thin wire, which she began to twist into a rope of bronze. The metal seemed to flow under her hand. When she stopped, a twisted rope bracelet lay in her palm. Lifting her wide eyes to Sean's, the shock and wonder on her face spoke volumes.

"It seems I'm not the only dual Shaper in this village," he said with a broad smile. "I do believe you are more than you ever suspected."

Lips parting, cheeks burning, her breath came in small pants. "You've changed me—"

"No," Sean said simply, holding up his hand to forestall her. "All I did was show you a possibility. You stepped through the door and accepted a gift from me. It was the least I could do for the gift you gave me last night. I would call us even in this exchange."

"No! We are not," Fiona disagreed, shaking her head sharply. Pausing as she tried to find the words, her chest heaving with the excitement of success. "I might be Shamed in the eyes of society, but if I let this be known, then even nobles would crawl over each other for my services. While I might have shown you a dormant Talent that resided in you, you have shown me a new side to me—not just in ability, but also a new way of seeing myself as a person. I am indebted to you, Sean MacDougal. I will honor that debt in some way before you leave this village, as this village is surely too small a place for you to stay."

Sean stalled by downing the tea in his cup, buying the time he needed to get his words lined up. "While I disagree with how much value you place on what I've done, I won't try to dissuade you, Fiona. I would ask for two things to call us even, and one of them is quite personal."

"I will do them," Fiona said, leaning forward to place the bracelet in his hand, "if you accept this gift in return."

Using the simple clasp, he put the bracelet on. "Fair trade." Meeting her eyes, he could see excitement in hers, as well as a touch of hope. "The first is an easy thing to ask; will you continue to teach me until I leave this village?"

"Of course. As you are also teaching me, that is an easy request and should almost not count," Fiona replied quickly.

"The more personal thing..." Sean trailed off for a second, breaking eye contact with her. "I want you to embrace this new facet of yourself wholly; leave Silvershame behind and become Mithrilsoul."

"Oh," Fiona said, the disappointment loud in that single word. "I will try, Sean." Getting up, she went to her bed and pulled a small chest from under it. "If you'll excuse me, I have some things I need to do." Her voice was odd and she wouldn't meet his eyes.

Thinking he might have overstepped himself by asking her to change her name, he got up and went to the door. "I'll see you for dinner, I hope," he said as he opened the door.

"Of course," Fiona said flatly.

The silence stretched for a moment before Sean left, berating himself as he went. *Idiot. You knew she hated that name, but you brought it up again and then named her like she's some kind of pet*, he cursed inwardly. Shaking his head, he found the village seemingly empty, but the sun was just past midday. He went to use the single outhouse, not looking forward to the rough leaves that were used for paper, and found the women in the small farm area, tending the crops.

"Afternoon, ladies," Sean greeted them with a smile.

"Works all day and all night, then goes to a woman's home, and greets us like everything is normal," Tamaya said archly, a single brow raised as she stood up from where she had been working. "What wonders are you going to accomplish today, Sean MacDougal? You seem to have bewitched all of our husbands into thinking you are some powerful ally here to help us get the village started."

Blindsided by her greeting, Sean stood there blinking at her, "Err... huh?"

The women broke into laughter at his dumbstruck expression. "You really got him with that one, Tamaya," Enna snickered.

Tamaya came over to the fence that had been erected around the garden, her grin wide and full of crooked teeth. "I was just having you on. We're thankful you've helped them all find a bit of fire again, as well as Fiona, it seems." Lips curling into a salacious smirk, Tamaya leaned in a bit more, "So, is her metal side warm to the touch?"

Stepping back as he stared at her, he was at a loss for words. "Oh, the silent lover type, are you?" Rylee chuckled at him.

"We didn't do anything of the sort," Sean protested. "Fiona and I only slept, her in her bed and me on the floor."

Booing, the women all shook their heads at him. "A shame. We thought maybe you had melted her icy heart a bit," Tamaya sighed. "Ah well, maybe it was a bit too much to hope for."

"You're all cracked, you know that, right?" Sean asked.

"No," Tamaya said. "We've been less than accepting of her and, while she bears a Shame, so does Darragh, and we don't shun him. With how accepting of her you've been, we realized it was time that we tried to do the same, and not keep her at arm's length like we have been."

"Oh," Sean said, turning over her words in his mind. "She would probably welcome your friendship. She's not doing much at the moment, maybe you could head over and talk with her a bit."

"Not going to go back and help her test her new bed a bit first?" Tamaya grinned at him.

"Really?" Sean exhaled loudly. "That's it, I'm using the outhouse, then going over to speak with Darragh. You're all as crazed as I thought!" Laughter trailed after him as he walked away, comments about him being the crazy one trailing after him.

Using the outhouse was worse than using a modern day port-a-potty, like those found at most outdoor events. Grabbing one of the leaves to finish up with, Sean frowned, a strained smile coming to his lips as he focused on it. Its texture began to change, becoming softer and more pliable. He couldn't quite match the softness of the toilet paper he was used to, but it was better than it had been. Using two pieces, he finished up and left the box. With a thoughtful look, he took the basket with him when he left, walking over to the nearest house and leaning against the wall. It only took him a few minutes to transform all of the leaves into the more comfortable version he'd used. He returned the basket, then headed off to see Darragh, wondering if anyone would mention the leaves later.

CHAPTER FOURTEEN

Misa opened the door of Darragh's home shortly after he knocked. "Afternoon, Misa. Might I speak with Darragh for a while?"

"He hasss been waiting for you," Misa said as she let him in, left him with Darragh, and went to the kitchen.

Darragh was seated at the head of the table, so Sean took the chair to his left. "Afternoon, Darragh."

"Good day to you as well, Sean," Darragh replied. "What can I do for you?" he asked as Misa brought them both tea.

"I was hoping to learn more about the world, and maybe learn magic from Misa," Sean said, sipping the tea which had a strong berry flavor. "This is delicious, Misa."

"Ward brought the tea back from town with him, along with the repaired hand axe lassst night," Misa told him.

"What information do you seek today?" Darragh asked, bringing the conversation back on track.

"You've told me of Agreements, and what follows them. Fiona told me a little of the Quadital and how the capitals are laid out, how the Queens move from capital to capital, and about their meeting once every century. Knowing that, I was wondering what the average person's life is like?"

"Interesting. Not a question I had anticipated," Darragh said. "I would think the average life is the same everywhere. Wake, work, family, and then sleep. Maybe once a tenday, they go to the pub to see friends. Most people will never enter a serious Agreement that might bring them to the Queens' attention. What were you seeking with that question?"

"I'm not sure, really," Sean said after a minute. "I just wanted an idea of how I could fit in easily. I don't want to draw attention to myself."

Darragh nodded, "A very worthwhile endeavor. Unfortunately for you, you seem to have the Talent to Shape, and Shapers are sought after as long as they bear no Shame. Any of the nobles would be interested in retaining your abilities, if for no other reason than to deny others access to your Talent."

"Letting it become known I can Shape would be something to avoid, then, if possible. Good to know," Sean said. He sipped the tea, enjoying the flavor more than any of the others he'd had previously, while he put his thoughts in order. "Considering your village out here, on the edge of the map, as it were, is there a living to be made off exploring the wilds?"

"Yes, and no," Darragh replied. "If you have the ability to draw accurate maps, you can make some money off that. You might also find something of value in your travels. It is said this world was not always under the sway of the Queens, and that the wilds still possess things they would pay well to have or know about. From my younger days, I can recall a band of explorers that traveled far to the east and found a ruined city built of basalt. The Winter Queen lavished the group with their hearts' desires for the location of that city, along with the Agreement that no other would learn of that site from the group. Or, at any rate, that is how the rumor goes. I did once speak to someone who, while not a Fey, lived like a noble. He would only say he found something that he sold the location of to the Winter Queen."

"Risk and reward is what I'm hearing," Sean said.

"Indeed, any venture poses such a dilemma," Darragh chuckled, holding out his cup for Misa to refill.

"Do the explorers have a group or guild that they all collectively belong to?" Sean asked.

"They do, but it is very difficult to gain entry. Only those who can prove they've found something worthy of the guild's attention are accepted," Darragh replied. "The only other option is to have a Talent that they seek."

"Good to know," Sean said. "Might I excuse myself to ask Misa to train me in magic?"

"I will be glad to, Sssean," Misa said as she came around Darragh's chair. "I ssshall take him to the kitchen, ssso asss not to bother you."

"That is fine, Misa. I hope you can learn at least a small something from her, Sean," Darragh said, closing his eyes while he sipped his tea.

The kitchen was small, with limited storage space and a fireplace taking up most of the room. Sean took in the room, seeing the bronze knives and wooden cutting boards. The edges of the cutting boards were covered in dried blood. "This is where all the food is prepared?"

"Yesss," Misa said catching his tone. "Problem?"

"Bacteria. This is a breeding ground for things that can make people sick."

"What isss bactara?" Misa asked.

"Tiny organisms, so tiny they can't be seen with the naked eye. They carry disease and sickness with them, and spread through unsanitary food preparation areas, among other things."

"No one hasss gotten sssick," Misa replied, bridling at Sean's words.

"Yet," Sean sighed. "Bacteria grows, and the problem becomes worse the longer they have to breed. I really want to clean this place up."

"My kitchen isss clean already," Misa said, her tail lightly thumping the floor in annoyance.

Shaking his head, Sean bit back his knee-jerk reply. "Misa, your food is delicious. It is something I look forward to. With that said, though, I would really like to scrub down your prep area, please."

Tail thumping, Misa glared at him, tongue flicking out a couple of times before she replied. "If... if you can sssummon water today, then yesss, you can clean. If you fail, you will never talk about my kitchen again."

"We have an Agreement," Sean said, feeling the weight of the words settle over him. Turning his attention to Misa, he waited for her to teach him.

"Ssso eager to learn," Misa hissed with laughter as she brought an empty pot over and motioned him to sit. Looking at the floor, he saw that it was mostly clean and did as she bade him. "For ssstartersss, you will need to chant the wordsss. It helpsss to focusss the energy you will ssspend to sssummon the water. Lisssten to my wordssss carefully," Misa told him sternly, "From water comesss life, without water there issss death. I bessseech the Queensss to hear my call to let me sssummon forth the most preciousss of all liquidsss. Come now water, anssswer my call and bring forth your esssssssence for me." While she said the words, her arms moved in a counter-clockwise circle above the pot as her three-fingered hands motioned a complex pattern. When the words ended, a stream of water flowed from her hands into the pot. After a minute, Misa pulled her hands further apart and the water stopped flowing. "Did you hear the wordsss?"

"Yeah," Sean said before repeating the words back perfectly, dropping the excessive hisses that seemed natural to Misa.

Misa nodded, "Very good, but did you follow the arcane pattern that I created with my handsss?"

"I know the pattern of your arms, but your fingers were a bit faster than I was able to follow the first time," Sean admitted, as he hadn't been expecting Misa's fingers to be as nimble as they appeared to be.

"Watch, thisss time without wordsss," Misa waited for his nod, then swept her arms and fingers through the pattern again. Water spilled out from her hands and into the pot again, which she stopped a moment later. "Did you sssee?"

Sean could see the pattern in his mind and tried to replicate it, but his fingers weren't quite able to match hers. "I know what you did but..." he spread his five-digit hands out, "how do I account for the extras?"

Misa hissed another laugh, "Very good, you asssk the right quessstion. You can't make the sssame motionsss." Her middle finger bent backward at a sharp angle without her touching it. "Naga are more flexible than humansss," she said, with more hissing laughter.

"Fair enough," Sean said with a faint smile. "How do I manage to make the correct motions, then?"

"Practice," Misa said as she settled in, her vertical pupils focused on him. "I will wait."

Shaking his head with a wry grin Sean chuckled, "Okay, here we go."

He wasn't sure how long he worked at trying to perfect the motions, but he stopped when his fingers started to cramp. Misa handed him some tea when he paused, "Drink."

Taking the cup, he sipped at it, "Thanks. What am I doing wrong?"

"Nothing, and everything," Misa said as she settled back into her spot.

"Vague, not very helpful, and slightly condescending," Sean said.

"Yesss. I don't get to be ssso often," she replied with amusement as her tongue poked out from her snout slightly.

"You were just waiting for me to give up?" Sean asked with a raised brow.

"Yesss," Misa nodded. "Now I will tell you the trick. Neither the wordsss nor the motionsss are what makesss the magic happen. They are only foci that helpsss one bring the energy inssside, out to impossse your will upon the world. Sssome use carved wandsss or ssstavesss to help focusss their mindsss; my people teach by wordsss and gesssturesss."

"So just focus, and believe I can make it happen? That's it?" Sean asked with a frown. "It can't be that easy."

"Easssy, no. Imposssing your will on a world is not easssy. Like ssswinging a sssword, the more you do it, the more natural it isss and easssier to accomplisssh. If your mind waversss on the magic, it will fail."

"Okay, so I should set my own words and motions to use as a focus until it becomes second nature, then I can start trying to drop one or both of them, like you do."

Misa nodded, "Yesss. Try again?"

Downing the tea, Sean nodded, "Yeah."

Closing his eyes, Sean felt for that vibration he related to Shaping. After a minute, he felt a small vibration near his heart. Focusing on that, he held his out left arm, his hand parallel to the floor and his elbow tucked to his side. Breathing slowly, he put his right hand, curled into a fist on his hip, letting the elbow flare out wide. Taking a few deep breaths, he began to chant.

"I'm a little teapot, short and stout. Here is my handle, and here is my spout. When I get all steamed up, I just shout. Now tip me over and pour me out." He felt the vibration in his chest surge out along his left arm as he tilted sideways. The draining of his energy was more pronounced than it was with Shaping, but not excessive. Misa's gasp and the splashing of water brought his eyes open. Water was indeed pouring from his left hand.

"Holy fuck," Sean laughed. He let out a surprised yelp as the steaming hot water hit his leg. Rolling away from the water made him break the teapot position and the magic stopped. "Why was it hot?" Sean asked Misa as he rubbed at his leg.

Misa stared at the steaming water before tentatively touching it. "It ssshould not be..." she trailed off and brought her eyes back to him. "You do thingsss that ssshould not happen," Misa stated simply her tongue flickering rapidly. "You did what you sssaid and sssummoned the water, ssso now you can clean my kitchen."

Sean considered what just happened with a frown. *Maybe because*

I was specific that it's when the teapot shouts, which is when the water boils, Sean mulled over internally. Shaking his head, he gave Misa a grin, "Thank you, Misa. Do you have any soap?"

CHAPTER FIFTEEN

Stepping out of Darragh's house, he saw the lumberjacks just coming into the village with a log on their shoulders, wearing exhausted but smiling faces. "Cian, good to see you had a good day," Sean said as he went over to talk to them as they dropped the log.

Cian nodded, "It was a bit rougher without the extra body. Seems we might have forgotten in the last few days what trying to get two trees down used to be like."

"He's not kidding," Walden added, "we rotated who was using Dark Cutter but it was not as easy as the last two days had been."

"Glad to know I'm useful," Sean chuckled. "I had a question, as I wasn't paying attention over the last few days. Where do the regular axes get stored?"

Brow furrowing, Cian replied, "I keep them in my home. Did you need one for tonight?"

"Can I see all of them until dinner?" Sean asked, keeping a blank face.

"Sure," Cian said, shucking the axes off his shoulder and setting them down next to the log. "Here you go." He handed over the hand axes, which were attached to a belt he was wearing. "We just got the one axe back from town, from your misadventure with it, so please don't break it again."

Sean laughed, "I promise."

"We'll see you at dinner," Tamaya said, taking Cian's arm and leading him away.

"At dinner," Sean replied as he draped the belt over his shoulder, before knocking on Fiona's door.

"Who is it?" Fiona called from inside.

"Sean. I'm hoping you'll let me step inside for a few minutes."

A minute passed before the door opened. "What did you need, Sean?" Fiona asked as she stepped aside for him to enter.

"I wanted to look over these axes, but Darragh said that if my ability to Shape gets around too much I could be sought after, which I'd rather avoid at least for now."

Eyes scrunching as she looked at him, she let out a sigh. "Are the others outside?"

"The axes? Yeah," Sean said.

Fiona brought them inside, shutting the door behind her. She placed them gently on her table before taking a seat. "I see they brought me a log again. Are you going to help me Shape it tonight?"

Hearing the hint of hope, Sean paused before he answered. "Fiona…" he paused as he looked at the hand axes he had placed before him. "I upset you earlier. I want to apologize for that before anything else." Lifting his gaze from the axes, he found her heterochromatic eyes watching him. "When I suggested changing your name earlier, I didn't mean to hurt you."

Fiona let her head bow so her hair fell forward, creating a curtain between them. "I know. I was being foolish. I'm sorry if my reaction caused you distress, Sean. It wasn't my intent."

"To answer your question, I would love to spend the night with you laughing, talking, and spending time enjoying your company," Sean said. "I don't know if Darragh would consider that fair for the Agreement we have in place, though. I'll be going out with Cian and the others tomorrow again, and seeing what we can do now that I can do something with the trees because of what you taught me."

"I see," the two words contained a mixture of sadness and joy. "I don't wish to cause you to break an Agreement," Fiona said after a brief pause. "I do hope we can Shape something again in the future."

"Want to help me check the axes?" Sean asked. "We can both Shape wood and metal, and it would go faster with a friend's help."

"Friend..." the word seemed to linger on her tongue for a moment. "I will be happy to help you, Sean. Might I request something in trade?"

"Of course," Sean said with a smile, happy she had accepted his apology for earlier. "Did you have something specific in mind?"

"Not yet, but I'll give it some thought," Fiona said. "I'll ask for something later."

"Fair enough," Sean said, "now let's look over these axes and see if we can improve them."

"Sounds good to me," the happiness in her voice was clear, and was made more clear when she brushed her hair back and her radiant smile was on display.

That made Sean smile in return. He didn't understand why she was so happy, but her smile was among the most beautiful things he had ever seen. Pulling his eyes away from her face, he focused on the axes, as he had something to do and she would distract him to no end if he didn't focus.

Picking up one of the axes, he placed the bronze head across one of his palms and held the haft in his other hand. Reaching into his middle, he felt the vibration he associated with the energy he used for Shaping and magic. The vibrations filled his body quickly as he touched that core. Focusing on the axe, he didn't try to Shape it, but looked into the tool, to determine if it had flaws or deficiencies and whether or not he could make it better. The weapon seemed to turn translucent in his hands, the flaws in the blade and haft standing out as red spots in the pale blue image. Before he could start trying to fix them, another image appeared over the top of the tool.

Bronze hand axe
Common tool

Poor quality

"Game menus. Probably Oghma, he is the god of knowledge, after all," Sean muttered under his breath. "Maybe Morrigan. She did say I would like it here."

"What was that?" Fiona asked as she continued to stare at the axe in her hands.

"I can see the flaws, and was wondering if you can see them too?" Sean asked, to forestall having to explain his muttering, and out of genuine curiosity.

"I can feel them, but the axe looks the same as it did. Do you see it differently?" Fiona asked as she glanced up to Sean.

"Yeah," Sean said, concentrating on the ugly red line halfway down the haft of the axe he held. "The axe looks like glass and the defects are red discolorations."

"Hmm. It would be helpful to be able to really see the flaws instead of just feeling them," Fiona said as she set the axe down. "Do you think you could teach someone that Talent?"

After he fixed the red streak on the edge of the blade, he removed all of the red splotches. As he stared at the axe in his hand, another tool-tip appeared.

Bronze hand axe
Common tool
Uncommon quality

"Neat. It's much better now," Sean said, turning to Fiona. "I wouldn't even know how to try to teach you. I don't even know what I did."

"If I asked, would you try for me?" She tilted her head to the side a fraction, brushing her hair back behind her ear and letting her blue eye be seen again.

"I will try, if you'll tell me more about your heritage," Sean countered.

Her playful demeanor shifted to uncertainty, eyes shifting side to side as she licked her lips. "That is not something worth the trade," she said.

"I think it is, and when bartering, the value of what something is worth is flexible," Sean said evenly. "If you don't want to, that's fine. I just wanted to get to know you better."

Licking her lips again, she took a deep breath, "Okay. If you try to teach me how to see into an object, I will tell you something about myself." She grabbed the next hand axe, keeping her eyes locked on it. "You're so different," Fiona murmured in a soft whisper that wasn't meant to be heard.

"I try," Sean said.

Fiona jerked her head up and stared at him with wide eyes, "You heard that?"

"Yes. Was I not supposed to? I've noticed all my senses are sharper here than I previously had. I've heard everything said in my presence."

"We have sharp hearing in common then, at least," Fiona smiled.

"And Shaping, but that's because you showed me how," Sean pointed out, setting aside his second axe once he'd fixed all the flaws in it.

"Two things are a good place to start," Fiona said as she picked up her third axe.

"A place to start?" Sean asked.

"I think we can finish these before dinner," Fiona said, dodging his question.

Nodding, he focused on the task he'd asked her for help with, grateful that she was willing to help him. By the time he picked up the last axe, he could easily see how to fix all of the flaws. Fiona set her last axe down and sat back, letting her head hang off the back of her chair as she let out a deep sigh.

Setting down the last axe, having finished it quickly, he looked over at Fiona and felt his heart beat harder for a moment. Swallowing hard, his eyes traced the graceful lines of her neck, then trailed down her figure as she arched her back, stretching her arms over her head.

Tearing his eyes away just as she sat back upright, he coughed. "Ready for dinner?"

Glancing at him, seeing his nervousness and his flushed cheeks, her lips turned up at the corners. "Is that an invitation?"

"Huh?" Blinking, Sean met her eyes and found a knowing look in them as she smirked. "Umm, I mean, yes?"

Standing, Fiona put the hand axes back into the belt loops. "We need to drop these off with Cian, as well."

"Right," Sean agreed as he gathered up the first of the six large bronze axes. As he did, he smiled at how sleek and sharp each of them looked. With pursed lips, he focused on the axe and tried to get it to change as Fiona had done with her staff the other night.

The vibrating core inside him surged out along his arms, and the weapon seemed to become coated in the energy, wrapping a faint sheen of green around the blade. Imagining the haft lengthening and the blade slimming down to a point, he willed the weapon to change for him. A few seconds later, the axe had become a spear with a sharp tip and a thin coating of bronze covering half of the shaft.

"You are impossible," Fiona said softly. "It took me years to reach that level of control."

Grinning, Sean split the spear into two short blades of bronze covered wood. "This is amazing." Chuckling, he brought the two blades together and fused them into a single blade.

"I thought you were taking me to dinner?" Fiona asked.

The axe quickly replaced the blade. "Sorry, I got distracted."

"It happens, when men begin to play with their tools," Fiona fought to keep a grin off her face.

"Sharper than a serpent's tooth," Sean chuckled, "but accurate."

Outside, Sean waited for Fiona to shut her door before they started towards Cian's house. The two fell into step unconsciously as they crossed the village.

"How cute, Silvershame is on a date with the Outsider," Whelan sneered. "I guess that isn't too surprising, it's not like anyone who knows her would want to get close to her. I heard in the city she was as cold inside as her metal exterior. Is that true, MacDougal?"

Fiona's steps faltered for a second. Sean's free hand touched her elbow, steadying her. "Ignore him," Sean said, softly enough that only Fiona would hear him. "He'll get his in time. He wants a confrontation right now, and you don't fight people on their terms."

Fiona nodded as she kept walking, Sean's hand on her elbow. "It doesn't bother you? The idea of being on a date with me?" She also carefully pitched her voice too low for most to hear.

Turning his head a bit, he grinned at her. "Why would I object to dating a beautiful woman?"

"Just going to ignore your better, are you?" Whelan scoffed.

Raising his voice, Sean replied, "Not at all. Darragh wasn't talking to me, though. Neither was Fiona or Cian."

"What?" Whelan snarled as they walked away from him. "We will see who is whose better soon, MacDougal." Whelan stalked off towards Darragh's house, his fists clenched.

"What happened to ignoring him?" Fiona asked.

"I'm only human," Sean chuckled.

CHAPTER SIXTEEN

Cian and Tamaya weren't at home, so Fiona set the axes just inside their door before heading over to Darragh's. Being the last two to enter, all eyes turned to them. All of the wives smiled at Fiona with speculative gazes. Fiona stopped just inside the door under the concentrated, inquisitive eyes. "I-I'll go help Misa," Fiona stammered, darting into the kitchen as soon as the words left her lips.

Sean watched her go before taking his usual seat. "Cian, I'll be going back out with you tomorrow."

"We'll be glad to have you," Cian said. "We'll be holding off on four trees, though."

Sean chuckled, "Oh come on, don't you want to do it again?"

The other lumberjacks all shook their heads with various sounds of disagreement. Cian grinned, "Seems like we have a majority."

"Fine," Sean replied.

"You can keep him," Whelan snorted. "He doesn't have the skills to help us do the hard job."

"We'll see after tomorrow," Sean said. "I planned on learning from Myna tomorrow afternoon, and then going out with you the day after."

"We'll try to keep you safe," Whelan replied. "Myna, when we get back tomorrow, you are to train him as best you can. You will also be responsible for him when we hunt."

"Yes," Myna said simply.

"It is decided," Darragh stated.

"Food," Misa said before anyone else could add anything.

Misa and Fiona placed a soup mostly consisting of broth, a handful of diced vegetables, and a few pieces of meat before each person. Once everyone was served, Cian mumbled under his breath, "Seems someone failed getting meat for us again."

"What was that, coward?" Whelan seethed, staring daggers at Cian.

"Nothing," Cian said, taking a mouthful of soup.

"Not at the table," Darragh interjected before Whelan could say more.

The broth was bland, the meat was tough, and the vegetables were mush. Sean ate without complaint, but he thought about all the ways it could have been improved. He briefly wished James was with him; James had been a cook for years, and could have turned even this meal into something amazing. Finishing his soup, Sean wondered if Misa would let him make some suggestions. He wasn't James by any stretch of the imagination, but he might have a tip or two for her.

As soon as Fiona set her spoon down, Whelan stood and left the house, followed swiftly by the rest of the hunters, except for Myna. Myna's brown eyes went to Sean, "Tomorrow afternoon, training."

"I'll come back to the village, then," Sean told her.

"Only a half day with us? We might have to tax you a bit," Cian chuckled.

"We'll see what happens. I want to try something different tomorrow."

Cian paused on the way to the door, "That sounds either wonderful, or ominous. Guess we'll see which it is tomorrow."

"I will see you later?" Fiona asked as she helped Misa gather the dishes.

"I'll be along," Sean told her.

Once everyone was gone, Darragh spoke up, "What did you wish to learn tonight?"

"Tell me about the currency of this world—what does an average laborer make in a year?"

Darragh launched into an explanation of the world's currency; copper, bronze, silver and gold coins. The breakdown was familiar to Sean- one gold equaled 100 silver, one silver equaled 100 bronze, and one bronze equaled 100 copper. The average laborer would earn around eight bronze during the 360 days of the year. A Shaper could make over four silver a year from commissions, if they weren't Bonded.

Thanking Darragh for the lesson and finishing the tea Misa had provided, Sean excused himself to go meet with Fiona before he turned in for the night. Fiona was kneeling next to the log, Shaping a cot. Sean slowed his steps, watching her use both of her hands to mould the tree. A smile formed as he considered her rapid change. The confidence she felt now was obvious to him, even focused on her work. Before, she was slightly hunched from trying to hide her metallic limbs, but now she didn't seem to care.

Waiting for her to finish the cot, Sean leaned against the house and tried to see into the log, like he had before with the axes. The energy inside him responded to his intentions, but the log didn't seem to want to respond to him. Focusing, he strained, trying to force the sight to kick in. With a rush of energy, he felt a wave of vertigo and his vision swam out of focus for a moment. When his vision steadied, he could see the flaws inside the wood and was surprised to see the vivid green energy filling Fiona and flowing gently from her fingers, changing the wood and fixing its flaws.

Straightening up, Fiona smiled broadly as she looked at the finished cot. Her mithril hand stroked the wood with the gentlest of touches, like a lover. Sean was loathe to bring himself to her attention as he watched her. She was obviously pleased with her work, which finally prompted him to speak.

"You do wonderful work," Sean said softly, startling her.

"I didn't see you show up," Fiona said as she caught her breath.

"You were busy and I didn't want to interrupt," Sean said as he felt his energy continue to drain. "I need to try this quickly, though. It seems to be more taxing at range," he told her as he took a knee next to her.

"What do I need to do?" Fiona asked quickly, her eagerness to learn apparent.

The drain ebbed to a trickle as he knelt closer to the log. "I'm not sure, but we're going to try the idea I had earlier. First, close your eyes for me, then picture your energy filling your eyes."

Her eyes snapped shut as soon as he asked. Watching her carefully, he could see the energy in her core surge up in her, but as it reached her neck it seemed to hit a wall. "I... can't," Fiona murmured, seeming to strain to force her energy past the block.

"Okay, I'm going to move your hands. Don't do anything, just let your hands rest there," Sean said. She didn't fight him as he positioned her hands, though she continued trying to push her energy past the block around her throat. "I'm going to put my hands on you, is that okay?"

Her energy flared wildly for a minute, before calming. "Yes."

Placing his left hand on the back of her neck, he tried to see if he could connect his energy to hers. Slowly and gently, he tried to push his energy into her, only to be rebuffed by an unseen force. Frowning, he pushed a little harder, only to have that same force push back just as hard. Chewing his lip, he put his other hand over Fiona's eyes, and she let out a soft gasp. "Did you want me to stop?"

"No, I just wasn't expecting your hand over my eyes. It's a little intimate, don't you think?"

Blinking, Sean took stock of his body. He was only an inch away from her, with both of his hands controlling her head. "I guess it is..." Sean said, trailing off as his imagination provided other ideas of ways he could control her head intimately. Coughing, he shook the thoughts aside and focused on what he was trying to do. "I'm going to see if I can create a channel between my hands. Maybe if I can impart some of my energy into you, you can see the same way I can."

"Ah," the acknowledgement was soft. "I was curious why you were doing things this way."

"I'm about to start," Sean said as he pushed energy from his right hand towards her eyes and tried to draw energy with his left. The attempt failed utterly. After a minute, he removed his hands from her head. "It's not working."

"What shall we try next?" Fiona asked, keeping her eyes closed.

"I don't know. You seem to have some kind of block right about your neck, which is stopping your energy from progressing up to your eyes."

Fiona leaned back, pressing her back into his chest. "Hmm, so we've reached an impasse?"

Swallowing as her warmth seemed to heat his body, Sean stammered, "U-Uh, y-yeah... it seems."

"You feel warm," Fiona said softly.

"You're the warm one," Sean replied, afraid to move.

"Can I try something to see if it helps?" Fiona asked as she pulled away from him.

"Sure," the word came out in a relieved, yet disappointed, exhale.

Fiona stood up and went around him, then knelt behind him. "Close your eyes. I'm going to try what you just did," she said, her breath tickling his neck as she whispered the words.

Placing his hands on the log, Sean closed his eyes and tried to focus on what they were doing, and not Fiona behind him or her warm breath on his neck. Her slender fingers cupped the back of his neck as her other hand covered his eyes, just as he had done to her. He could still feel her energy swirling inside of her, even though he couldn't see it. An almost unfelt pressure seemed to press in on his eyes and neck before it vanished. The pressure returned, increasing by a fraction before it stopped again.

"Wait," Sean said, "before you try again, tell me just beforehand."

"Okay," her words tickled his ear.

Gulping, as his brain conjured up images of what she could do with those lips and his neck, Sean fought to maintain his focus on what they were trying to do. When she began to count down from three, he was able to ignore the distractions. As she got to one and began to try pushing energy into him, he pulled in unison. A sharp pain seared his mind.

"Ngh!" an involuntary gasp of pain escaped him.

That was enough for Fiona to immediately stop what she was doing and caused Sean to lose his concentration on seeing energy.

"Are you okay?" Fiona asked as she pulled her hands away.

"I'm fine," Sean said as the pain vanished and a lingering discomfort took its place. Rubbing at his face, he sighed as the discomfort faded away. "Okay. Not trying that again."

"Maybe it's not possible to learn," Fiona said, a hint of disappointment clear in her tone.

"Maybe," Sean said, but he didn't like giving up so easily. "I'll try to think of something else."

"That's fair," Fiona said as she moved away from behind him and knelt by the log again. "I'm going to work, if that's okay?"

"It is. I should be going to get some sleep as it is," Sean replied.

"I promised to tell you about my lineage..." Fiona said uncertainly.

"Oh, right," Sean said, shifting to kneel a little further up the log. "I'll help you Shape while you talk."

"Thank you," Biting her lower lip, she took a deep breath. "My mother is half Dryad," she began slowly. "Which, of course, means I am also part Dryad. That is the source of my Talent for Shaping wood. My father was a good man and tried his best to provide for us, but he died in an accident when I was five. Mother didn't have much Talent for Shaping, but she did have some, which is what provided for us. When I was eight, she was Bonded by a rich merchant to Shape the goods he sold. It was a decent life. Mother was paid a fair, if not lavish, wage, and I don't recall ever wanting for anything. When I turned twelve, I was sent to Southpoint to be tested at the Academy. When my Talent and its strength was discovered, I began to be courted by the noble families at the Academy."

"You're part Dryad, huh? That would explain your natural affinity for plant life," Sean said as his hands ran over the wood, Shaping another cot.

Brow furrowing, she glanced at him. "You don't care?"

"Why should I?" Sean snorted softly. "No one chooses their family. Besides, I think you're pretty amazing."

Blinking slowly, Fiona shook her head. "What Whelan said earlier, about us on a date. Would you consider actually doing so with me?"

His hands wobbled as he Shaped the wood, and he had to go back and fix the spot. Taking a minute to let her words sink in, he took a deep breath. "It's been a long time since I went on a date, Fiona, and this village isn't exactly the best spot for one. If I can get a reprieve from Darragh and can take a day off again, then I would love to." He felt his cheeks heat and hoped he wasn't making a fool of himself.

"I'll talk with Darragh tomorrow, while you chop more supplies for me and train with Myna." Fiona's words were bubbly and full of happiness, "I'm sure he will agree to my request."

"Why me?" Sean asked, still off balance.

"You treat me as if I'm more than I am. My mixed blood doesn't bother you, my Shame doesn't bother you, and I have seen you being a good man. The better question would be, why me? Why would you agree to date someone like me?"

"You're gorgeous, inside and out, and you're getting over your low self-esteem, which is crazy sexy. I think you're smart, which I've always liked in women. I've seen you handle weapons—so I know that you can protect yourself, and others, if needed. Neither your blood nor your Shame will deter me, as they mean nothing to me."

They stared at each other for a moment before Fiona leaned in and placed a soft kiss on Sean's cheek. "You need to get some sleep for tomorrow, Sean. I hope you have pleasant dreams, and I look forward to seeing you in the morning."

Absently touching his cheek, a broad smile split his face. "I'll sleep like a babe now, Fiona. Don't overwork yourself, and I'll see you at breakfast." He felt like he was floating as he walked to Darragh's to sleep.

Fiona watched him go, her cheeks ablaze. She couldn't believe she'd been so bold. Shaking her head, she tried to go back to work, but her mind continually strayed to the outsider who had so quickly turned her world upside down and made her heart flutter like a young girl. "Tomorrow..."

CHAPTER SEVENTEEN

Waking from a sound sleep filled with dreams of wandering a city and sightseeing with Fiona, Sean stretched and yawned. The only interruption during his sleep had been when Misa snuck off to Darragh's room, and the ensuing sounds of pleasure, but he got back to sleep easily enough.

Sean went through a few exercises to limber up his back, still not used to sleeping on the floor. Nodding to Misa as she came out of Darragh's room, Sean had to ask, "Sleep well?"

"I wasss jussst waking Darragh," Misa replied.

"Of course," Sean said. "Can I help with breakfast this morning?"

"Yesss," her voice held a questioning tone as she led the way to the kitchen.

Sniffing, Sean realized that he could smell himself. "Misa, when and where does everyone bathe?"

"Once a tenday, on Oneday, we go to the river to bathe and wasssh clothing. Tomorrow isss that day," Misa replied as she grabbed a cauldron. "Breakfassst isss porridge," she told him, setting it next to the embers in the fireplace.

"Can we try something different this morning?" Sean asked.

"What?"

"Can I get some of the berry tea? I want to use it as the base liquid for the porridge."

"It doesssn't work well," Misa said. "I've tried it before."

"Damn," Sean said, "ah well, it was worth a try. Do the hunters at least forage while they're out?"

"No," Misa's voice was flat and disapproving, "Whelan thinksss it beneath them. Idiot, he doesssn't undersssstand how much better thingsss could be if he ssstopped being obssstinate."

"He seems to be a big problem. Why does Darragh put up with it?"

"Commanded to ssshepherd him," Misa said as she put the grainy porridge mixture into the cauldron. "Sssummon hot water, pleassse," Misa asked him.

Nodding, he moved to the pot and tried to summon water without the words or motions, but after a minute he gave up. "Not yet, it seems," he muttered.

"It takesss a long time," Misa told him.

"Never hurts to try," Sean shrugged. "I'm a little teapot..." Sean began to sing and formed himself into the teapot. At the end of the song he poured hot water from his hand into the cauldron. He could feel his core draining as the water poured from him. Once he had the cauldron filled to the point Misa wanted, he stopped and took a seat. "That was a big pot."

"Yesss," Misa said as she stirred the mixture, "not many could fill their sssecond time working water magic."

"I'm a freak," Sean chuckled.

"But a good one, who calls me friend," Fiona said from the doorway. "Morning Misa, morning Sean. I see that I'm not needed this morning."

"He asssked to help," Misa said. "He isss the only one in the village besidesss you who treatsss me asss an equal."

"All of us Shamed, Life Bonded, and Outcasts need to stick together," Fiona said. "Besides, you are a thousand times better a person than Whelan."

"That'sss like sssaying the sssun isss hotter than a torch. It'sss not hard," Misa hissed in laughter.

"Too true," Sean chuckled along with her.

"Did your guest leave, Darragh?" Whelan's voice carried easily from main room.

"No, I'm just being useful and trying to learn from your example, Whelan," Sean said from the kitchen doorway.

Eyes narrowing, Whelan's lips flattened out, "Ahh, I see. You shall need to be a quick learner when Myna trains you."

"I'm sure I'll be okay," Sean chuckled. "But thanks for thinking of me."

"Whelan is thinking of you?" Cian asked as he entered. "Color me surprised, here I always thought he only thought of himself."

"Wood lover," Whelan snapped.

"Enough," Darragh sighed. "Take your places, food will be served soon."

The hunters and lumberjacks all took their seats at Darragh's words. Misa came out of the kitchen with Fiona and Sean, all of them bearing bowls which they set before the people waiting. The meal followed the same pattern as those before—limited, if any, conversation, and as soon as the meal was done, Whelan and his hunters all left the room. Except for Myna, who stayed behind.

"Not going with them?" Sean asked Myna.

"Training you," Myna stated. "I will go with you to the stream, wait for high sun, then train you. This is what Whelan told me this morning."

"Works for me," Sean said. "Cian, you okay with that?"

Grim faced, Cian nodded. "It will help. Today is the last of the tenday, so we will be attacked on the way to the water. Make sure to have an axe in hand."

"Will do," Sean said.

"Sean," Fiona called out as they all got ready to leave, "can I have a moment?"

"I'll be right there," he told the others, and waited to speak with Fiona. "What's up?"

"It has been the Red-eyes every time they've been attacked before. They are feral beasts that are relentless when angered. Unless you strike hard, your blows will likely not penetrate their hides. Be careful, okay? You promised me a date."

Her concern filled Sean's chest with warmth. "I'll do my very best, but the date isn't guaranteed unless Darragh agrees to it. Which you're going to be asking him about soon, I believe." Smiling, he met her dual-colored eyes and could see the hope in them. "I earnestly hope he says yes. I need to go, though. I'll see you later today, Fiona Mithrilsoul."

Her cheeks flushed as he used that name, but she nodded. "Of course, Sean MacDougal. Stay safe."

Hurrying off to catch up with the others, he could feel her eyes on him. "Sorry guys," he said when he found them waiting by the path. He took an axe from Cian and frowned slightly, "If we know we're going to be attacked, why don't we have spears?"

"We don't have any," Cian muttered. "We're just starting to build up a bankroll in Oaklake. We might be able to afford more from town in the next tenday or two."

Myna stepped off the path and, in short order, seemed to vanish into the trees. "That is amazing," Sean said.

"It's a Talent," Byrne told him. "That is what really sets them apart from us. You're going to be hard pressed to keep up with them."

Thinking of his many gifts from the gods, Sean shrugged. "We'll see," his smile was enigmatic, "I think I'll be okay."

"Keep your eyes open," Cian said firmly. "They will come for us soon."

Dropping to the back of the line, Sean focused on the axe and shifted it into a bronze tipped spear, hardening the bronze, sharpening the edges, and making the wood denser to keep it from cracking.

A hellish yip came from their left, and all eyes turned to see Myna standing over a wolf-like body. "There are more," she said, stepping behind a tree.

Not two seconds later, a mournful howl came from the right,

making Sean's hair stand on end. Spinning, the lumberjacks stared aghast at the three Red-eyes barreling towards them, froth coating their mouths.

"They are enraged," Cian said, stepping back and getting ready to swing.

Sean could feel the hatred radiating off the beasts as they neared. Stepping past the others, he angled out to the Red-eye on the right side, his spear held low and ready to attack.

"Sean, get back here," Cian snapped.

"Be right there," Sean said absently. He could almost see himself stepping forward and lunging at the Red-eye. Following that instinct, his lunge was almost textbook perfect in its execution. It was also much faster than the creature had expected, so the spear punched clean into its chest and sliced through its heart.

Yanking the spear out in a shower of blood, he pivoted, finding that the next closest Red-eye had turned to come after him as well. Time seemed to slow as Sean brought the haft of the spear up to club the attacking Red-eye as it passed.

"Sean!" Cian yelled out a second later as the third Red-Eye ignored Sean and attacked the woodsmen. Sean kept his attention on the Red-Eye he'd clubbed, which had leapt away and turned to face him.

The beast's brightly glowing red eyes focused on Sean as it growled. Settling on his back leg, Sean waited for it to attack, but the creature lowered its body and waited as if thinking about what to do next.

Screams and yells behind him made Sean twitchy. He wanted to go help the others, but couldn't, until he dealt with the creature before him. "Come on, puppy, let's play," Sean growled.

With another howl, the creature came forward, fast and low. Something made Sean pull back instead of lunging forward. That proved to be the right idea, the Red-eye twisting its body to dodge the aborted attack. As it contorted, Sean jabbed down, pinning the beast through the neck and stopping it just short of his leg.

"Tricky fucker," Sean exhaled as he yanked the spear from the dead beast. Turning, he ran for the others and found them surrounding the beast, harrying it like a pack of wolves. Cian and Byrne bled from several wounds as they worked to keep the beast spinning between them all.

As he ran to join them, he Shaped the spear back into its original axe form. "Cian, go left," Sean called out as he ran up behind the wounded man.

Sidestepping on reflex at Sean's command, Cian was surprised when Sean went past him and sank his axe into the beast. He cleaved cleanly through it, the axe burying itself in the ground as the two halves toppled.

"Nice strike," Walden said with wide eyes.

"Why did you leave us?" Cian asked as he spun, looking for the other two Red-eyes, then seeing their dead bodies. "Did you do that?"

"Yeah, and it was the right thing to do," Sean replied. "Sorry I didn't warn you, but I just felt the moment was right to strike and followed through on it."

The others all looked at the dead Red-eyes with shocked expressions, staring from the corpses to Sean and back. After a minute of that, Sean frowned. "What?"

"We've only been attacked by one or two of them before today, and even then, we'd have taken wounds dealing with them," Cian said as he pulled a bandage from his belt pouch and began wrapping it around a deep bite on his arm. "You killed all of them, two of them without any help. But you stand here without a single scratch to show for it."

"It's not natural," Byrne said as he wrapped his leg.

"Just what are you?" Eagon asked.

"Unique," Sean sighed. "Look, I have a Talent or two, and I don't want them exactly known. I'll share one with you while we do the job. Are you two going to be able to work?"

Cian nodded, "Darragh gave us these bandages. They stop the bleeding immediately, and close up the wounds in a few hours. We won't go spilling your secrets, Sean, though it does feel like you don't trust us right now."

Looking around, Sean raised a brow pointedly and locked gazes with Cian. "It's not you."

Cian looked at the woods then nodded slowly, "Ah, I see. That makes me feel a little better. We need to get on with the day, but we also need to take the bodies back to the village. Whelan will be beside himself when he sees the haul we have."

"I will take one," Myna said, appearing behind Cian.

Spinning, Cian let out a strangled gasp. "Myna, please don't do that again."

Bowing her head, Myna picked up the halves of the bisected wolf. "I will gut this one first."

"I'll get the other three," Sean told the others. "I'll catch up as soon as I can."

"But—" Eagon began, but Cian clapped a hand on his shoulder, interrupting him.

"That will be fine," Cian said. "At least the trip will be safe now."

"I hope so," Sean said as he went to collect the other dead bodies.

Tossing one over each shoulder, he carried the third under his arm and started for the village. Myna fell into step beside him, but was having difficulty carrying the halves of the fourth Red-eye.

"Will you switch with me?" Myna asked.

Dropping the one corpse from under his arm, Sean held out his hands for the bisected halves. "Sure thing," he said, taking each half by the neck and starting off again.

With a grunt, Myna slung the Red-eye corpse across her shoulders, and staggered after him. "How do you carry them so easily?" Myna asked as she trailed him.

"They aren't heavy to me," Sean said, stopping himself from shrugging. "How do you vanish so easily among the trees?"

"It is a Talent I have," Myna managed to say as she staggered under the weight of the body.

"I take it you don't normally carry the dead?" Sean asked with a raised brow.

"Yes, but normally we lash them to a pole and carry them back to the village two to a corpse. We've never encountered more than two Red-eyes before, either. Normally we find the Fawntin, which are much less dense than these."

"Fawntin?" Sean asked, slowing to match her pace.

"You don't know what the Fawntin are?" Myna asked as she staggered again, almost dropping the body.

Stopping, Sean sighed. "No, I don't. I'll carry that one, too, if you'll answer my questions about the creatures near the village."

"Agreement accepted," Myna said.

Rolling his eyes, Sean knelt next to her, allowing her to stack the body on one of the others across his shoulders. "Keep them steady while I get up," Sean told her. At her nod, he got back to his feet. "Okay, so about these Fawntin?" He started walking, not seeing the blank look of astonishment on her face before she wiped it off and fell into step beside him.

"Fawntin are four legged beasts with hooves. The males have massive antlers that they use to fight with. The antlers are much prized by bowyers skilled enough to Shape them. They are herbivores, but can outdistance most predators with unmatched grace."

"Deer," Sean chuckled softly. "What about these Red-eyes?"

Lips pursed, Myna gazed at him for a moment before answering. "Red-eyes are woodland predators. They have keen senses, and once they're on your trail, they can always track you. They are ferocious fighters, and take killing blows to put down. The older ones have patterns in their fur that help them blend into the forest. They normally work in pairs to bring down their prey."

"How did you manage to kill the first one so quickly? I didn't see you with anything other than those two blades on your back."

"I cut its throat before it knew what was happening, then pierced its heart to make sure it was dead. One can never be too careful with Red-eyes."

"I'll keep that in mind," Sean said.

"I will keep your secret as well," Myna said after a moment. "I know what it is to be wanted just for your Talent. Whelan dislikes me because I'm not a proper hunter in his eyes. My Talent to Vanish is unmatched by the others, though, so he uses me to scout for our prey."

Sean nodded as he listened, realizing that her soft tone fit her like a glove. "And that's why you got saddled with me. He hopes that I won't learn, which will get me injured or killed, and all the blame will fall to you."

"Yes," Myna agreed. "Is Fiona your type?" she said after a pause, catching Sean off guard.

Blinking, Sean's mouth hung open for a moment. "Left field much?" Snorting, he considered Myna's question. "I think she is. She's beautiful, smart, funny, and now that she's starting to value herself again, she has the self-confidence I like."

"And she is a Shaper, like you," Myna said.

"Her Talent has nothing to do with it. I like her for her."

"Even with her Shame?" Myna pressed, her head turning so she could focus her eyes on him.

"I couldn't give a fuck less about her Shame. If anything, her Shame has made her stronger than before," Sean smiled. "She is a friend who intrigues me."

"You seem to treat Misa like a person, as well," Myna pointed out.

"She is," Sean shrugged, shifting the double stacked Red-eyes and dropping them off his shoulder. "Fuck me," he sighed.

"Kneel, I will stack," Myna told him.

"Glad I can be a pack mule, at least," Sean snorted, but did as he was asked.

Myna quickly had the bodies back on his shoulder, and they continued on towards the village. "You aren't from here, are you?" Myna asked as they reached the outskirts.

Sean didn't get the feeling she was trying to fuck him over, but she was in Whelan's group, so he hesitated. After a moment, he went with his gut. "No, I'm not."

"My grandfather wasn't either," Myna said softly, eyes darting around to make sure that nobody was close by. "Outsiders are viewed with suspicion, and he had a hard life because of it."

"Good to know. Thank you Myna," Sean said as she led him to Darragh's house.

"I'll get Misa. Wait, please." With that, Myna darted into the home.

CHAPTER EIGHTEEN

Misa followed Myna out of the home, her eyes growing large when she saw the bodies Sean was carrying. "I owe you an extra portion of meat tonight," Misa said to Myna after a moment. Turning back to Sean, she beckoned him to follow her, "Around back isss the area I need them taken to."

Sean followed her around to an area with tables set up for butchering. The area also held several racks for curing hides. Of the four, only one had a hide stretched on it. "So this is where the hunters bring their meat?" Sean asked as he placed the wolves on one of the tables.

"Yesss," Misa told him. "I ssskin and ssset hidesss for tanning. Then I butcher the meat before sssmoking the majority of it. I will be taking a haunch in with me for tonight'sss food."

"Good to know," Sean said, as he looked at the one hide that was tanning. "Myna, is this from a Fawntin?"

"Yes, it's the one we killed a few days ago," Myna replied.

"Misa, are you going to be okay? Are we good to leave?" Sean asked the Lesser Naga.

"Yesss, go cut sssome wood," Misa said absently, already busy making a cut down the length of one Red-eye corpse.

"See you later," Sean told her, heading back to the path that would lead them to the stream.

"Do you want to try melting into the woods while we travel?" Myna asked as they left the village.

Shrugging, Sean nodded, "Sure. How do I do it?"

"Since you can Shape, you should know where your energy is stored. You need to harness it, then focus on using it to blend in with your surroundings." As Myna spoke, she stepped next to a tree and her body began to fade away.

Squinting at her, Sean could see where she and the tree seemed to blend together. He was reminded of a chameleon, the way her skin and clothing took on the color of her surroundings. "Okay," he breathed, concentrating on the vibration at his center and focusing his mind on blending in as he walked over to a tree.

Myna's eyes widened, "Interesting."

Looking down at his own body, Sean had to agree with her. "Guess I have some Talent for this after all."

"We shall see," Myna said as she vanished completely. "Can you move unseen?" Her voice floated to him from a different place than where she had been.

Keeping his mind focused on blending in, he moved towards the next tree. He paused next to it and was startled by a tap on his side. His camouflage fell away as he jerked in surprise. "What the hell?"

Myna appeared next to him, "You shimmer when you move. You need to work on moving in sync with the energy, and step more lightly while you do it. If you can perfect it, you can become a shadow that stalks its prey."

"Well, we can keep practicing on our way to the stream," Sean said, as he focused on blending in again.

"Good, but you must also learn to spot your target. I will go easy for this first part. If you can follow me, I will be impressed. Are you ready?"

Sean knew this wasn't going to be easy. Taking a deep breath, he nodded. "Let's do this."

Myna faded mostly from view, only a very hazy outline remaining visible. "Follow me after three seconds," she told him as she moved away.

Counting to three, he kept his eyes focused on the faint shimmer that was all he could see of her. Concentrating on blending into the forest, he followed after her, acutely conscious of how much noise he was making.

He lost her twice, once when she picked up speed unexpectedly, and once when she zigzagged around two closely set trees. Each time, he was able to find the shimmer that marked her and began following it again.

Myna appeared just short of the bank, her normally impassive face cracked by the smallest of smiles. "You did very well for your first time at seek and sneak," she said.

"I have a very good teacher," Sean said with a grin. "It was fun. Did I improve my own sneaking?"

"Somewhat," Myna nodded. "With a few years of practice, you might approach my Talent."

Snorting, Sean shook his head. "Only a few years?"

Her face went blank again, as if he had insulted her, "It is no small thing to match my skills."

Knowing he had goofed, Sean bowed his head. "I didn't mean it as an insult, Myna. It is just that a couple of years can last a lifetime."

After a moment, she nodded. "I accept the apology. You have work to do for a few hours. I will look for forage that Misa can use for dinner while you work. I will be back at high sun."

"Thanks for the early practice," Sean said as Myna vanished from view. Shaking his head, he looked around and failed to spot her, "A few years? I wonder if I'll have that long to practice."

Stepping out of the tree line, Sean headed for the men. "Sorry for the delay, guys," he called out.

Cian waved at him, "Good. Let's start trimming this log up."

He joined them at the fallen tree, and they went to work trimming it. Sean used Darragh's axe, which helped them get the log trimmed quickly. The others all looked at him in disbelief as Sean was shaking out his arm.

"You're spoiling us," Ward chuckled.

"Who rides this one?" Sean asked.

"No one," Cian said. "Today is one of the two days we don't send anyone downstream. Tomorrow is bathing day and no one wants to miss that."

"I thought you sent someone each day?" Sean asked.

"Eight of the ten," Cian replied. "It's all part of our Agreement. We enjoy one day off every tenday. No worries about being attacked, no sending someone downstream, and no work to be done."

"Bathing can't take all day," Sean snorted.

"It doesn't, but it gives us the chance to work on our crafts or other hobbies," Eagon said. "I like to carve knick-knacks from some of the branches."

"I'll get to check on my barrel," Ward grinned.

"Barrel?" Sean asked.

"I've got some berries fermenting," Ward said.

"The last batch was rank," Byrne shuddered.

"You still drank your share," Ward sniffed, "so your comment is not valid." The others laughed at Ward's put-upon airs.

"What are you going to do with your day, Sean?" Walden asked.

"How far away is town?"

Cian shook his head, "That's a good eight hour walk, a bit far for the one day we take off."

"Well, fuck," Sean sighed. "I don't know now."

"You want to go to town that badly?" Cian asked.

"I kind of agreed to see about going to town in the near future, if Darragh agrees to let me go," Sean muttered.

All the guys turned their heads to stare at him. Cian wore a knowing grin. "I take it someone asked you to go with them?"

Raising a single brow, Sean's lips pursed. "Maybe."

Everyone began to chuckle easily, seeing his evasion for what it was. "Oh, come on now, Sean, why try to hide it?" Cian chuckled. "It's obvious you two are interested in each other, and you've spent a fair amount of your short time here so far with her. The only question really is who asked who."

Shaking his head, Sean didn't reply. Instead, he walked over to a nearby tree. "Oh, look at that, break time is over." He began sizing up where to make his cuts and ignoring the others, who had stopped chuckling.

"Sean," Cian called out, his voice serious. "We don't mean to cause problems. Most of us have no issue with her, and even our wives seem to have mellowed toward her over the last few days. So don't go thinking we look down on her. We don't—how could we, when we follow Darragh? We're mostly surprised that she is willing to open up at all."

Sean glanced at the quintet. "Okay. I told her I would take her to town, if Darragh gave me the time away from our Agreement to do so."

"Good for you," Ward said first. Similar sentiments from the others swiftly followed.

"We should get back to work," Sean said. "I'm going away at noon and you're all going to have to toil on without me."

"You mentioned wanting to try something, earlier," Cian reminded him.

"Oh, right," Sean said, having forgotten.

Putting the axe down, he touched the tree, trying to feel it well enough to Shape it. The vibrating energy came to him a little more quickly, and he wondered if it was like a muscle that was becoming accustomed to being used. Shaking the thought off, he focused on the tree and tried to weaken the areas he was going to chop.

Frowning as the tree resisted his Shaping, Sean wondered if it was because it was a living thing. Pushing harder, he could feel the tree begin to change but the energy seemed to pour out of him, similar to when he summoned water. Once he had weakened the tree a bit, he stopped and stepped back.

"What were you trying to do?" Cian asked.

"Clear out of the way guys," he replied with a tight smile. "I want to see if it worked."

Once they were out of the way, he swung the axe with all his strength. The wood shattered where he had weakened it, like he was chopping through particle board. The tree began to creak as the weakened wood began to give way.

"Fuck," Sean said as he darted around the tree.

Sean moved just in time as the tree shivered and then, with a loud crack, toppled. All five of the guys with him stared at Sean with wide eyes, a sight he was quickly becoming accustomed to.

"You felled it with a single blow?" Cian finally managed after a long pause.

"Maybe it was rotted inside?" Sean suggested halfheartedly. He kept his face blank as best he could, almost as surprised as they were. He wasn't prepared to explain his Talent.

With a raised brow, Cian went over to check the log. After a minute, he looked back at Sean. "I'm thinking one of your secrets might be similar to Fiona's."

The other men went to look at the tree. Eagon picked up a piece of the cut section, which crumbled in his hand. "I think Cian is right."

"Keep it under wraps, please," Sean said.

Shaking their heads, the five woodsmen grabbed their hand axes and went to work without comment. Sean joined them a moment later with Dark Cutter, making short work of trimming the branches. Sean took a break when they were done.

That prompted the men to all take a moment to rest as well. "You're just full of surprises, Sean," Cian said after a minute. "Anything else you want to warn us about?"

"Not right now, no," Sean said, looking away.

"You're not planning on staying, though, are you?" Walden asked. "How long are you planning to be around for?"

"Maybe a few weeks," Sean said. "This was just the first place I got to."

Nodding slowly, Cian sighed, "An Outsider, alright. We don't hold any ill will towards you, Sean, but you're going to catch a lot of attention if you do this kind of thing in other places."

"Which is why I'm trying to figure out as much as I can," Sean said.

"That's fair," Ward said. "You don't mind helping us out until you go?"

"Good people are hard to find, so no, I don't mind at all," Sean replied.

"Means we'll get a lot done in that time," Cian said. "Thanks again for helping us."

Sean shrugged, "You all want one more? I'm not going to be around to help cart them back to town, after all."

Glancing at each other, the men exchanged knowing looks. "Maybe we should drag these two back now, and work on our third for the rest of the day," Cian finally said.

The others quickly agreed and got to their feet. Sean got up along with them and dusted off his pants. "I've been meaning to ask, do you guys use all these limbs?"

"We use them for firewood, mostly," Cian said as they picked up the first log. "They're harder for her to Shape than proper logs, but we do what we have to until we get everything we need made."

"I want to try something on the next log, if I'm still around when it drops," Sean said as they began to cart the first one to town.

"Oh goodness, more surprises," Eagon said, causing the others to laugh.

CHAPTER NINETEEN

No one was in the village when they dropped the logs off, nor when they dragged back the branches, which they left next to the logs. When they got back to the stream, the sun was just cresting high and Myna sat on a stump at the edge of the woods, waiting for them.

"Looks like I'm done for the day, guys," Sean told them.

"We'll probably get one more today," Cian said. "Good luck on learning the skills she can teach."

"It'll be fun," Sean said as he met Myna where she was waiting.

"Are you ready to continue our lessons from earlier?" Myna asked.

"I hope so," Sean said. "What's the plan, more seek and sneak?"

"Yes, but with added incentive," Myna smiled with a hint of dark humor as she picked up a wooden sword and tossed it to him. "We're going to train harder. Hunt me. If you can find me, then hit me. I will be doing the same." She picked up two shorter wooden blades, "Between here and the village, the width of the village, is our training area."

Sean focused on the sword, but couldn't find any flaws in it. Looking up at Myna, he nodded. "Learning to hunt the hunters is the lesson?"

"Yes," Myna said, stepping around a tree. "We begin in one minute."

"I think I'm going to get bruised," Sean muttered, as he let his energy flow and walked into the woods away from where Myna had, fading from casual sight as he went.

Slipping from tree to tree, Sean kept his head moving, trying to find any hint of Myna. With a growing sense of dread as the minutes ticked by, Sean got the feeling Myna was close. A shimmer appeared right next to him as two wooden blades crashed into his side.

"Fuck," Sean hissed as he bounced off the tree he was next to. His ribs ached dully where he'd been struck. Sean looked for her, but she was already gone. He silently cursed, rubbing his side as the pain began to fade.

"One for me," Myna's voice drifted to him, but he couldn't guess the direction.

Keeping score. That doesn't bode well for me at all, Sean thought. Taking off at a run, he slipped through the woods as best he could, getting snagged once or twice by branches. Once he thought he had put a bit of distance between himself and Myna, he put his back to a tree and focused intently on being completely gone.

Determined to wait, Sean breathed easily as he moved only his eyes. *I should have been a little winded from that sprint. I wonder why I wasn't?* Sean pondered as he scanned for Myna.

Minutes later, Sean blinked as he saw the faintest hint of distortion a few feet away to his left. It was pressed against the trunk of a tree, and appeared to be searching for something. Resisting the urge to go for an attack in that moment, he waited, making sure to keep his gaze on the shimmer.

After another minute the shimmering figure moved forward, passing a couple of trees before pausing again. Now that he was behind it, Sean slowly and carefully began to creep up on his target. Freezing in place next to a tree as the shimmer seemed to turn towards him, Sean held his breath. After a minute, though, the figure seemed to go back to looking elsewhere.

Holding back a deep sigh of relief, Sean began to creep forward again, wooden sword held ready to strike. Once he was close enough, he rushed the last two feet and tapped the middle of the shimmer with his mock sword.

She tried to dart away, but the tip of the blade grazed her and a grunt came from Myna as she briefly appeared, a wince on her face. Sean darted away from her, focusing on hiding and not on the look of anger that had flared in Myna's eyes.

Hunkering down, Sean waited for the next attack to come. Minutes ticked by slowly, each second feeling like ten. He had no warning when two hard points dug into his chest with vicious strength. Myna appeared before him as he gasped.

"Do not hit me at full strength, understand?" Myna said grimly.

Blinking, Sean shook his head, "I didn't hit you at full strength. I pulled the strike."

Eyes narrowing, Myna kept her two wooden swords against him. "You almost cracked my rib with that grazing blow," she hissed. "Do you really think I can believe what you say, with that as proof?"

"I can prove it," Sean said. "Let me go."

Stepping back, Myna raised a brow, "How are you going to prove it?"

Casting about, Sean found a broken branch a few dozen feet away. "I need that branch," he said, grabbing it. Seeing Myna a few feet away when he turned around, Sean sighed. "Sorry about the hit, but I'm still getting used to my strength." With that, he took the inch thick limb and cracked it across the trunk of the closest tree.

Shards of splintered wood went flying, and Myna shielded her face from them. Looking at the tree a moment later, her eyes widened and her head shook from side to side. "That…"

"Yeah, I know. I'm getting used to hearing people say things aren't possible," Sean said after she trailed off.

With a distant look, Myna seemed to be thinking. Nodding, she turned back to Sean. "I was wrong. I apologize."

"It's fine," Sean told her. "Can we keep this display just between us?"

"I will agree to that," Myna said. "We shall go back to the training, but maybe with just light taps instead."

"I'll do my best to temper my strikes, but you're quick, which makes it hard to connect without trying to get to you before you dodge."

"Fair," Myna conceded. "I will not dodge if you strike. I will concede the blow if you can get close to me."

"Back to the hunt?" Sean asked.

"I will give you a minute to flee, and I will be vanishing even more, so be prepared for even less warning of my approach."

"Less than when you pinned me to the tree, or less than when I snuck up on you? Because I never knew you were there when you pinned me to the tree."

A faint smile touched her lips. "Less than the pinning, more than your sneaking. Now hurry, for your time is quickly running out."

Bolting away, Sean grabbed at his energy and wrapped it around him. A small thrill of excitement ran through him as he did. Myna really did want to teach him, and she was ready to press the training further.

Myna proved to be hard to spot once she upped her camo Talent. During the next two hours, Sean only found her sneaking by once. She noticed him just as he closed the distance and dropped her cover, acknowledging his point without him having to attack. The rest of the two hours proved a valuable lesson in what someone who had trained their Talent could do. Myna found and attacked him over a dozen times in that span.

Shaking his head, Sean sighed as he rubbed his ribs where Myna had hit him. She hadn't hit hard enough to bruise, but it still stung. "I don't know if I'll ever train to the degree you have, Myna, but I hope I haven't been a complete disappointment."

"No, you have been an apt pupil, and I do not think you will hinder the others in the least. We should move on to your ability to track prey," Myna said, handing him a canteen. "I will leave a trail behind me, and I want you to follow it to where I hide."

"Okay," Sean said as he took a sip from the canteen. The warm water eased his dry throat. He hadn't realized how thirsty he had gotten during their training. Handing back the canteen, he nodded. "How long do I give before I follow?"

"Count to three hundred," Myna said, stepping into the woods, "then come for me."

"Three hundred seconds is five minutes," Sean muttered as he began to idly count. Once the time had passed, he looked at the forest floor and found distinct footprints. "She's letting me start easy, that's good," Sean chuckled and began to trail after her.

After a few minutes of following the prints, he found a place where two sets diverged from each other. Kneeling down, he examined the tracks that appeared almost identical. Further examining them, he found two footprints atop each other, but not perfectly lined up, heading north.

"That's the false trail she laid before she backed up to here and went the other way," Sean muttered, wondering how he knew that. Another minute of following the tracks brought him to a fallen tree. No tracks appeared on the other side of the tree, though. "Think, Sean, think. She probably used the trunk to break her trail, but where could she have gone from here?"

He looked up at the limb above the fallen log, his eyes drawn to a fresh scuff, like something heavy had marked it. "She went up the tree, and not down the fallen log, so she probably came down on the other side of the tree."

Circling the tree, he eventually found a deep set of prints where Myna had dropped out of the branches of the tree. He set off after the tracks, which slowly faded away as he went. "No, it's not a trick, she's just upping the difficulty again," Sean told himself after pausing to check the prints. "There's still tracks, just not so obvious now."

Another few minutes brought him to another divergence in the tracks, and he instinctively knew which set to follow. He stopped, the trail having led to a hard packed smooth piece of ground that didn't appear to have any tracks at all across it.

Kneeling next to where the last sign was, he could see very faint scuffs along the hard earth. It took him a couple of minutes to pick up the trail again, the tracks having faded even further, but he could see them clearly. Shaking his head, he knew he should thank Cernunnos for his gift. He came to a sudden stop as the tracks ended abruptly before him. Looking immediately up, he found Myna resting on a branch with her back to the tree.

"Not horrible," Myna said as she dropped down. "I didn't expect you to follow me so easily." Lips pursed, she studied him intently, "Now we will flip it and I will track you. Do your best to keep me from finding you."

"Well, fuck," Sean said as he set off at a run, not waiting for her to tell him to go. After a hundred yards or so, he slowed and started walking carefully, even though he knew she would probably find him easily. Coming across the same log Myna ignored earlier, he walked gingerly down the length of it before gently stepping off and walking to the closest tree. It had a decently low branch of sufficient size that Sean thought might support him.

Crouching, he jumped for the limb and was surprised to go past it. He grabbed the branch above the one he had been aiming for and hauled himself up onto it. Blinking, he looked down to find himself fifteen feet up. "I really need to figure out what my baseline for physical abilities is," Sean muttered. He got carefully to his feet and walked along the branch, mentally measuring the distance to the next tree. He backed up a couple of steps and took a running jump for a limb near the one he was on.

His feet found purchase, and he wavered for a moment before catching his balance. Once he was certain he was good, he walked along the branch to the trunk. Grabbing the large trunk, he shimmied around it to the far side then looked up and found another branch higher up. Springing up, he grabbed the limb and pulled himself up, putting him almost twenty-five feet above the ground. Settling onto the branch, he leaned against the trunk and pulled his energy out of his core. He covered himself and focused intently on becoming completely invisible. Breathing slowly, he waited for Myna, knowing she would eventually come.

Time seemed to crawl by as he waited. Eventually, he thought he saw a faint shimmer walk below him. It vanished in the same instant he thought he saw it. Gritting his teeth, he wished he had some way to beat Myna's Talent. He continued to wait, and the thought of being able to see into objects when Shaping made him wonder if he could do something similar here. He focused on seeing into the tree he was sitting against in the same way he'd done with the logs and axes before.

It took a few minutes, but his normal sight was eventually overlaid with the energy imagery he'd gotten used to seeing when Shaping. Lifting his eyes from the branch he sat on, he looked out into the woods and his mouth dropped open. Stretching out before him was not the woods he'd seen all day, but a shimmering panorama of life of different colors and intensities, all glowing to his sight.

"Fucking beautiful," Sean whispered.

In awe of the sight, he didn't see Myna looking up at him, nor did he see the small stone that she flung. Snapped out of the moment by the rock hitting him in the chest, he looked down and his vision swam for a moment. He found a shimmer, shaped like a human and a vibrant black in color, staring up at him. He tossed his wooden sword down to her.

"You win," Sean said before he started down the tree, after dismissing the overlay on his sight. He missed Myna's shocked expression when he tossed her the sword, which she'd caught without thinking. When he dropped to the ground, he turned to find her inches away from him. "Err... hello?"

"How did you spot me?" Myna asked, staring into his eyes with an almost feral intensity.

"It was an experiment. How did you see me?"

"Your camouflage, when I went past originally, was better than I'd anticipated. When I turned around to examine the tree you were in from a different angle, your shimmer was noticeable. Now, how did you spot me?" Her tone was as intense as her eyes, boring into him.

"I was trying to adapt a Talent into something new, which is probably why my camo flickered, but it let me see your energy."

Stepping back with pursed lips, Myna seemed to be deep in thought. "How do you manage it?"

Licking his lips, Sean's head tilted slightly to the side as he took in her posture. She looked angry, and it was the first time Sean had seen her so aggressive. When she'd pinned him to the tree earlier, she had been upset, but not about to rip his head off. "What do you offer in trade?" he finally said, and hoped he wasn't overplaying his hand.

Myna hissed, but took a step back. "I've already trained you as Whelan told me to. There isn't much I can give, besides trying to train you further in the skills I've been showing you."

Sean looked around before nodding. "I'll offer a trade. I'll try to explain what I did, and in return, you tell no one that I can do it or how it's done. On top of that, I want to know if there's a trick to how well and easily you're able to camo."

Her hands twitched, as if she was thinking of throttling him. Instead she exhaled loudly. "That would require explaining my family, something I've been loathe to do. I will agree to your terms, if you do the same for me. No telling others about what I say here."

"Agreed," Sean said, the weight of the agreement settling on him like a heavy cloak.

"You first," Myna said as she took a seat on the ground, ready for his explanation.

CHAPTER TWENTY

Taking a seat, Sean ordered his thoughts. "Okay, how do you reach the energy you harness to use your Talent?"

Myna frowned, "It's just there. I wish it to happen and it does. It's an innate Talent from my mother's lineage."

"Crap," Sean sighed. "Well, here goes anyway. When I Shape, I can see into the wood, see the energy and all of the flaws. I decided to try that and lost focus on my camo, but I was able to see the underlying energy in the woods as well as the energy you'd wrapped yourself in. You looked like a bright shadow that stood out against the pale greens of the forest."

Lips pursed, Myna's head tilted slightly and her eyes narrowed as she considered what he'd said. "You have Mage Sight," Myna finally said softly. "That is a very rare Talent, which means I won't be able to duplicate it."

"I'm not sure about that," Sean shrugged. "Fiona has learned a thing or two from me. Besides, there's nobody saying I can't try to help you learn it."

Eyes focusing on him, Myna considered his offer. "What would your teaching cost?"

"I truly have no idea at the moment, but I'm not opposed to trying to teach it to you. We can come back to it in a bit. You were going to tell me about how you manage such excellent control over your camo."

Looking away, Myna frowned and reached up to remove the leather cap covering her head. Sean frowned as two small, furred points came into view, mostly obscured by her hair. "My mother's lineage. I told you my grandfather was an Outsider. He took an... unusual wife, one of the Feline Moonbonded. The Feline Moonbonded are known for their excellent hunting Talents, but to take one to wife is just not done. My grandfather was shunned for it. My mother had almost none of the physical traits of the Feline Moonbonded, but did inherit all of her mother's Talents. I inherited those Talents as well, but was born with these ears. They proclaim my heritage, lowering any possible status I might ever hope to attain. Luckily for me, I have neither the tail nor fur, making it easier for me to hide my blood."

"This village is full of people with interesting pasts," Sean smiled.

"Two Shamed, a Life Bonded Lesser Naga, and me," Myna nodded. "We have an unusual collection in such a small village."

"There is no trick to better camo, then? It's just your bloodline that has strengthened your Talent?"

"Correct," Myna said. "If I could teach others, I might have been able to find a different path in life. Instead, I am here, under Whelan's command." The last few words were said in disdain, her lips twisting into a sneer.

"I see he's popular with everyone," Sean chuckled.

"He once tried to get me into a wager, with me bedding him as his reward. I have no such desire for that. When I turned him down, he attacked me and pulled my cap from my head. I've been shunned by the others since then. Moonbonded are considered barely above animals, after all."

"Such an ass," Sean sighed. "This world seems to have many prejudices, maybe even more than my last. Anyway, we should be getting back to town."

"Wait, what about trying to teach me Mage Sight?" Myna said, stopping him from getting to his feet as she put her cap back in place.

"I have nothing to ask for in return," Sean told her. "Unless you're willing to give me a favor of equal value to be called in later?"

Myna sucked at her teeth for a moment. "That could be tantamount to giving over my life." With a sad shake of her head, she got to her feet. "I cannot accept that trade at this time."

"If I can think of something later, or if you do, I'll be more than happy to see if we can come to an Agreement," Sean told her as he stood.

Both of them turned to face the east, as the voices of the women could be heard singing in the distance. Exchanging glances, Myna seemed puzzled again, "You hear them?"

"Yeah," Sean said.

"You truly are unique," With another shake of her head, she vanished into the trees.

"You're the first catgirl I've met, which makes you unique to me, too," Sean muttered. Pulling his energy around him, he headed towards the sound of the song.

Sean came out on the trail well behind Taavi, who was following the women. Dropping his camo, Sean focused on bringing his Mage Sight back into being. Blinking against the sudden increase of input as everything took on soft glows of various colors, he looked around to find Myna. Ahead of the group, Myna's outline was pressed against a tree, her head turned toward Sean. Making a motion from his eyes to her, he watched her head dip a fraction. Smile in place, he was about to drop Mage Sight when his eyes caught another darker black outline off to the right. The outline was a little over four foot in height, with a gently swaying tail stretched out behind it. Staring, he caught sight of another four silhouettes further back. Sean got the impression of bipedal cats, who seemed to be enjoying the music.

Glancing back to Myna, he stepped off the path and stopped next to her once he caught up. "Myna—the Moonbound, do they stand about four feet?"

"Those of feline blood do," Myna replied softly. "They come to listen to the songs."

"You know they're there?"

"I met with them shortly after we arrived here; one of them sought me out. Darragh asked me to work out an Agreement with them. As long as we do not hunt them, they will leave the village alone."

"Seems reasonable," Sean said.

"Feline Moonbound are the best at remaining unseen. It is considered a great feat for a hunter to find one, and an even greater feat to kill it. Only those with Mage Sight can reliably find us, but most of those with Mage Sight don't have the physical prowess to best one of us."

Sean smiled at her use of the word 'us' when speaking of the Moonbound. *As much as you try to downplay your heritage, you're still proud of it*, he chuckled internally. "I should just leave them alone, then?"

"Unless you wish to kill all of us," Myna snorted.

"I'm fond of living, so I'll pass."

Myna dropped her camouflage. "Shall we follow the singers?"

"Sounds good," Sean said as he followed Taavi, who had gotten further away during Sean's brief conversation. The forest seemed almost drab when he dropped Mage Sight, his vision wavering. He blinked several times before it cleared.

"Comes with a downside?" Myna asked as she walked along beside him.

"When you push it away, it causes a bit of vertigo," Sean said. "It stabilizes quickly though, so maybe that will fade in time."

"That is good to know. Don't release the sight until you are safe," Myna nodded.

The sounds of the wives and husbands greeting each other was enough to bring Sean's attention back to the path before him. "Cian, have you finished that tree yet?"

Cian laughed, "Of course we did."

"Three trees again?" Tamaya asked. "We noticed the other two laid out next to Fiona's home."

"Sean is a bit of a madman, when it comes to knocking trees down," Eagon said.

"Aye, he's a bit unique," Ward said, hurriedly adding, "at least in that regard."

"Are we carrying the tree back to town, or standing around talking?" Sean asked, eager to change the subject.

"The branches are gathered already, to make things easier for you, wife," Cian said, motioning to the bundles that were neatly laid out.

"It's only taken years, but it seems my training is finally paying off. Girls, there's hope for your husbands as well," Tamaya said, prompting laughter from the rest of the women. "Let's show the men what it means to support them."

Sean joined the guys at the fallen log. Hoisting it up, they followed along after the women, who were singing again. Sean chuckled when he realized the song was a back and forth between the women and men. The song was a comedy, about wives trying to get their husbands to work, and the husbands coming up with various excuses to avoid working. Their singing came to an end as they dropped the log at Fiona's home.

"Tomorrow is wash day," Cian reminded Sean.

"I remember. I'll have to figure something out," Sean replied.

"I have a suggestion," Fiona's voice came from inside her home as the door opened. "Sean, may I have a moment?"

"Off you go," Cian laughed, giving Sean a nudge. "We'll see you at dinner."

Tamaya slapped Cian on the back of the head. "Knock it off, and let them speak to each other alone, you lackwit."

The other guys chuckled as they walked off with their wives, eager to avoid being slapped as well. Sean watched them all leave with a smile. He was growing attached to them, faster than he would have thought possible. Turning to the open door, his smile broadened. "Evening, Fiona. We've kind of stacked you up on work again."

"So I see. Do please come in, Sean," she replied.

He caught the scent of berry tea as he stepped inside. "Borrowed some of Misa's tea?"

"No, Myna brought me some things earlier today. Apparently she had some time before the sun was high, so she brought Misa and me some herbs and berries."

"Ah, before she ran me through the wringer."

"Exactly. Please, sit," Fiona told him as she went past him and took a seat herself. "I spoke with Darragh this morning," Fiona said, pouring their drinks. "He was hesitant, but said he would consider letting you take an extra day off the day after wash day."

"What do I have to do to tip that to a yes instead of a maybe?" Sean asked as he sipped the fresh tea.

"You brought back four Red-eyes earlier today, Misa told me," Fiona said, ignoring the question for the moment.

"It wasn't just me," Sean told her. "Myna killed one and the guys basically killed one."

"Which means you killed two all by yourself, if what Misa told me is the truth."

"Who told her?" Sean asked with a frown.

"Myna, when she dropped off the plants. Misa then told me when I went to speak with Darragh again a few hours ago. She'd already told Darragh about the Red-eyes and the two logs outside my hut, which has now become three. Darragh was impressed and graciously granted a day's reprieve to your Agreement, unless you would like to break it, he said."

"I'd rather not break it yet," Sean told her. "I've met a number of kind people here and would like to stay longer."

Cheeks turning pink, Fiona nodded. "In that case, if you are willing to forego wash day, we can head to Oaklake. We can spend the day showing you around, take a room at the inn there, and come back the next day. If you'd like?"

"Two days with you?" Sean asked.

"Yes, it's just—"

"I'd love that," Sean cut her off. "Two days with my friend, to see new things and learn more from you. I'd be the biggest fool in the world to pass up the opportunity."

"So it's a date then," Fiona said.

"Indeed," Sean said, then paused. "You're going to be exhausted if you work all night."

"I was going to ask if you would help me for part of the night," Fiona said. "Darragh is fine with me going, as long as I finish up a few things first. Then we can get a good nap in and head out after breakfast."

The setting sun came through the window, highlighting her sharp cheeks and different colored eyes. "I'll be glad to help, Fiona," Sean said, putting his hand on the table palm up.

Hesitating for a moment, Fiona licked her lips and set her hand in his. "I'm looking forward to the next couple of days," her voice was soft, tinged with hope and fear.

Giving her hand a small squeeze, he smiled. "Maybe as much as I am?"

Her smile bloomed, dazzling him. "We should go to dinner."

"After we finish our tea," his thumb traced the edge of her palm.

Shivering at his touch, her eyes met his. "Did your training go well?" The question was weak, as her breath caught in her throat.

"I learned a bit from Myna, and we're trying to come to an Agreement about learning more from each other."

Lips compressing, Fiona nodded. "What will you be teaching her?" Removing her hand from his, she sipped her tea.

"Remember how you asked me to try to teach you to see into things?"

"Of course," Fiona said, her eyes hopeful. "Did you have another idea?"

"Yes and no," Sean told her. "When I was training with Myna, I was trying to think of a way to see past her Talent for camouflage. I used the same idea, but differently, and it let me see the energy she uses to cover herself."

"Mage Sight," Fiona said softly. "Oh, I didn't think that was what you did the other day," she frowned. "I guess I won't be able to learn it after all."

"Is it so rare?" Sean asked.

"It's said that less than a thousandth of the people who can reliably use magic can harness their energy in such a way," Fiona told him.

"Fuck," Sean sighed. "I'm not sure the Dana did me any favors by giving me so many gifts."

"You do seem especially blessed, which will make it difficult if you wish to avoid the attention of the nobility."

"We tried to have you bring energy up to your eyes and it didn't work. I was curious, though... Is there a way to imbue an item with magic?"

"Of course, but most imbued items don't last long. Imbuing energy into an item causes it to weaken, making it break after repeated uses."

"Do you have any silver?"

Frowning, Fiona finished her tea, then got up to retrieve something. Reseating herself right next to him, she placed a couple of small silver coins on the table. "Why silver?" she asked.

"An old myth on my world is that silver was a metal much sought after for its ability to hold magic," Sean said as he frowned. "I don't want to use your money, though. I know that's a tidy sum."

"Are you going to make it vanish?" Fiona giggled.

"No, but it might break," Sean told her.

"Do what you will. I think you'll surprise me again," Fiona told him, laying her hand on his arm.

Licking his lips as his heart sped up, he nodded and stammered, "O-okay." Coughing as he stumbled over the word, he picked up the coins and focused on them.

Calling his energy forth, he melded the coins into a ring, large enough to look through with one eye. Once he had it Shaped, he focused on bringing the Mage Sight to his eyes. The room lit up, soft blues and greens dominating almost every inch of the small home. Placing the monocle to his eye, he focused on pushing the energy from his eye into the monocle, trying to saturate the metal with it. As he did, he could see the silver beginning to develop small flaws. Holding the energy where it was, he Shaped the monocle, fixing the flaws, before pushing more energy into it. That caused more flaws to appear, which he fixed again. Stopping there, he released his energy and wobbled in place for a moment as his vision swam.

"Are you okay, Sean?" Fiona asked.

Taking the monocle from his eye, he nodded and handed it to Fiona. "Try this," he said, before draining what was left of his tea.

Fiona took the monocle and placed it before her eye, her forehead creasing with lines as she peered through it. A moment later, a sharp intake of breath came from her. "Oh…"

"Did it work?" Sean asked.

"I can see everything," Fiona whispered as she looked at the room. Head turning, she looked at him, and her jaw dropped. "You're… goodness…"

"What?" Sean asked.

"You're saturated in energy, every strand of your being holds so much…" Shaking her head, she reached out and touched his chest. "Here. Most of it resides here, next to your heart. But even your hair," her hand gently touched his hair, "each strand holds energy. What you'll be capable of, if you learn to harness it all…"

"I'll need a good teacher for that," Sean said. "Want to help me?"

Fiona's eyes snapped wide, causing the monocle to fall and bounce on the floor. She suddenly slumped to the side, her head swimming as the connection to the Mage Sight broke. Sean caught her, worried at her suddenly pale face.

"Fiona? Fiona, are you okay?" Sean asked quickly, checking the pulse in her neck, finding it racing.

"Hmm," Fiona blinked as she came to. "What happened?" She slowly sat upright, assisted by Sean.

"You passed out when the monocle fell off," Sean told her.

Eyes blinking rapidly, she looked at him, then at his arm holding her. "Umm…" Getting to her feet, she walked away from him, stumbling a little. "I'm sorry about that. Your item takes a lot of energy to use, and when it stops, it causes the head to swim."

Sean picked up the monocle from the floor and got to his feet. About to step towards her, he stopped, as he didn't want her to feel like he was pressuring her or being clingy. Instead, he set the monocle on the table. "I'll go over to Darragh's. I'll see you there, right?"

"In a few minutes," Fiona said, not looking at him. "I need to collect myself first."

"I'll be waiting. I hope you're okay, Fiona Mithrilsoul," Sean said, before leaving her house.

"I'll be okay in a moment," Fiona said into the empty room.

CHAPTER TWENTY-ONE

"I don't trust him," Whelan's voice carried from Darragh's open door. "No one with the abilities and skills he possesses would just happen to show up. He has to be in the employ of a noble, or perhaps one of the Queens."

"Oh, come off it, Whelan," Cian scoffed. "You're just mad that he's putting your *efforts* to shame."

"I will hurt you, Cian, if you mock our attempts to keep you fed," Whelan snarled, his words accompanied by the sound of a chair being thrown back.

"Enough," Darragh said. "He is a guest, and he isn't with either Queen, nor is he sent by their sycophants."

"How can you be sure?" Whelan asked.

"There are some things that I know, Whelan," Darragh replied. "Tomorrow is wash day. He will be taking the day off, and the day after as well. I suggest that you focus on your own tasks during this time. Maybe having him out hunting with you on Threeday will help you view him as an ally."

"Of course, Darragh," Whelan said dismissively.

"Evening," Sean said as he stepped inside.

All eyes turned to him; the lumberjacks and wives with friendly smiles, while Whelan and most of the hunters all gave him scowls. Myna sat there with a neutral expression, giving him a brief nod.

"It was a busy day. Thanks again for teaching me what you could, Myna."

"You're a passable student," Myna shrugged.

"Passable," snorted Whelan. "We'll see on Threeday when he hunts with us."

"Maybe you can keep the Red-eyes from our trail," Cian said.

Eyes narrowing, Whelan glared at Cian. "We'll just have to see."

"I'm just glad Myna and Sean were there today," Cian continued. "I hate to think of what might have happened otherwise."

"Food," Misa said from the kitchen, just as Fiona came in. "Help, Fiona?"

"Of course," Fiona replied, heading to the kitchen as Misa came out, carrying a tray with plates on it.

Each plate held a steak that had been seared on the outside, along with a small chunk of rye bread and two green husks. Sean nodded his thanks to Misa when she placed his before him.

Sean waited until everyone had been served to start eating. The bread was warm and pliable, and vegetable husks were just as they had been before, but the steak was a different matter.

Everyone at the table had belt knives they used to slice pieces off their steaks with. Frowning at his lack of cutlery, he grabbed the small blade he had carried without using the last few days. Focusing on it briefly and holding it out of sight, he Shaped it into a knife like the others used.

Fiona glanced at him when he cut into his steak, her eyes dipping to the empty sheath on his waist. Lips pursed, she stayed quiet, even though it was obvious she wanted to say something.

The meat was well into medium, but still leaked pink juice as it was cut. The flavor of the first bite was intense, carrying a smoky hint of the fireplace along with a sharp, spicy tang. Chewing, he found the meat a little on the tough side, but not too bad.

Experimenting with the flavors, he alternated bites of steak with the bread or veggies. The plant increased the tang of the meat and helped highlight an underlying flavor of sweetness he had missed earlier. The bread, on the other hand, mellowed the tang and helped dampen the smoky flavor.

Sated as he finished his meal, Sean finally looked up to discover he was the last one eating. "Err, sorry about that."

"Freak," Whelan muttered as he got to his feet and left, followed by the other hunters.

"Haven't had steak in a while," Cian said as he sighed happily. "Our thanks for helping us kill them, and for the meal, Sean."

The others agreed as they also stood up to leave. With a few friendly parting words, they all shuffled out, leaving just Darragh, Misa, Fiona, and Sean alone in the room.

"I'll see you in a bit, Sean?" Fiona asked as she began to help Misa clean the table.

Licking his knife clean carefully, Sean nodded as he held the knife under the table. "After I speak with Darragh for a few minutes." He quickly Shaped the knife back to its original form and sheathed it.

"Okay," Fiona left after a few moments, and Sean settled into a chair closer to Darragh.

"I take it Fiona already told you?" Darragh asked.

"That I have two days off, yeah," Sean said. "Thanks for modifying the Agreement for me."

"You kept my grandson alive today, gave us meat for a tenday, and helped bring in three logs again." Shaking his head, Darragh smiled sadly. "I have the feeling that you won't stay for much longer, but I'm happy that you've helped as much as you have."

"I will leave eventually, Darragh, but I don't think it'll be soon."

"We shall see what fate brings," Darragh said. "Now, what did you want to learn today?"

"I don't know if you know anything about Mage Sight, but I'm interested in hearing more about it," Sean said.

"Misa," Darragh called out. When she poked her head out of the kitchen, he spoke again, "I need your assistance on a topic."

Misa came out of the kitchen a moment later with a kettle and cups. "What do you need my assssissstance for?"

"Mage Sight," Darragh said as he took the cup she handed him.

"Mage Sssight isss a rare thing for the Naga, and rarer ssstill for other racesss," Misa said as she put a cup before Sean. Taking a third for herself, she coiled into a comfortable position across from Sean. "What knowledge did you ssseek?"

"Anything you know about it, but especially, can it be taught to others?"

Misa swayed slightly back and forth, "Sssome of what I could sssay isss sssecret knowledge that my race keepsss."

"I won't ask for anything that would cause you issues, Misa," Sean told her quickly.

"Very well," Misa said, bowing to him. "Mage Sssight can be taught to othersss, but only if they have the aptitude for it. It isss a very taxing thing to do, and comesss with ssside effectsss. The most common isss vertigo. Othersss might experience nausssea or even temporary blindnessss."

"Is there an easy way to learn how to use it, provided one has the aptitude for it?"

Misa swayed back and forth, "I can't anssswer that."

"How about a yes or no, then?" Sean said. "Do you know of a way for a mage to teach someone Mage Sight, that *doesn't* involve Naga secrets?"

"No," Misa said, tilting her head back and pouring some tea into her open mouth.

"Myna told me that you slew three of the Red-eyes yourself," Darragh said into the silence that followed Misa's answer. "How'd you manage it?"

"I turned one of the axes into a spear, then got the jump on two of them," Sean replied with a shrug. "The third was going to be killed by Cian and the others, but I stepped in to help out, so they wouldn't get hurt too badly before they killed it."

"You slew that one with an axe, sheared it clean in two," Darragh said as he set his cup down.

"Lucky strike," Sean said levelly.

"Luck is what a person makes of it," Darragh said. "Sean, I won't press you for answers, but I feel you're more than you're letting on. I have to ask, though, were you brought here by someone connected to *Fate*?"

"I'm not sure I should answer that, Darragh."

"Very well. Might I inquire what you've thought of us?"

"I have had pleasant interactions with everyone but most of the hunters. Myna was quite pleasant to train with."

"You learned of her heritage, she tells me," Darragh's blind eyes seemed to pin Sean in place. "She said you treated her well, much as you have Fiona and Misa. I will remind you that such actions are outside the norm. You'll invite attention to yourself if you continue to act in a similar manner. Keep that in mind when you go to town tomorrow. You'll see many things you might object to. Those who are Life Bonded are not free to talk to those who are not, for instance."

"How do you tell if someone is Life Bonded?" Sean asked.

Misa placed both of her arms on the table. The light of the single lamp above the table glittered off her yellow and black scales. "Look at my wrissstsss and neck," Misa hissed softly.

Inch wide black bands encircled Misa's wrists and throat. "So black bands on the wrists and neck indicate someone who's Life Bonded?"

"Yes," Darragh said. "Lesser Bonds encircle one or both wrists."

"Being Life Bonded is a type of slavery?" Sean asked.

"Yesss," Misa replied, "but voluntary."

"Huh?"

"To be Bonded at all, one must agree to it," Darragh said. "It is said the Queens can Bond people against their wills, but I've never met anyone who could, or would, verify that."

"Why Bond to anyone?" Sean asked, trying to process what he was being told.

"There are... benefits," Darragh said, his lips creasing into a smile. "At the time of Bonding, rules can be set about what benefits are granted to each other." Taking a deep breath, Darragh paused. "I have a small bit of sight due to Misa being Life Bonded to me. I should be completely blind, but I can see a very faint shape where you are. I have also been able to learn magic from her."

"I have increased physssical abilitiesss. I am now much deadlier than I wasss," Misa said.

Sitting back and sipping his tea, Sean looked thoughtful. "Are there other benefits? What are the downsides?"

"Bonding can last as little as one day, one's entire life, or anything in between," Darragh explained. "For anything short of a Life Bond, the percentage of energy and Talents that are given to the Bond Holder are Agreed upon. The Holder can take as little, or as much, of that as they wish at any given time. They can also give the same in return. Flooding someone with too much energy can damage them in various ways." Reaching out to gently touch Misa, Darragh continued, "Life Bonded give up everything they are to their Holder, and their soul becomes tied to the Holder's soul. If I die, Misa will not survive a single day. Life Bonded are special in other ways, as well, but that's personal."

"Interesting," Sean said as he stood up, feeling the awkward tension that suddenly filled the room. "I do need to go. I promised to help Fiona finish with her work so we can get some rest tonight."

"Sean," Darragh said, "do you think you can best Whelan, when he challenges you?"

"We'll find out," Sean said with a grim smile. "I don't like bullies. Why did you even pick a man so ill-fitted to the rest of you?"

Darragh sighed, "I owed an old friend a favor, and that resulted in Whelan and the others in my village as hunters. Myna is different. I owed a favor to her mother. She asked me to bring Myna with me, to spare her some of the pain she was experiencing in the town she lived in."

"I see. I'll see you in the morning for breakfast."

"No," Misa shook her head and darted into the kitchen, returning shortly with a small sling bag. "Travel food for tomorrow. No need to come to breakfassst."

"Very well," Sean chuckled as he took the bag, placing it over his shoulder. "We'll see you when we return."

"I have grown to like that one," Misa's voice was soft as Sean left, but he still heard her words.

"He's destined for a harsh life, full of decisions that have no good answer," Darragh replied, equally softly. "Do you think we have time for..."

Sean left the area quickly, not wanting to know what Darragh was about to ask Misa. It was bad enough just listening to the somewhat muffled sounds from behind the curtain that led to Darragh's room at night. Fiona sat beside the logs, Shaping a chair. She smiled as he drew closer. "Evening, Fiona," Sean said as he sat down beside her. "What do we need to finish tonight?"

"Chairs for everyone, so they have places to sit in their own homes."

"Okay," Sean settled in by another section of log and started Shaping a chair to match the one Fiona was working on.

"What did you converse with Darragh about tonight?"

"Mage Sight and Bonding," Sean said. "I was wondering if he had any ideas how to teach the Talent to another. He only knew of one way," Sean focused on the chair.

"Bonding," Fiona said. "It's a drastic option to share Talents. There is even a rumor that says the Queens' personal guards are all Bonded to them, which is why they're so feared. They share the Queens' abilities."

"The bodyguards that travel with the Queens?"

"Yes," Fiona said, her hands gliding over the wood she was Shaping.

"I'm still trying to think of ways to share Mage Sight with you," Sean told her, his hands mirroring hers.

"We haven't agreed on a price for you to teach it to me," Fiona uttered softly.

"Everything in this world is bargained for, isn't it?"

"Yes, it is as the Queens have decreed. There are no free gifts, all exchanges must be balanced."

"Hmm," Sean muttered as he mulled over her words. "That

explains why Myna was hesitant to make an Agreement about learning Mage Sight from me."

"Of course. Mage Sight is very rare, so the price needed to balance the scales would be enormous," Fiona said as her hands slowed.

"Huh. But if I can't teach it, the point is moot," Sean muttered.

"That is true," Fiona agreed.

"I thought we'd Agreed on me teaching you already," Sean said after a moment.

"No, the Agreement was for you to try to teach me, which you already did," Fiona replied, setting the chair aside and beginning to Shape another section of the log.

"Can't I just gift you the knowledge?"

"No. You can offset the cost to a degree, but only those who are married, or children of the one gifting, are exempt from needing to bargain."

"The more I learn of this world, the odder it seems," Sean sighed.

"I would probably feel the same on your old world," Fiona said.

"Fair enough," Sean chuckled. "Shall we finish this up so we can get some sleep? We've got a busy day ahead of us tomorrow."

"That sounds like a good idea," Fiona agreed.

CHAPTER TWENTY-TWO

Sean heard Fiona's soft snores coming from her cot when he woke the next morning. Sitting up from his spot on the floor, he glanced over and saw her face relaxed in sleep. A smile creased his lips as he got to his feet. Opening the kettle on the table, he saw it was empty, and focused on what he was about to do. Getting his body into position, he began to softly sing the song he used to conjure hot water. As he poured water into the kettle, he felt Fiona's eyes on him and his cheeks heated. Once the kettle was full, he stopped the spell and looked over at her.

"You use a child's song to conjure water?" Fiona asked.

"Yeah," Sean said as he looked around. "Where are the leaves for the tea?"

"I need to heat it first," Fiona said, gathering her blanket around herself while getting out of bed.

"It's already steaming," Sean said, looking away from her.

"Really?" With a soft giggle, Fiona shook her head. "Why am I surprised when it's you? You always seem to do things differently." Changing direction, she retrieved a tin from under her bed and brought it over to the table. "Take three leaves and crumble them into the water. I'll get dressed, so we can get going."

"Sure," Sean said, taking the tin and making tea. While it brewed, he pulled bread and jerky out of the bag Misa had given him. Glancing over, he watched as Fiona pulled a jerkin over her head. Her body was at an angle to him, but gave him a decent view of one of her firm, high breasts, the mithril gleaming in the little bit of light that leaked in around the shuttered window. Quickly looking away, he felt his mouth go dry as his body reminded him just how long he had gone without being near a naked woman. Closing his eyes, he rubbed at his face and tried to think about something else as the image of her danced before his eyes.

"And breakfast as well," Fiona said from behind him. "Misa was nice to us, indeed."

"Tea should be good," Sean managed, though his words were strangled.

Raising a brow, she walked around him to her chair, her eyes on him the whole time. "Did you peek while I dressed?"

"I didn't mean to," Sean said, not looking at her as he took the other chair available. "I was going to tell you it was ready, and... you hadn't quite gotten your top on yet."

"Ahh," her cheeks pinked slightly. "I'm sorry for causing you discomfort. I tried to make it quick."

"It's not your fault," Sean quickly told her. "I shouldn't have assumed you were done."

"It was my left side, wasn't it?" Fiona asked, pouring the tea.

"Yeah," Sean said, taking the cup she offered him. His hand shook lightly, causing some to splash from the cup. "I'm sorry."

"I—" Fiona began, then shook her head. "I know it's not something that men want to think about. That half of my body is no longer flesh," she looked at the cup in her hands.

"No," Sean exclaimed. Coughing, he met her heterochromatic eyes, "It's not that, it's just not normal for men to see women naked on my old world if they're not in a relationship."

Lips turning up, Fiona giggled. "It's a good thing we aren't joining the others for bathing, then."

Nibbling his bread, Sean frowned. "Why?"

"Everyone bathes in the stream together," Fiona said, her smile fading as pain filled her eyes. "In the cities and towns, there are public bath houses for the masses, and every inn has a washroom. Only nobles have the luxury of personal baths."

"I..." Sean paused, then pressed on, "I thought your body was amazing. The detail, and the way your body moves, is beautiful." Holding a tight smile as he said the words, he waited for her rebuke but felt the need to tell her.

Her cheeks flushed at his words, and she looked away from him. "So strange," Fiona mumbled. "We'll have to bathe at the inn later today," she said a little louder. "Maybe I'll ask you to wash my back, since my body doesn't repulse you."

"I'm not sure if that's the best idea in the world," Sean said as he swallowed the last of his jerky.

"Oh? I didn't mean—" Fiona began.

"No. It's like putting a steak before a starving man. Self-control only goes so far," Sean interrupted.

"Oh," the single word was full of something Sean couldn't decipher. "Once we finish, we'll head out. Can I ask you to tell me about your world while we walk?"

"Of course," Sean said, grateful for the change of subject. "I'd like to hear any story you wish to share in exchange," Sean said, popping the last of the bread into his mouth.

Fiona nodded, eyes full of hope. "I agree."

Finishing up, Fiona gathered a few things into a messenger bag that she slung over her neck and shoulder. Sean stepped outside as she gathered her things, pulling a length of wood from one of the logs and making a walking staff for himself. Fiona came out with a bounce to her step and a broad smile.

"Sean," a voice called out to him as they turned to start walking.

Pausing, he turned to find Myna jogging towards him, "What's up Myna?"

"Will you grant me a small request, since you are going to town?"

"Sure, what is it?"

"Drop this letter at the general store. It is for my mother," Myna said, holding out a small scroll tube. "I have an account with them, so it will cost you nothing."

"No problem," Sean said, taking the case and tucking it into his belt.

"In exchange, I will give you this," Myna said, her voice lowering as she stepped closer to him. Before he realized what she might be up to, she kissed his cheek. "I look forward to working with you when you get back."

"Right," Sean coughed as he stepped back from her. "Until later."

He missed the narrow-eyed gaze Fiona shot him and Myna. Myna didn't, her lips twisting into a smirk as she met Fiona's gaze. "Take your time," Myna said, "and thank you again."

"We need to get going," Fiona said, starting down the road.

"Later," Sean said again and hurried to catch up to Fiona.

The two walked in uncomfortable silence for a bit. Eventually, Sean decided to speak up, "You wanted to hear stories, right?"

Looking at him out of the corner of her eye, she nodded. "I do. I was wondering though, when you were training with Myna, did she do anything else like that?"

"Nope. That was straight out of left field," Sean said.

"I see," Fiona mumbled. "Please talk to me, then. Tell me something of your old world."

"I'll tell you a story about my friend James, the friend I left behind. We'd known each other for years, met at the shooting range..." as Sean spoke, he couldn't help but smile and wonder again about his friend. He did offer some small thanks that both of his parents had already passed, as his dying would have been too much for them to handle.

The walk was pleasant, even with the weather on the chill side as winter approached. Sean found himself explaining the idea of cell phones and cars to Fiona, some of which could be found in this world, with magic as the base instead of electricity or internal combustion engines. Such things tended to be in the hands of the rich and powerful, the way the Queens liked it. Fiona, for her part, told Sean about her early life before her Shame. Sean was interested to hear about the Academy that trained those with Talents to excel at them. It was where many nobles found those that they would eventually employ. Fiona avoided any stories of her graduation or her family, and he didn't ask.

Sean was in the middle of telling a story of how James had gotten them both shot down by a bartender a few years before, when the town came into view as they walked around a bend in the road. Faltering in his telling of the story, Sean took in the sight. An eight-foot-tall wooden palisade surrounded it on three sides, with the fourth side bordered by a lake of beautiful blue water. A couple of small islands were visible in the distance, one dominated by a tower that rose a few stories into the air. What he could see above the wall were wooden structures with wood shingle roofs.

"How many people live here?" Sean asked.

"A few hundred," Fiona said, her cheery demeanor shifting to wariness as they approached the town.

Seeing the shift, Sean reached out and took her hand. "Come on, can't have my guide all gloomy."

Her hand twitched in his before it stilled. "They'll look at you oddly if you're so free with me."

"Fuck'em if they can't understand friends," Sean shrugged. "Besides, I just think they're going to be jealous that the most beautiful woman in town will be with me."

"Incorrigible," Fiona murmured, but her smile returned.

A guard leaned against the wall next to the open gate. He watched them walk up, clearly bored with his job. "State your names, where you're from, and your business here in Oaklake," the guard told them as they got close enough to talk.

"Fiona Mithrilsoul and Sean MacDougal, of Oakwood. We're here to sell some of my items, and will be buying some things for the village before we head back tomorrow," Fiona said clearly, though her hand twitched in Sean's when she said her name.

Lips twisting at her words, the guard sneered. "Silvershame, everyone knows who you are. Darragh normally sends the lads on the logs to buy stuff. Why did he send you instead?"

"I asked to come," Sean said, his voice frosty. "Darragh told me how hospitable the town was and that I should take in the wonders of the bountiful lake. Maybe he meant a different town, hmm?"

The guard came off the wall, his face frozen, "Sean MacDougal, you say? I don't recall ever seeing you in the last three months. Where did you hail from before Darragh's village? There's nothing else close by that I know of."

"I came from the town of Waterrock. It's a bit far, but I like to wander," Sean smirked. "Can we enter now?"

"Of course, but the mayor just instituted a new law. Every first-time entry must pay a copper," the guard's sneer changed to a sly smile.

"Of course," Fiona said, removing her hand from Sean's to extend a copper. "I'll need a receipt, though, for Darragh."

The smile vanished, and the guard's hand was rapidly withdrawn. "I just recalled, the law doesn't go into effect until Fiveday."

"Right," Sean chuckled. "Have a good day, officer." Turning his attention to Fiona, he took her metallic hand again, "Which way to the store? We have that letter to drop, after all."

"I'll show you," Fiona said, ignoring the scowling guard as they entered the town.

After a few dozen feet, Sean snorted, "Corruption and idiots, the same in every world."

"People are people everywhere," Fiona added, her own lips perking up.

Looking around like a tourist, Sean was pleased to see that the dirt streets were cleaner than he'd feared. He didn't see any waste littering the roads, and wondered about it. When he asked, Fiona explained that Fire Mages were employed to help control litter. They oversaw the offal gatherers, then burned the collected waste. Sean nodded, seeing it as just another form of sewer and trash collection.

The store Fiona led him to was in the middle of town. A sign reading "Gern's" hung from two bronze chains above the door. The first floor was stone and the upper floors built of wood, much like the other large building across the square from it. Sean looked around as they entered the shop, expecting shelves full of goods like almost every video game he'd ever played. Instead, the large main room had a comfortable sitting area, and just one long counter. An older, grumpy-looking man with thinning hair stood behind the counter, leaning on it.

"Silvershame," the man greeted her evenly. "Never thought Darragh would send you to town. That must mean you have wares to sell. Let's see them."

Placing her bag on the counter, Fiona began to unload small wooden knick-knacks. While she did, Sean placed the scroll tube on the counter. "Sir, Myna asked us to deliver this tube to you," Sean told the man.

"I can do that. She still has money in her account, though she did get a letter yesterday. Can I trust you to deliver it to her safely?" the man asked, eyeing Sean with deliberate care.

"I will gladly do so. I do owe her, after all," Sean said.

"My name is Gern, and this is my store. Who might you be?" Gern asked, taking Myna's letter and placing it in a bag.

"Sean MacDougal," Sean replied. "I'm a friend of Fiona and Myna."

"I see," the man said evenly, barely holding back contempt at Sean's admission of friendship with the women. "Here's Myna's letter. I'll need your Agreement to deliver it only to her hand. I'll give you a copper to do so."

"The copper is Myna's, isn't it?" Sean asked.

"Of course. Why else would she have an account for mail?" Gern smirked.

"I Agree to your terms," Sean said, feeling the now familiar weight of an Agreement settle on him.

Pushing the tube and copper to Sean, Gern turned his attention back to Fiona, who stood waiting patiently. "Okay, let's give them a look," Gern snorted as he pulled a pair of Pince-nez spectacles from under the counter and placed them on his nose. Gern took his time searching each item for flaws, and eventually, he put his glasses away.

"Your work is still good, despite being half of the woman you used to be. I'll give you ten bronze for the lot."

Sean's hands clenched at the way Gern causally insulted Fiona. He knew he would be hearing similar insults all the time if he stayed near Fiona, but he didn't understand how she could accept it so calmly. When Gern stated the price, something made Sean want to vehemently disagree, but he held his tongue.

"Twenty," Fiona said simply.

"Where else could you even try to sell your wares around here?" Gern snickered, "Eleven, and not a single copper more."

Lips compressed, Fiona nodded stiffly. "Agreed."

"Pleasure doing business with you," Gern laughed as he counted out eleven small bronze coins. "What else can I be doing for you today?"

"We need some essentials," Fiona managed with some civility. "A set of bronze utensils, a warm jacket, good boots, travel clothing to fit my friend, a wool blanket, a striker, a canteen, and a bag to carry it all in."

Gern looked from Fiona to Sean and began to laugh, "You sold me all of that just to give this guy some basic essentials? What did he do to earn that, eh? Finally make you a woman?"

Sean's knuckles popped audibly as he stared at Gern. "Did you just imply that she's buying me things because I slept with her?"

"Not implying," Gern smirked, "flat saying. What backwater did you crawl out of, that you don't know Silvershame's dirty past? I'm surprised you're still breathing, considering the fate of the last guy."

Fiona touched Sean's arm, "Don't. This is my life, and I don't need someone trying to shield me from my Shame."

"That's the way a Shamed should act. Pay attention, boy," Gern snickered. "Now, what you're asking for will cost you six bronze coins," his words aimed at Fiona.

"That's more than double what I should pay," Fiona replied.

"Your *friend* drove the price up by irritating me," Gern said. "Either pay, or go find someone who'll sell you used goods, instead of my new wares."

"I wish to see the items first," Fiona said.

"Of course." Gern rang a bell, bringing a small creature flying out of the back at speed.

The blur of silver settled on the counter next to Gern, "Yes, master?"

"Have Olaf put together a winter travel set, along with some bronze utensils," Gern said, not even looking at the androgynous being standing next to his hand.

"Right away," the creature said, before zipping off in a blur that took it around Sean for a moment.

"Pixie?" Sean asked.

Gern snorted, "Never seen a Messenger Fairy?" Sean snapped his mouth shut, which only made Gern laugh. "I was right, some backbirth shithole must be where you hail from."

Sean stayed quiet, not rising to the bait this time. The last time he'd risen to provocation he'd been killed for it, after all. The silence stretched out until the curtain that separated the front of the shop from the rest was moved aside.

A being with grey fur and a wolf's head came out of the back carrying a bag. Black ring markings stood out in the fur at its wrists and around its neck. "The items, master," it said, though the words were difficult to understand from the canine's mouth.

"Spread out the items for inspection, Olaf," Gern said dismissively.

Nodding its head, Olaf opened the leather bag and pulled items out of it, laying each of them on the counter. Once they were laid out, it stepped back and waited.

"Well?" Gern said.

"Make sure the clothing fits," Fiona told Sean.

Sean started with the fur lined jacket, which proved to be just a little big, but not enough to hinder him. Next, he pulled off his own footwear and tried on the calf high boots. The soles were tough, thick leather, while the upper part was made from much softer leather. The fur lining encased his feet in warmth. Taking a few steps, he was amazed at how well the boots fit. He put his other boots back on, returning the new ones to the counter.

"The clothes are fine," Sean said, beginning to check the rest of the gear laid out in front of him. Everything was of good make and serviceable, if not exceptional, quality. "Everything is fine," Sean finally told Fiona.

Placing six of the bronze coins on the counter, Fiona nodded to Gern. "Thank you for your time, Gern."

"Thank you for the profit, Silvershame," Gern grinned, his blackened teeth horrible to see.

"We have other places to visit, Sean," Fiona said, motioning to the gear on the counter.

Sean began to pack everything back into the bag, which he promptly slung over his shoulder after it was packed. "Good day, Gern," Sean managed as he turned to leave with Fiona.

Stepping out into the town square once more, Sean mulled over Fiona's earlier words to him. *Maybe I should try to adapt to the world. It's not like it'll change because of me.* Shaking the thought from his mind, he looked to Fiona. "Fiona, about what happened inside—"

"Don't," Fiona cut him off. "It's as much my fault as yours. Back at Oakwood, I let your words influence me more than I should have. You're one of the very few who treats me as if my Shame is nothing. That's not the way the world works, and I should have made sure you understood that long before now." She started walking away from the store. "I'm sorry for snapping at you, but this is the way the world is, and you need to accept that."

Trailing after her, he grimaced. He knew she had a point, but didn't like it at all. "I'll try, but it's going to take a lot of adjusting," Sean said as he fell into step beside her.

"For both of us," Fiona muttered. "You didn't mind me telling you to back off?"

"No. Like you said, it's your life. I haven't even known you for a tenday, and it's wrong for me to impose my values on you, or the world. If you'll continue to teach me, I'll do my best to learn."

A smile appeared, before quickly vanishing from her lips. "I'll do what I can, while we're together," Fiona said. Her hand bumped his and he took it, bringing another smile to her lips. "Besides, maybe Gern was closer to the truth than he knew."

Sean stumbled a step, bringing a giggle from Fiona. "What?" he choked out.

"The lake is just ahead. You should see the Naiads at work and play," Fiona said, ignoring his question.

CHAPTER TWENTY-THREE

The docks for the lake were bigger than Sean had expected. Boats of various sizes could be seen, tied up or plying the waters. The biggest of the ships was just getting underway, with a deep drum slowly pounding out a rhythm that helped the oars move in unison.

"Slave galley?" Sean asked.

"Just a galley," Fiona said. "The rowers might be paid, or they might be Bonded."

"Why would a ship that size be here?"

"The lake connects to one of the major riverways leading to Southpoint," Fiona said, pointing at the keel of a ship slowly coming to dock. "A Naiad," she said softly.

Sean squinted where she was pointing, and could just make out a darker fluid shape in the water that seemed to hug the keel. "What's it doing?"

"She's leading them into their berth," Fiona told him.

"Why do you say she?" Sean asked as he walked with Fiona down to the docks.

"All Naiads are female, as all Satyrs are male. It is just the way the world is," Fiona said simply.

Sean looked back, seeing a number of people rush up where the ship was just touching the dock. "Tying her up?"

"Yes, some of them. Others are offering their services for unloading," Fiona explained. "Dock hands are a simple lot; they get a copper per boat they help unload. Perhaps two, if the captain is generous."

"Small pay for hard work," Sean muttered.

"Being without a Talent or any magic, means you either learn a craft, or you get relegated to menial labor."

"The way of the world, no matter what world it is," Sean chuckled darkly.

"I've been meaning to ask," Fiona began, before dropping the volume of her voice, "how do you speak the language so fluently? Many Outsiders spend years learning to converse properly."

"A gift from those that brought me here," he said just as softly. "I seem to know Naga as well."

Lips pursing, Fiona nodded. "I see. They seem to have invested quite a bit in your welfare. Why did they do that?"

"They said something about setting some mistake right," Sean shrugged. "They also hoped I would find a way to eventually allow them to show up here."

Fiona slowed for a step, before walking normally again. "They want you to be the Harbinger."

"Huh?"

"An old myth. It's said that the Harbinger will force the Queens to make the world fairer for those who aren't of the courts."

"Every world has a similar story," Sean said, trying to dismiss her words, feeling a shiver run down his spine.

"Of course," Fiona nodded. "Look at the last dock," she said in her normal tone.

Looking where she indicated, Sean blinked and his jaw fell open slightly. One of the most gorgeous women he had ever seen was lounging on the end of the dock. A simple, transparent white gown was barely covering her body, doing far more to accent than conceal. "W-wow," Sean stammered.

"Naiad," Fiona said as her thumb dug into his hand, snapping his gaze from the woman. "They use their looks and words to convince men to kiss them. If someone does, a bit of their energy goes to the Naiad. If she continues to kiss them, they eventually end up suffocating. You can't breathe when kissing one."

"I take it the kiss has some kind of aphrodisiac effect that makes the victim want to keep kissing?"

"Of course," Fiona said. "The Agreement in place that allows us to use the stream is that a kiss lasts for five seconds, and no longer—unless the villager asks for it."

"Cian said something about the kisses being addictive."

"That's what people say. I don't know, never having kissed one myself," Fiona said.

"They don't like women?" Sean asked, the image of Fiona and the Naiad making out popping into his mind.

"They aren't picky at all, I just haven't," Fiona said, digging her thumb in again as she saw his blank expression. "Is there anything else in town you'd like to see?"

"I don't have any coin, so it's a moot point," Sean chuckled. "I trust you to show me the things I should see."

"Maybe a quick tour," Fiona said, leading him away from the Naiad, who had turned her head to focus on Sean.

"Come back later and see me," the woman's voice echoed eerily as she arched her back, pressing her impressive breasts against her garment.

Shaking his head, Sean frowned. Her voice, while seductive, also held a nails-on-a-chalkboard quality. "Maybe later," Sean said, letting Fiona lead him away.

Fiona looked at him worriedly until he spoke, then her eyes narrowed as she stared at him. She didn't say anything until they were away from the docks. "You didn't seem interested in her offer."

"Her voice was unpleasant," Sean said. "I thought they were supposed to be persuasive?"

"They are," Fiona said. "I wanted to listen to her offer, even though she wasn't focused on me. I think she's one of the older Naiads that inhabits the lake."

Considering Fiona's words, and thinking of the undertone to the Naiad's, Sean became lost in thought. Fiona stopped, pulling him from his thoughts. "Huh?"

"We're here," Fiona said as she led him around the side of a nearby building.

Passing through the double doors, Sean saw a very broad, but decidedly short person loading an ingot of bronze into a forge. Sean let his gaze dart all over the smithy, taking in the crafting space. Different ingots were stacked along one wall, another wall held different chests with small signs on them. Near the massive double doors that served as the smithy entrance were three different colored fifty-gallon barrels.

Turning to get something else, the man saw them and stopped, his eyes narrowing as he looked at Fiona. "What does Silvershame want with me?" His voice was much higher-pitched than Sean expected, but still masculine.

"I'm showing a friend the town," Fiona said simply. "As you are the only smith here, and my friend is interested in metalwork, it seemed prudent to bring him here."

The person turned his full gaze to Sean, seeming to weigh him. "You're not a smith," he said evenly, "so what could you want with me?"

"I would be honored if you would just let me watch you work for a bit, but I'm not in need of anything specifically."

"I would get nothing out of allowing that," the smith said with a snort.

"Fairly said, and true," Sean nodded. "I wanted to watch a smith who knows their craft work, was all."

"Trying to sway me with a silver tongue, eh?"

"A little flattery can open closed doors," Sean chuckled, "it was worth a shot."

"Stay out of my way, and you can watch for a bit," the smith finally said and grabbed the hammer he had been looking for.

Stepping back, Sean leaned his head towards Fiona, "Does he have non-human blood?"

"Maybe Dwarven blood," Fiona whispered. "The Dwarves in the Quadital are the best smiths, and are all known for having a high Talent for Shaping metal."

"I always thought of Dwarves as bearded," Sean whispered back as he glanced at the clean shaven, short-haired smith.

Pulling the ingot from the fire, the smith laid it on the anvil and began to hammer the metal. When the metal cooled to a point he was unhappy with, he put it back in the forge and pumped the bellows, ignoring his audience.

When the smith went to pull the metal from the fire again, Sean pulled up Mage Sight to see if the smith was using any Talent or magic. The faintest sheen of silvered-gold ran from the chest of the smith, down his right arm, and to the hammer. Sean nodded, watching the worst of the flaws being erased from the metal with each strike of the smith's hammer.

Shaking the Sight off, Sean waited until the smith paused again before clearing his throat to gain the man's attention. "Sir, it has been a pleasure to watch a serious crafter intent on plying their trade. My thanks for allowing me to watch your work."

Snorting, the smith shook his head. "Not that I did anything of note, but sure. If you need anything made, make sure to come and see me."

"Gladly," Sean said. "I wish you the best day."

As they left the smith's shop, Fiona glanced at Sean. "Was he?"

"Was he what?"

"Was he using a Talent?"

"Very weakly, but yes. I don't think it was conscious, though; it was the faintest use of energy I've seen up to this point and it only happened when he was hammering."

"I was thinking of going to the mill, and maybe the woodworker, before going to the inn," Fiona told him.

"That sounds fine," Sean said, taking Fiona's hand again as they walked down the road.

The sawmill was impressive, for the fact that they had an adamantine blade. The woman in charge of the mill was cool, but not cold, to Fiona. When Sean asked about the blade, the foreman explained that the Lord of Southpoint had had it delivered so that the wood could be milled faster for the city.

Briefly using his Mage Sight, he saw that two Bonded females were a deep green when they helped guide the log to be cut onto the cutting area. The dark green hair of each gave clear clues to their nonhuman nature.

When they were leaving, Sean asked Fiona about the two. "Were the two Bonded workers part dryad?"

"Deeply so," Fiona nodded. "Maybe as much as half-blooded. The sheer energy they radiated when lifting the logs was staggering. If they could harness even a tenth of that into Shaping, they wouldn't be there."

"That explains it," Sean nodded, but wondered if Talent itself couldn't be trained in time.

The woodworker's shop wasn't far from the inn. The large building's interior exhibited almost every type of craft possible with wood. Tables, chairs, cabinets, and even bread boxes were on display.

"Welcome..." The thin angular man trailed off as he saw Fiona. "Silvershame, what are you doing in my shop?" The question was delivered with a sneer, speaking of the hatred the man harbored towards Fiona.

"Sean here is a guest of Darragh, Venar. When Sean expressed that he wished to visit the town, I was tasked with bringing him. He spoke of an interest in woodworking, so we ended up here."

"You aren't wanted in my shop. I'll not have it sullied by a Shamed," Venar hissed.

"I'll wait outside. Please take your time, Sean," Fiona said as she disengaged her hand and left.

"Holding hands with Fiona Silvershame? How low you must be," Venar sneered at Sean. "Can't find a real woman, or even a whore, to take an interest in you?"

Sean's knuckles cracked, but he held to Fiona's warning and bit back his comments. "Who knows?" he managed through clenched teeth. "I was interested in how you craft your wares."

"The same way Silvershame used to, before she lost much of her Talent," Venar snickered. "Now I'm the far superior Shaper." Raising his chin, the man seemed to preen. "What Talents or skills do you possess, if any?"

"I'm a hunter," Sean said as he looked around the shop. "Nothing in here is of any real use to me, but seeing how beautiful the items Fiona crafts are, I thought the person here in town could surely produce better."

"And as you can see, I d—" Venar began with a haughty smile.

"Sadly," Sean cut the man off, "I see she's still your superior in every way. I'm sorry for taking up your time. I'll be going now."

Sean walked out as Venar was still spluttering and purpling in the face, unable to form coherent words over the insult that Sean had delivered so easily. Finding Fiona standing outside looking at the sky, Sean crossed the street to her. "I'm ready to go now."

"So soon?" Fiona asked.

"He doesn't Shape half as well as you, and his attitude sucks," Sean said as he took her hand. "Let's see about some food, and maybe a bath, shall we?"

Her eyes had narrowed when he started speaking, but she smiled when he asked the question. "Of course," Fiona said and led him back to the town square.

Neither of them noticed Venar leave his shop to stare after them with an ugly expression on his face. "You'll pay for that," the man hissed softly, before stepping back into his shop.

CHAPTER TWENTY-FOUR

The inn's sign proclaimed it to be the Oaklake Respite. The main room was a tavern, with a long bar along one side of the room, a handful of large casks and numerous bottles and jugs taking up the wall behind it.

The stone floor was smooth, seemingly made of a single large block of grey granite. The room held numerous tables of various sizes, all of them crafted in the same plain style.

Since it wasn't yet nightfall, the room was mostly empty. A group of four rough-looking men sat in a corner, nursing their drinks in silence. Another smaller table near the large windows dominating the front of the building held two older men, who were playing a game of chance.

A single woman, in well-made but not ostentatious clothing, sat by herself. Her eyes flickered to them as they came in. Her unblemished face creased with a frown as she saw Fiona, but went blank again as her eyes found Sean.

Fiona had released Sean's hand before entering the inn, and went to the tall, rotund man behind the bar. "Gosrek, we require a room for the evening, a meal, and use of the bathing room."

Gosrek's lips went taut, but he nodded. "Silvershame. Never thought Darragh would send you to town. Who's this with you?"

"My name's Sean MacDougal," Sean said. "Your inn is the nicest I've seen, Gosrek."

"You've clearly never been to any of the Quadital's inns, then," Gosrek chuckled. "I do thank you for the compliment. Two rooms and such will—"

"One room will suffice," Fiona said quickly, placing a bronze coin on the counter.

Brows rising, Gosrek looked from her to Sean and back. "It's not my place to question a patron's choice of partners. I'll have one of mine show you to your room. Did you want food right away?"

"No, we'll wait for the normal evening meal," Fiona said. "I would like to put my bag in the room, though."

"Fair enough." Gosrek took the coin, replacing it with five large coppers and three small ones. "If you need anything else, just ask." Having said that, he turned his head and shouted towards the open doorway next to the bar. "Matilda, customers."

A short blonde woman with broad shoulders came out of the back. Her hair was in long, thin braids that were gathered into a tail behind her head, except for two that trailed down her cheeks and hung to her shoulders. "Right away, master," Matilda said as she came hurrying out of the back. Turning her attention to Sean and Fiona, she gave a small curtsy. "Follow me, please."

Trailing behind the maid, Sean was glad that this world didn't seem to have the standard maid outfit his world knew—it would have looked out of place on Matilda. She wore what he had always thought of as Ren Faire garb. Her chest wasn't overly exposed, though that would have been difficult as her chest seemed more muscle than fat. He noted that the dress went all the way to her ankles as well.

Matilda led them up to the second floor, down a hall lined with doors. She stopped before the room with a 9 on it. "Here is your room," Matilda said, opening the door and walking in. While Sean and Fiona trailed her into the room, she set out a pitcher and basin, along with a washcloth, on a sideboard. "If there's anything else you need, please don't hesitate to ask."

"We will," Fiona said, holding out a copper to the maid, who quickly accepted it. Sean noticed a single thin black band encircling her left wrist as she took the coin.

"Have a good stay," Matilda said, her smile a little more genuine than before.

Sean looked around the room as Matilda left. A small table and two chairs sat in the middle of a mostly empty room. A bed that would be snug for both of them took up one corner, and a window, too small to be more than an arrow slit, provided some light.

"Cozy," Sean said, turning to see Fiona's cheeks turning pink as she looked from him to the bed.

"You don't mind, do you?"

"Not in the least, the floor will be fine," Sean said.

Face scrunching up, Fiona's eyes began filling with unshed tears. "Oh, I... see. I thought—"

"Wait, Fiona," Sean said, cutting her off. "It's not what you think. You're a wonderful person and absolutely gorgeous. I'm not saying I'm not interested, not at all. I'm just not sure if we should, so soon after having met."

"I see," Fiona sniffled as the first few tears spilled from her eyes.

Unable to watch a woman cry, Sean stepped forward and gently embraced Fiona. "I'm sorry, this is a me issue. I don't know what might happen between us later. I just want you to know, I'm not going to be able to stay in the village. It would feel like I was taking advantage of you if I accepted your advance and then left."

Her hands went around him hesitantly, then clung to him like a life preserver in a winter lake. "I... I had men after me when I was younger. I was sought after for my beauty and Talent. When I earned my Shame, though, they all vanished overnight. I never once felt for any of them what I feel with you. Our energies seemed to harmonize with each other so fluidly; I thought maybe you were what my mother always talked about."

Holding her as she clung to him and cried, Sean rubbed her back.

"I don't want you to be hurt, Fiona Mithrilsoul," he whispered. "I think you're worth much more than the little I can offer."

"What if that's all I want?" Fiona sniffled. "If I said I was okay with just tonight, and won't expect anything in the morning, would you consider it, for me?"

Swallowing the lump in his throat, Sean nodded. "Yes."

She pressed herself against him a bit more firmly, and he could feel a certain tension leave her. "Thank you," she whispered as she held him.

He just held her, waiting for her to break the hug. The moment stretched on, and Sean became increasingly aware of her body. Shifting, he eased the hug, indicating he was ready to move away. Fiona held on a moment longer, before releasing him.

"I'm going to head down to the taproom for a bit," Sean said, stepping back once the hug broke.

"Wait," Fiona said, grabbing the small pouch she kept coins in and drawing out one of her bronze pieces. "Take this, so you can get a drink or two. You can repay me later."

Taking the coin, he put it into the small pouch on his waist. "Are you going to come with?"

"No," Fiona said, turning away as she wiped at her eyes. "I'm going to stay up here, for a bit at least."

"Okay," Sean said, "but don't stay up here too long."

"I won't," she said, a hint of happiness apparent in her voice.

Without saying more, Sean exited the room and wondered if he'd made the right decision. He was attracted to Fiona, that wasn't in doubt, but he had never been the kind of guy to love them and leave them. *Maybe I'm overthinking things, and she's just wanting a make-out session later*, Sean mentally sighed to himself.

Downstairs, he found a couple more people in the room. A man in fine silks was sitting with the lady from before, and a third old man had joined the other two by the window.

"Gosrek, what drinks do you have?" Sean asked, seating himself on one of the stools at the bar.

"Light ale, dark ale, mead, brandy, and hard cider in the kegs. If you want the fancy stuff, I've got that too, for a price," Gosrek said. "Which do you prefer?"

Sean wasn't much for beer, but he knew he'd be fine with a darker ale. "A dark ale to start with, please," Sean placed the bronze coin on the counter. "Can I run a tab on that?"

Gosrek snorted, "Of course. I'm a fair man who doesn't skimp on the change due at the end of the night." Taking the coin, he grabbed a large stein, which he filled from the second keg. "Here you go. Enjoy."

The tankard was full to the top, though the ale's head wasn't as pronounced as Sean was used to seeing. He took a sip, and found it thicker than any drink he'd ever had, and sweeter than any beer he'd drunk. The flavor was rich malt, with hints of blackberries. Gosrek wandered down the bar to refill the steins of the four men in the corner, who'd called for another round.

Turning around on the stool, Sean took a moment to gauge the four men better. Their clothing was thick, and looked to be made of coarse material. Each of them also wore hardened leather chest guards and had a weapon on their hip. *Adventurers or guards of some kind*, Sean thought.

Matilda came out of the back and loaded the drinks on her tray. They all ignored her like she was furniture. *No remarks and no touching. I didn't expect that,* Sean frowned. *Why do they ignore her?* Taking another sip of his beer, he tried to puzzle out the reasons for their behavior. *Maybe because of her mixed blood? Or is it just more civilized than I thought it would be?*

Shaking his head, he turned his attention to the three old men at their table. They were playing a game of some kind, involving dice and a cup. Interested, he waved Gosrek over to him, "Gosrek, a round of whatever those three are drinking on me, please."

Raising a brow, Gosrek nodded and moved off to fill the order. As he filled the tankards, Sean stood up and waited. When the third tankard touched the bar top, Sean slipped his hand through the handles and carefully picked up all three.

"Don't be making a mess," Gosrek said, but otherwise didn't object.

"I'll do my best," Sean said as he carefully crossed over to the trio. "Gentlemen, might I join your table? I've brought drinks."

The three men looked over at him speculatively. The largest of them, who still had some black coloration to his mostly grey hair spoke up, "We won't turn down the drinks, but we're not keen on playing with strangers."

"That's fair," Sean said as he set the tankards down. "Do you mind if I just watch for a bit?"

"For the drinks, you can watch as long as you want," one of the others laughed.

"Easy now, Gert," the third said as he took one of the tankards, "he might just be trying to dull your already dull wits."

"Always so quick to insult, Jay," Gert snorted, "but we all know it's you that has the dull wits."

"Don't mind them, they've been like this for years," the first man said to Sean. "That's Jay Porter, and Gert Lowenhamn, and I'm Bill Murphy. Who might you be?"

"Sean MacDougal," he said, extending a hand to Bill. "A pleasure. I'm just wanting some company for a bit, and out of all the tables, yours seemed the most inviting."

Looking at the other two tables, Bill chuckled, "I would say so. Velin and her lackey would not welcome one of lower status than themselves. As for her guards, unless you can prove your strength, they won't accept you."

"Seems I chose wisely, then," Sean grinned.

"Not really. Now you have to put up with Gert," Jay snorted.

"We have company, tone it down," Bill sighed. "Fifty years and they still act like damn kids."

"And you're still not my dad," Gert snapped, "so mind yourself."

"What variant are you playing?" Sean asked, hoping to find out more about the game without being pegged as an Outsider.

"No variant, just plain old Knuckles," Bill said.

"Ah, I thought you were playing something a bit more complex," Sean said as if he understood.

"We're too old to try keeping up with whatever nonsense the Lords come up with every year," Jay said.

"Ain't that the truth," Gert agreed. "I watched them playing Bones once, where the lowest toss was the winner. What is the point of that?"

"Who knows what the Lords think?" Bill shook his head as he collected the dice and placed them in the cup. "Now let's see if our guest can bring me luck for the Quadital drop."

"Get real," Gert laughed as Bill shook the cup before upending it on the table.

"It seems no such luck today," Bill chuckled. "Still, five eyes are a damn good drop. I'll stay with that."

Jay picked up the cup and dice, and began to rattle them around. "I would say so; five anything is hard to beat."

After a few rounds of the game, Sean thought he'd figured out the rules. It was close to Yahtzee, except that each game was a single round, with the best hand taking the pot. They could reroll any number of dice once before their turn was over. Oddly, it wasn't five sixes that were the best hand possible, but five fives.

Making a note to ask Fiona about that later, he just watched them play and ordered them all a second round. Almost an hour after he came downstairs, the inn began to fill as the sun sank below the horizon.

"Well, it looks like the night has come," Bill said as he gathered up the cup and dice, stowing them in his pouch. "It was good to meet you, Sean. We'll see you here tomorrow, if you're still about." The other two drained their mugs and stood, agreeing with Bill.

"Leaving before dinner?" Sean asked.

"Oh yes. The night crowd can get a little rowdier than we care for, and each of us has dinner waiting for us at home." Bill clapped a hand to Sean's shoulder, "If you're game tomorrow, you can join us."

"I'll be heading out early tomorrow to make it back to the village," Sean said, standing and shaking hands with the others. "If I make it back this way again, I'll make it a point to stop by and say hi."

"Fair enough," Bill said. "I take it you're down south, with Darragh?"

"Yup, it's slowly building into a fine village," Sean said.

"I hear he has more than a few unusual ones with him," Gert said.

"A few," Sean agreed, "but they're better people than others I've met."

"Isn't that always the way?" Jay nodded. "Good travels to you tomorrow, then."

"Good travels," Gert agreed as he and Jay headed for the door.

"Safe travels," Bill added, following the other two.

Sean smiled as he watched them go. The three men had been some of the most normal people he'd met so far in this world. They reminded him of the old army buddies his father had over for poker when he was little.

The bar was filling up, so Sean shifted to a smaller table, freeing the larger for others. When he'd gotten settled, Matilda came over to see if he wanted another mug. "Maybe something a little less potent this time?" Sean asked.

"The light ale it is," Matilda said as she walked through the growing crowd to get other orders.

CHAPTER TWENTY-FIVE

By the time Matilda brought Sean's ale, the seat across from him was the only empty one in the room. She walked away before Sean could thank her, her tray full of drinks for other tables.

The light ale was even sweeter than the dark had been, tasting of pears instead of blackberries. His internal musings over the ale were cut short when the room went quiet. Looking up, he saw Fiona at the bottom of the stairs, and the center of attention. Quickly taking in the dropping temperature of the room, Sean raised his hand. "Over here, Fiona," he called out in a clear tone.

When she started toward him, all eyes left her and turned to Sean. She took the seat with a weak smile. "Thank you."

"Never leave a woman in distress, my dad always told me," Sean said. "What are you going to have?"

"Probably mead," Fiona said as she looked at his mug. "I hope you haven't had too many."

"Less than a handful. The light ale is much lighter than the dark."

A sardonic smile came to her lips, "Really?"

"Words are hard," Sean sighed, earning him a giggle from Fiona.

Conversation began to pick back up around them, letting both of them breathe a little easier. Not long after that, an overly endowed waitress came over to the table. "Are you ready for dinner, and can I get you a drink?"

Sean looked over, directly at the expanse of freckled skin on display, scant inches away. He blinked and looked away, feeling his cheeks burning. -That- is the outfit I expected to see, Sean coughed internally. Caught up in his thoughts, he missed what Fiona said. He looked up to find both of them staring at him. "Err…"

"I asked if you were ready for food," Fiona said again, noting his coloring cheeks.

"Yes," Sean managed, keeping his eyes on Fiona. "As well as another light ale, please."

"Two dinners, one mead and one light ale. I'll be right back," the waitress said as she swayed away from the table, dodging a number of reaching hands from other tables as she went.

"You like them chesty, do you?" Fiona asked.

"I wasn't expecting so much skin, is all," Sean said, looking into his mug. "The maid earlier wasn't flaunting what she had."

"Of course she wouldn't. That's not in the nature of her bloodline," Fiona told him. "The waitress, though, is Life Bonded, and probably wears the outfit to advertise other services that Gosrek charges heavily for."

"She's a whore?" Sean blinked, having half expected it, but still taken by surprise.

"She'll have sex with whoever pays the price that Gosrek sets. It happens. It's a reason to be aware of who you Bond to, especially a Life Bond. The Holder can have you do anything; you give them your soul, after all."

"Okay, no Life Bonding for me," Sean said.

The waitress returned, setting down their drinks. "Food will be out in a moment."

"Thanks," Sean said, meeting the nearly lifeless eyes of the waitress. As she walked away, Sean sucked at his teeth. "She hates her life."

"Who can blame her?" Fiona said softly. "Look at the table near the door."

When Sean spotted the table of obese men all leering at the waitress, he shuddered. "Exactly," Fiona continued, "she'll end up with one, or more, of them—if they pay Gosrek for her time. Who would want that life? For her to end up here, something terrible must have happened. Either a debt too large to pay off, or perhaps something similar."

"Shit," Sean muttered as he finished off his mug. "The more I learn, the more I wonder why I'm even here."

"I'm glad you are," Fiona said quietly, sipping her mug.

"I'm glad to have met you, and happier still you're helping me learn. I'm just not sure if I'll be able to adjust to what this world is and how it works."

"I'll help as much as I can," Fiona said, placing her hand on the table.

Covering her hand with his, Sean smiled. "Then I'm in good hands. With you helping me, I'm sure things will work out."

"Your food," the waitress placed two platters before them, her tone cold.

Glancing at the waitress, he found her eyes locked on their hands. "I'm sorry," Sean said sincerely. "I wish I could help."

Eyes snapping to his and seeing only honesty, the waitress looked away. "There's no help for me now. Even though she's Shamed, she still has someone who actually cares for her..." Touching the band on her neck, the waitress let the sentence fade. "Is there anything else I can get you?"

"No," Fiona said softly. "I do hope Gosrek charges heavily for you, at least, to keep most of them at bay."

"It depends on the week," the waitress sighed, but gave them both a nod. "If either of you wishes *anything*, please tell me." Walking off before they could respond, the waitress deftly avoided more hands on her way back to the bar.

"Poor girl," Fiona said as she looked at the meal.

"Life is full of hard choices and worse outcomes, it seems," Sean agreed.

The platters had pieces of cubed meat and mashed potatoes covered with gravy, as well as small, still steaming, green shoots. The meat and potatoes were about what he expected, though the gravy was thicker and had a bitter note that enhanced the meat and potatoes. The green shoots turned out to be something he hadn't encountered before. Crunchy and firm, they vaguely reminded him of snow peas, but the flavor was a mixture of asparagus and honey dew. Pushing the veggies to the side, he made a face at them.

"You don't like aspon?" Fiona asked as she watched him.

"Tastes awful," Sean said. "Do you want them?"

"I'll take them," Fiona smiled as she edged her plate next to his.

The rest of the meal was eaten in silence. Sean was listening to the surrounding conversations, but other than the occasional comment about Fiona, nothing of note was said. Sean idly noted the other two buxom waitresses that had appeared during dinner. The trio of servers with black bands on their necks had their work cut out for them, avoiding the roaming hands of the patrons.

Sipping the last of his ale while Fiona polished off the last of her food, Sean caught a commotion starting by the doors. A trio of rough looking men were scowling as they looked around the room, one of them arguing with a server. Frowning at the idiots, Sean was about to look away when the lead tough locked eyes with him and sneered.

Wondering why the man was focused on him, Sean missed seeing Venar, who was watching the scene with a smirk from his seat at the bar. Before Sean could figure out what was going on, the men shoved past the waitress and headed right for their table.

"Trouble," Sean warned Fiona, who was just pushing her empty plate away.

Looking where he was staring, Fiona saw the toughs a few feet away. Before she could speak, the leader slapped his hand on their table.

"Why is Silvershame preventing proper, upstanding folk from getting a table?"

"Maybe because she's still worth four of you," Sean replied out of reflex.

The room, which had been paying attention, went dead silent. All three of the men stared daggers at Sean. "What did you just say?" the leader asked in a snarl.

"We've just finished and will be going," Fiona said, briefly pulling all eyes to her.

"Shut it," the leader snapped, turning his gaze back to Sean. "Did you just say that she's worth four of me?"

"I apologize," Sean said as he got to his feet, "I was wrong. She's worth six of you at the very least."

The thugs all went red at his words, and a collective intake of breath was heard in the silence. "You'll pay for that," the leader snapped and pulled his arm back.

As soon as the man pulled back, time seemed to slow down for Sean, just as it had with the wolves. The leader's punch came forward at the speed of someone throwing a mock punch. Slapping the arm up and away, Sean transitioned the block into an attack, resting his hand briefly on the man's chest before shoving him backwards.

The other two toughs had started to come forward, but stopped to catch their leader, who had been thrown off his feet into them. A startled murmur was heard throughout the inn at the casual show of strength Sean exhibited.

"Stop it, and leave us alone," Sean said coldly as the trio untangled themselves.

"Like hell I will," the man snapped, scrambling to his feet. "Flank him," he hissed to his two followers, who started edging around the table.

"Sean, don't kill them," Fiona said worriedly, her eyes darting from Sean to the thugs.

One of them snickered, "As if he could."

Taking her warning seriously, Sean knew he would have to pull his punches. Myna had mentioned that he'd hit her far harder than he should have been able to the other day. Not waiting for the other two to get into position, Sean lunged forward and grabbed the leader by his shirt.

Hoisting the man up, Sean turned and tossed him lightly at one of the others. The two men went down in a tangle that rolled to a nearby table as the third rushed Sean from behind. Knowing that the man would attack his back, Sean didn't turn, but kicked out lazily behind himself. A gasp confirmed what Sean's foot told him as the third man went down hard.

"Stop it. No one needs to get hurt," Sean said, backing up to bring the men all into view.

"Take it outside," Gosrek snapped, pulling a crossbow from under the bar.

Sean looked at Fiona and bowed his head to her. "I'll be right back. I'm sorry about my mouth. I'll try to do better."

Shaking her head at his apparent flippancy, Fiona covered her face with a hand. "Just don't get hurt and don't kill them."

"Sure thing," Sean said, heading to the door and waiting for the thugs to get to their feet. "You guys coming? Or are you done now?"

"Get him," the leader snarled as he and the others rushed at Sean, who was calmly walking out the door.

As the rest of the patrons rushed to the doorway and windows to watch the fight, Fiona slipped upstairs. A certain warmth had radiated through her at Sean's praise, but another part was angry that he still hadn't learned his lesson. Comments about her Shame would be commonplace, and he needed to learn not to react to them.

Sean was waiting in the middle of the square when the trio burst out of the inn. He'd never had any formal martial arts training, but when he fought, time seemed to slow for him, making control of the fistfight trivial.

The leader trailed just behind his two friends as they rushed at him. Waiting for them to close the distance, Sean slid to the right and put his shoulder into the first attacker's gut. The tough wheezed heavily as the wind was driven from his lungs. Tossing the winded attacker from his shoulder toward the leader, Sean sidestepped a kick from the third man.

The kick missed by inches, but it allowed Sean to grab the man's leg and pull him off balance. Using the leg as a lever, Sean flung the attacker at the winded guy that the leader had managed to dodge. "Are we done yet?" Sean asked with a smirk.

"I'll teach you to mock me and my boys," the leader snapped, drawing a bronze blade from his boot.

"Don't do that," Sean said, backing up a step. "This doesn't have to turn deadly."

"I won't be the one dying," the thug snarled and went after Sean.

Not seeing an option, Sean backed away, circling as he went. The leader rushed, but Sean slipped away, pulling in his gut as the swing went wide. Spinning, he came back at Sean again, only to find a body flying at him. Stabbing out of reflex, his eyes went wide as he found himself killing his friend.

"NO!" he yelled as his friend's body slid off the blade. Dropping the knife, he tried to staunch the gut wound. "Ungus, I'm sorry, Ungus stay with me. Get Doctor McFlynn, somebody!"

Seeing the leader panicking over his friend, Sean figured the fight was over and walked back towards the inn. Everyone backed away from him as he entered. "Someone needs to get that guy some help."

Without further comment, Sean went up the stairs to his room.

CHAPTER TWENTY-SIX

Entering the room, he found Fiona sitting at the table. "Sorry about that," Sean said as he closed the door behind him.

"I told you I don't need your interference when it comes to my Shame," Fiona said quietly. "I will always be targeted. My Shame is so obvious and too many people have heard skewed versions of what happened."

"I understand," Sean said as he stood across from her. "I still hold with what I said, though, you're worth six of him."

Fiona fought the smile that tried to come to her lips. "That isn't the point."

"It is to me," Sean said as he sat at the table. "I'll try, because you've asked me to, but I regard you that highly. Your Shame has no meaning for me, but I'll try to do as you've asked. I only ask you don't get upset with me when I slip up."

Not looking at him, her cheeks heated at his words. "Incorrigible," she muttered.

"I know you could've handled them, so why don't you stand up to that sort of thing?"

Shaking her head, Fiona met his gaze briefly. "Those Shamed are not supposed to act like those who aren't. You don't understand what it means to be Shamed, and I don't know how to explain it to you."

"Darragh is Shamed, but everyone still treats him with respect," Sean pointed out.

"Darragh is different..." Fiona trailed off, her eyes going distant for a moment. "Before his Shame, he was known throughout the Quadital. His Shame was... no, that is his story to tell." Shaking her head, she looked away from him again. "I might not have entirely deserved my Shame, but it helps remind me of my old pride and where that leads."

"Will you tell me?" Sean asked.

"Not today," Fiona said as she stood. "The inn might have calmed down some. I'm going to bathe before turning in. Come with me?"

Getting to his feet, Sean gave her a small smile. "Lead on."

Fiona led him away from the stairs that they had taken to their room. Down the hall and around the corner was another set of stairs leading down. Taking those brought them to a door that stood ajar to reveal a large, simple room. Tubs just big enough for a single person to soak in were set against the walls, and Sean felt a little relieved that it wasn't a giant tub. One wall was dominated by a series of stoves and racks of kettles. A hand pump for water was nearby.

Fiona crossed the room and picked up a kettle. Filling it, she set it on the closest stove. She filled another three before she filled a bucket with water and took it over to a series of small stone blocks. Turning, she saw Sean still standing just inside the doorway. "Get your kettles ready and grab a bucket. I'll teach you the proper way to use a public bathing area."

Doing as instructed, Sean finished after a few minutes and turned with bucket of cold water in hand to find Fiona nude. Jaw dropping and mouth going dry, his eyes roved over her body. "Uhm..."

"Clothing goes in this tub, we clean them first," Fiona said, her cheeks pinking slightly under his gaze. "Don't just stand there, set your bucket by the seats and come join me."

Swallowing hard, Sean set his bucket down by one of the stone seats and went to the tub. Stripping, he tried to keep his eyes and thoughts off Fiona, hoping to calm his libido. He couldn't help himself, though, and his eyes kept going back to her.

Standing an inch or two shorter than him, her body was more lithe than his. Her skin was a creamy white where the sun hadn't gotten to her, and a light tan where it had. The mithril side of her body gleamed in the lantern light that illuminated the room. Her small, firm breasts, a little bigger than a handful, stood proud, her nipples hard points that drew his eye. He didn't consciously notice that the reactions on her metallic side mimicked her flesh side perfectly as his gaze drifted down her toned body. The dividing line of flesh and metal was almost perfectly symmetrical, only wavering twice. The first was where it followed the line of her collarbone away from her neck to her shoulder, the second was where his eyes were traveling now, down past her navel. Just above her sex, the mithril veered to the left, leaving her womanhood unmarked by metal, though it did encompass her entire hip and leg.

"Gorgeous," Sean murmured without thought as he drew his eyes back up her body and pulled his shirt off. Noting the way her metallic side shifted smoothly as the muscles underneath moved, he marveled at her beauty.

"It's impolite to stare," Fiona said softly.

Blinking as he began to undo his belt, he found her dual-colored eyes staring at him. "Err... sorry..."

Shaking her head, she knelt down next to the tub and pulled her shirt from the water. "I understand, but please try not to stare."

Quickly stripping off the rest of his clothing, he dropped it into the tub, setting his boots and belt next to Fiona's. Kneeling next to the tub, he began washing his shirt, missing Fiona covertly checking him out and her eyes going wider as she caught full sight of his manhood before he knelt. The tub held cold water, and had small wash boards attached to the sides. Fiona handed him a small lump of soap to use on his clothing.

Focusing on the task helped Sean ignore the beauty kneeling opposite him. Fiona stood up with her dripping clothing and took them to the line that hung above the stoves. Draping her clothing on the line, she picked up her kettles, which should have been whistling by then, but weren't. She dumped them into a tub after plugging the drain with a cork. Sean did the same a moment later, following her example.

"Now we wash," Fiona told him as she placed the kettles back beside the stoves. Going to the buckets they'd set out before, she took a seat and began to wash herself.

Sean copied her example, forcing his eyes away from her every time they started to stray. He was red and acutely aware of the way he'd been responding to her ever since he'd stripped down. The water, which had been cold when it had been drawn, was simply cool now, after sitting in the warm room. He briefly wished it was ice cold to help quell his libido.

Light suds dotted Fiona's body when she stood. Picking up the bucket, she carefully poured some of it over her head, sluicing a majority of the suds from her body. Sitting back down, she started running soapy hands through her hair. Eyes closed, she hummed a song as she lathered.

Glancing over at her, Sean's lips turned up as he listened to the song. It was a happy, upbeat melody that was in time to her hands massaging her head. Pulling his gaze away, Sean rinsed himself. It took him less time to wash his hair, and they finished together.

"Good, you're done," Fiona said. "Now we get more water and fill the tubs the rest of the way, then we can relax until you're ready to leave." Moving with her bucket towards the pump, her body was a sight to behold. She didn't flaunt herself, but the sheer grace that she moved with was beautiful, in its own way.

Shaking his head, he knew it was pointless to worry about her knowing he was attracted to her. Sean filled his bucket as Fiona carried hers to her tub. When she returned, he handed her his bucket. "A bucket chain will fill your tub quicker," he said.

"That's not the proper way things are done," Fiona said, stepping aside. "Each person carries their own water."

Nodding, he carried his bucket of water to his tub, the hot water still steaming slightly as he poured in the first bucket of cold water.

Two buckets later, the tub was only half full. Checking the water, he found it cooling faster than he wanted. "Can we add more hot water to them?" Sean asked as he set his bucket down.

"Yes, but it takes time for the kettles to heat," Fiona said as she carried a fourth bucket to her tub. Testing the water, she frowned. "I see your point, though."

Stepping over to her tub, Sean murmured the song he needed and mimicked a teapot. Feeling the energy rush through him, he tilted to his left and poured water from his hand into the tub.

"I forgot about your ability to do that," Fiona chuckled. "Is there more you can do?"

Having poured a couple of kettles worth of steaming water into her tub, he released the magic. "I don't know," he said softly. "I get the feeling that the Tuatha Dé Danann gave me as much as they could. I've been able to pick up on a lot of stuff since I came here."

"You're so odd," Fiona murmured as she touched the water in her tub. "You did, however, make my water just right." Stepping into the tub, she sat down. "Thank you, Sean," she sighed.

Meeting her eyes, he smiled. "Thank you, Fiona."

As he went to his tub and magicked more hot water for himself, Sean didn't see Fiona's brow furrow as she watched him. Getting in, he sighed as the heat seeped into him. Laying back in the tub, he closed his eyes and relaxed.

Sean didn't know how long he had been soaking, but the sound of the door opening brought him upright. Wiping at his eyes, he found the lady from the tap room coming in. The cool gaze of the new arrival went from Fiona to Sean. Walking past them, she put six kettles on the stove and a bucket next to the washing stones, then went to the clothing tub. "Fiona Silvershame, I never thought I would see you out in this part of the world." The tone was cool, but not completely unfriendly.

"Velin. I wouldn't have expected to see someone connected to Lord Truestrike in this town, either," Fiona replied, her tone equally cool.

"What is the Shaper who lost half her Talent doing here, and with such an interesting companion?" Velin asked as she began to undo the buttons down the sides of her dress.

"I went with Darragh to establish a village south of here," Fiona said. "Sean is a friend who wanted to see the town. I had business here, and he was gracious enough to come with me, to make sure the beasts of the wilds stayed away."

"Ah. Darragh Axehand, such a tragic tale," Velin said mockingly. "Who would have guessed that he would have fallen so far?"

"What are you doing this far south?" Fiona asked, her tone cooling further.

"I have business here, of course. The person I'm expecting to meet will be along in no more than another day or two." Stripping her clothing away, she revealed a thin figure that bordered on skeletal. Kneeling, she began washing her clothing. "The small towns are such a bother. No one who can be trusted to care for one's clothing. Such drudgery is truly below me, but the Lord wills it, so I must endure. Sean—that is your name, right?" Sean nodded, looking away from her. "You seem to have some Talent for fighting, you would be wasted out here. I'm sure my Lord would be interested in hiring you. Would you care to come with me back to Southpoint, to hear his offer?"

Sean noticed the thin black bands encircling Velin's wrists. He'd missed seeing them while she was dressed, but against Velin's pale skin, they were easily visible when she was naked. Sean kept his head turned away, shaking it. "I have an Agreement with Darragh, and it would be wrong to break it."

Tsking, Velin shook her head. "A pity. I shall not accrue a bonus on this trip, then." Turning, she presented her profile to Sean. "Are you sure I can't entice you to change your mind? The Lord does offer some very good benefits to those who have Talents he's interested in."

Lips quirking up, Sean chuckled as he briefly met her eyes, "I'm sure he does, but I still have to decline." Standing up, Sean looked around for towels and popped the cork from the tub, allowing it to drain.

"The cupboard in the corner," Fiona told him as she also got out of her tub.

Retrieving a couple of towels, he handed one to her and let his eyes drink her body in one more time. "For you," he told her as he began to dry himself off.

"I see. So her Shame doesn't deter you?" Velin said casually as she hung up her clothing. "Or does that make it more exciting for you? The idea of having damaged goods, or maybe you like something exotic? I'm sure Lord Truestrike can arrange something that will catch your fancy."

Her persistent offers began to grate on Sean. "I doubt he has someone as singular as Fiona. If you will excuse me." He slipped past her, grabbed his clothing, and began to dress in the still slightly damp clothes.

Fiona did the same, her cheeks red as her eyes kept darting to Sean. They finished dressing at almost the same time, just as Velin began to lather herself. "Pity," she said with a smirk. "Oh well, I know it's impossible to have everything one wishes presented on a platter all the time. I do wish you a happy life, however long that may be." The last sentence seemed to hold a trace of dark humor and Sean paused briefly on his way out the door.

Shaking his head, Sean continued after Fiona, following her out of the chamber and back to their room. As the door closed behind them, Sean let out a deep sigh, "I wouldn't touch that with a ten foot pole. Something is wrong with her, to so freely offer that kind of thing to a complete stranger."

"She is a Bonded servant to a Lord," Fiona said, as if that explained everything.

"The more I hear about the nobility of the Fey, the less I like them," Sean said, looking out the window at the setting sun. "It's about time to turn in, isn't it?"

Fiona glanced from him, to the window, and then to the bed, "It probably is." Biting her lip, she began to strip off her clothing again. "About earlier... I know you just turned down Velin, but..."

Sean crossed the room, stopping inches away from Fiona. His heart was racing as she looked at him, their eyes meeting. "I would never consider her. You, though..." Trailing off, he tucked a few strands of hair behind her ear while he caressed her cheek. "It's been a long time for me and it's kind of quick to be doing this, with us only knowing each other a few days, but I won't say no."

Leaning her head into his palm, her dual-colored eyes seemed to search his for a moment. "Gern was wrong. I'd lain with men before my Shame, so it's been equally as long for me, if not longer." Swallowing, she pressed her hand to his, holding it against her cheek. "You make me feel like a young maiden all over again. My heart pounds, my hands go clammy, and I wonder if maybe I don't deserve this moment."

Acting on impulse, he brought his lips to hers. The kiss was tentative and uncertain at first, then his other arm went around her waist as the kiss began to deepen. Her arms went around the back of his neck as her body pressed against him. An almost electric current seemed to pass between them as their tongues met. Neither was trying to dominate the other—instead it was like being a teenager again, each of them uncertain, yet eager.

After a minute, Sean pulled his head back. His breathing was rapid, his face flushed. "Fiona, I don't want to hurt you…"

"Shh," Fiona said as she caressed the back of his neck. "Just give me this, tonight at least. I know you'll leave eventually, but you treat me like a woman, and I know your kindness isn't feigned. So please, don't push me away."

Arms tightening around her, Sean nodded. "As you wish."

This time, his mouth met hers with passion and a demanding need, to be met with the same from Fiona. Hands slipping lower, he pulled her against him by her tight ass, a small groan of need coming from her as the kiss continued. The moment became a blur to Sean as they kissed and stripped each other's clothing off. His hands roamed over her body, her mithril skin cool to the touch, but yielding like normal flesh to his hands.

Ducking his head to her left breast, the hard metal nipple had a faint metallic tang to his tongue. A moan came from Fiona as she arched her back, pressing her breast into his mouth. Glad that she could feel his ministrations, he continued to lavish attention to her breast. He traded off between both nipples as her hands found his erect manhood. She began to caress him much like she did logs when shaping, gently gliding her fingers along his length.

Pulling back, his passion filled eyes met her lust filled gaze. "Going to Shape me to fit?" he asked with a smirk.

"I just might try," Fiona said, dropping to her knees before him. "But maybe a little differently than normal." Tongue snaking out, she began to lick at him, happy noises coming from her as she lavished his shaft with attention.

His hands rubbed her back as she brought him pleasure with her mouth. He had never been a selfish lover, and all he wanted was to give her the same pleasure. "Fiona," he panted, "let me lay down and I can return your attentions in kind."

Looking up at him through her lashes, one corner of her mouth tugged up in a smile, then she took him into her mouth. Moaning, Sean's eyes rolled back as what little blood he had in his brain quickly fled south. Satisfied that he was indeed enjoying her attentions, she let his shaft go. Standing, she led him to the bed and pushed him gently, but firmly, down onto it. "I accept," she said as she climbed atop him, her legs to either side of his head as her mouth quickly resumed what she had been doing moments ago.

Fiona's sex glistened above him, the faint scent of honey wafting to his nose as he lifted his head and lapped once across her wet slit. Not quite honey, but it was sweet and delicious, more so than any woman he'd ever been with before. Grabbing her ass with both hands, he pulled her down to his mouth, eager to get more of her sweet nectar. It was only a few minutes later when Sean gasped, pulling his mouth from her sex, "Fiona, stop or I'll burst."

Happy to know he was enjoying her attentions, she wasn't about to stop. If anything, his words spurred her on. Forcing him as deep as she could into her throat, she choked, unable to take him all, but trying time and again regardless. Breath catching in his throat, he shuddered as his orgasm tore through him. The first spurt of his seed caught Fiona by surprise as it coated the back of her throat. Quickly pulling back, she kept his head in her mouth as she began swallowing all of his offering.

Body rigid as she suckled on his cock, Sean could barely remember to breathe. When his orgasm passed and he went limp under her, Fiona didn't stop. Her tongue went to work cleaning his length, which kept his manhood from flagging. Shuddering as small aftershocks coursed through him, he pulled her back to his mouth and viciously attacked her sex with his tongue. Fiona moaned around his shaft as he picked right back up where he had left off. Her own orgasm wasn't far off, and she eagerly rode his mouth as she kept him hard.

A sudden gush of fluid filled Sean's mouth a moment later as Fiona let out a soft wail, pressing her slit to his mouth. Swallowing, the sweet taste only grew stronger and he wanted more of it. As she collapsed atop him, Sean didn't stop, but licked at her folds with increased desire. Fiona didn't resist as Sean slid her body where he wanted it, giving him a better position to get to her clit more easily. When his tongue stroked across that small but sensitive part of her, Fiona gripped his body with her arms while her legs clamped around his head.

"Oh, Sean, if you do that..." she trailed off as he increased his attentions.

A longer, louder moan came from Fiona as the second orgasm crashed over her, and again Sean was rewarded with a mouthful of her nectar. Slowly and carefully, he cleaned her as she'd cleaned him earlier. She was still limp atop him when he finished. Carefully, he rolled her over onto her back and shifted around to position himself between her thighs. Heavy lidded eyes met his, her legs going around his waist while her arms reached up around his head.

"Please," Fiona whispered the word as she waited for him to enter her.

Bowing his head, he kissed her and shifted his hips forward, slowly entering her. The moan of pleasure was mutual as he sank inch by inch into her welcoming sex. Fiona thrust her hips up as she pulled him in with her legs, plunging the rest of his manhood into her in a sudden motion. Breath catching, Sean stared into her eyes as he went still, reveling in the moment.

Rolling her hips, she brought his focus back to what he had started. "Don't stop," Fiona whispered, enticing him to move again.

Bowing his head again, his lips met hers and their tongues tangled in a sensual dance as Sean began to slowly extract himself from her welcoming passage. Halfway out, he reversed direction and sank back into her, to both of their delights. The minutes seemed to become hours as they crashed together like the tide on the sands of a beach. The pleasure slowly built until both were again holding onto the edge, pushing back their orgasms and trying to prolong the moment of unity they both felt.

"Now," Fiona asked him, her nails digging into his back, "now, Sean, let it be now."

Her words were all he needed. With no warning, his speed went from the long slow strokes to a rapid, short, hard thrusting, like a woodpecker drilling a hole into a tree. His breath caught in his throat as Fiona gasped out a long exhale, her body surrendering to his assault. Fiona's orgasm hit first, causing her tunnel to clamp down on his shaft. That was the last straw, causing Sean to lose his control, his shaft swelling before he thrust one more time as his seed spilled into her. Their tongues came together again, breaths mingling as the last shuddering remnants of the moment washed over them.

Arms shaking, Sean held himself above Fiona. "Fucking gods, you are amazing."

Languid smile on her face, her legs slipped from his waist. "Thank you."

The bed was small for the two of them, but they managed, Sean laying on his side to hold her as his fingers trailed over her body. "Thank you. I never would have thought when I found myself on this world that I would ever find someone who would accept me, much less as readily as you have."

"I never thought I would reach out to anyone again," Fiona sighed as she turned to face him, her hand tracing his chest. "Your voice drew me that first day, and I don't know why. I'd never invited anyone into my home before that moment, and had resigned myself to being a recluse, even in the village. Your open, honest way drew me in and I wanted to know more about you, the person who didn't pull away from my Shame, but called it beautiful. That night, when we Shaped together and our energies mingled, then later when you opened another Talent to me... I knew then that I had to try, or I'd regret every day if I didn't at least take a step on a path I feared to walk again."

"Maybe I can stay in the village, for a while at least," Sean said as his eyes grew heavy.

"I will welcome you into my home, if you do," Fiona whispered as her fingers trailed up to his face.

"I would be the luckiest man in the village," Sean managed before his eyes closed and sleep overtook him.

"I would be the luckiest woman in the world," Fiona whispered, watching him drop off. She stayed there like she was for minutes before gathering up the covers to make them both comfortable. Her arms around him, she fell asleep with a smile and a sense of happiness she hadn't had in years.

CHAPTER TWENTY-SEVEN

A body shifting against his woke him. Blinking open his crusty eyes, he found Fiona spooned against him, her back to his chest. He smiled as he recalled their intimate night, until Fiona's body shuddered and a whimper came from her. "Fiona," Sean called to her gently, his hand lightly rubbing her flat stomach, "are you okay?"

"Die!" Fiona jerked upright, her eyes unfocused and wild as she spun on him. Her left hand clamped down on his throat while her right touched the wall, Shaping a wooden dagger from it in mere seconds.

Shocked by the sudden attack, Sean was barely able to grab her arm as she brought the dagger toward his chest. The wooden blade had a wicked point that he'd stopped a hair's breadth away from piercing him. "Fiona, stop it," Sean managed to get out as her hand tightened on his neck. "It's a nightmare, wake up."

Baring her teeth, she levered herself above him and pressed down with both arms. "Raping bastard, I don't care what it costs, you'll die for this!"

Sean knew he had flaws, but rape wasn't one of them—especially not when she'd invited him into bed last night. Using his left hand to hold the dagger at bay, he grasped her left hand with his right and dug his thumb into her wrist under the pad of her thumb. "I'm not your enemy," he spluttered as he felt her left hand begin to weaken in his grasp.

The pain of his thumb digging into her wrist helped clear some of the madness from her eyes. Realization came a moment later, and with a gasp of horror, the dagger fell from her hand as she let go of his throat. Tears began to pour from her eyes as she tried to stammer out a coherent sentence. The dagger dug a small furrow into his chest, but he ignored it as he released her arms to put his around her.

"Shh, it's okay. I know you didn't do it intentionally," Sean tried to calm her.

Crying with loud, hiccupping breaths, Fiona kept trying to apologize to him. Sean repeated his words in a calm tone as he rubbed her back and held her to him. Fiona eventually calmed enough to manage to speak. "I'm so sorry, Sean. I was having a night terror from my past. I wouldn't hurt you intentionally, I'm so sorry."

"It's okay, no harm done," Sean said calmly. He knew that she needed the reassurance, so he ignored the small part of him that was upset she hadn't told him of this possibility. "The past is done, it's okay now. Are you going to be okay?"

Laying her head against his shoulder she sniffled, "I don't know. I haven't had that terror in years. I thought that maybe I had moved past it, but I obviously haven't. I'm sorry I tried to kill you just like I did him."

Stroking her hair as the pre-dawn light began to fill the small window, Sean held her. "Do you want to talk about it? I understand if you don't. It sounds like somebody was forcing himself on you."

"Maybe later, when we're traveling. I don't want to think about it right now, if that's okay?"

"Sure," Sean told her, easing her away from him a bit so he could see her bloodshot eyes. "I don't think any person should be blamed for killing a rapist. It won't change my opinion of you for the worse. If anything, it makes me think better of you for defending yourself like that. Just, maybe next time, try not to kill me?" He tried for a bit of levity with the last few words, but her lips only faltered, as if she wanted to smile but couldn't.

"Maybe you shouldn't stay with me—" Fiona began, turning her head away from him.

"It will take more than a dagger to the chest to drive me off," Sean said, cutting her off. "As long as you'll have me, that is."

Puzzled eyes met his, "I almost killed you."

"No, no you didn't," Sean said, his lips turning up at the corners. "You only got that far because I wasn't prepared for an attack. Next time, you won't even come close."

Her lips wavered, "You're crazy..."

"Maybe I am, but maybe I need to be. My father once told me to never turn away from a friend in pain. I can see the pain in you, Fiona, and I care a great deal. I would risk being stabbed a hundred times over, if it means I can help you overcome that past hurt."

"I..." Shaking her head, Fiona seemed at a loss. "I don't understand you. You confound me so much. Your kindness, your willingness to overlook Shame or race to know the person, instead of the circumstance; your strength, both mentally and physically, your ability to forgive me trying to kill you in my terror."

Gently cupping her jaw, he brought her eyes to his again. "I've known infatuation, I've known lust, and I've known raw naked desire. When you taught me Shaping and I opened your eyes to being more than you were, that sparked something deeper inside me. I tried to resist it, but I couldn't. I want to know you, as much as you'll share with me. The depth of the feeling I have for you already is insane, and the more I'm with you, the stronger it becomes. I was afraid of what it might mean and I fought against it, but last night, I couldn't fight it anymore. Fiona Mithrilsoul, I believe I love you."

Her lips trembled as he spoke, tears forming at the corners of her eyes as she listened to his confession. The last three words broke the dam and tears of happiness began to flow from her eyes. Her lips met his softly, yet resolutely, as she accepted his declaration. Arms going around his neck, she pressed her naked body to his, letting the warmth his words had sparked flow through her.

When the kiss finally ended, Fiona managed to say what she'd been trying to express. "I feel the same. That moment when our energy connected was profound. When you opened my eyes to see my Shame as something positive, I tried to reject it. I always thought I deserved to be less than I was before. Your unflinching acceptance of me and my Shame made me want to hold you, but I resisted. When you spoke out on my behalf to Gern, I was angry. I thought you were trying to deny a part of me and who I am because of my Shame. I see it differently now. You see me as someone so much better than I am, and I have a hard time accepting it. But I will, if you'll keep trying to help me. Last night, I pushed away the last of my reservations and asked for you to give me life again, and you did. The last two decades have been hard. Shamed, alone, friendless, and unwanted, I've struggled just going on. Now I know that all my pain, all my troubles, have all led me to this point, this nexus of choice that stands before us. I know that you are far too good for the village. You can do so much more, and I want to see you do it. We can speak with Darragh when we return and ask if he'll free me from my Agreement so that I might go with you."

Gently pulling her in, he kissed her. Part of him was shocked at the breadth of the emotion they were sharing, and part of him reveled in it. It had taken death, gods, and a whole different world to find love, but now he had, and he would fight to hold onto it. Breaking the kiss, he rested his forehead against hers. "Yes. I would love for you to always be with me. I would ask for one thing." He paused, seeing her eyes grow wide with hope, "That you see yourself as I see you. No more letting others put you down, no more accepting their disdain. You are a wonder, a jewel that should be treasured, and I will not stand by and let them treat you as less than I see you. I would topple the Courts, if need be, so you will be recognized as the amazing person that I know you to be."

"Fool," Fiona sniffled as she kissed him again. She pushed against him so he lay back on the bed with her atop him.

The kiss, and ensuing passionate lovemaking, took hours to finally bring to a conclusion. Panting, they lay there spent, but happy, as the sun climbed higher into the sky. Fiona was tracing small circles on Sean's chest when she looked at the window and sat up abruptly. "Oh, it's late. We need to get going if we want to make it back to the village before dinner." Sean watched her scramble out of bed, enjoying the view as the sunlight came through the window and played across her skin. She was mostly dressed before she realized he was still laying there. "We need to go, or my Agreement with Darragh to have you back will be broken."

Getting out of bed, Sean began dressing quickly. "Can't have that. He might not listen to our request to let you go with me later."

"I'll get food for the road. Meet me downstairs as soon as you can," Fiona said, getting her boots on and slipping out the door.

Once he was dressed, Sean followed her downstairs and found her at the bar, assembling two sandwiches. "I have your change," Gosrek told Sean as he came to a stop beside Fiona. Placing a handful of copper on the counter, Gosrek gave Sean a tight smile. "Thank you for taking the fight outside last night. I explained what happened to the watch when they came to investigate."

Bowing his head, Sean replied, "Thank you, Gosrek. I doubt I could have explained it well. Did anyone say why they seemed so insistent on the confrontation?"

"Not to me," Gosrek said. "Next time, take it outside at the start though, please. You almost landed one of them on one of my tables."

"I'll try to end it faster next time. I kept thinking they would stop," the wry smile on Sean's face got a snort from Gosrek.

"The three you beat so soundly are known for bar brawls in town. Rumor says they can be paid to rough people up," Gosrek said the words casually, but he stared intently at Sean as he said them.

"Guess I upset someone in town, then," Sean laughed. "Good thing I'm leaving, isn't it?"

"Better for me," Gosrek agreed. "Next time, try not to bring trouble back to my place. If you can do that, then you'll be welcomed back."

"Deal," Sean agreed. Taking the sandwich Fiona offered him, he kissed her cheek. "Thank you."

Gosrek raised a brow, but held his tongue at the display of affection. Fiona gave Gosrek a tight smile. "We're done with the room, Gosrek. Our thanks for the clean room and the warm bath."

"My pleasure and your coin," Gosrek replied. "Fair speed and clear travel."

"May your purse fill with the coin you deserve," Fiona replied, the words having an almost ritual quality to them.

Nudging Sean with her hip, she headed for the door. Sean gave Gosrek another smile as he followed Fiona, taking a bite of the sandwich as he went. The meat was tough, cold, and held a hint of age to it, but the cheese was sharp and tasty, which helped make it a bit easier to eat. A brief wish for spicy brown mustard crossed his mind as a he contemplated what it could do for the meal.

Finishing their sandwiches as they got to the gates, they nodded to the guards on duty and headed back towards the village. "Can you believe Darragh sent Silvershame to town?" one of the guards muttered to the other as the pair passed them.

Fiona's shoulders twitched, but she kept walking. Sean looked back, locking eyes with the guards for a moment, keeping his mouth shut but making a mental note to remember them when he came back this way later. A few minutes down the road, Fiona sighed, "It's going to take me time to feel like I should speak up," she said softly.

"That's fine, as long as you try," Sean said as he took her hand.

They walked in silence for a bit, the sounds of the birds the only noise to be heard. Fiona finally broke the silence, "You asked about my night terror." Swallowing, she glanced at him, "Do you still wish to hear about it?"

"I want to know as much about you as you'll share with me," Sean told her honestly. "If you want to wait, though, I won't press you."

Closing her eyes, her smile was fragile. "I'll tell you. It might take me a bit to get through it all."

Squeezing her hand, he leaned over and kissed her cheek. "Take all the time you need."

Silence fell again, as Fiona nerved herself to share her Shame with him. Sean didn't press, just held her hand and waited for her as they walked. The silence, broken only by bird calls, stretched on for minutes. Wondering if he had asked for too much, he opened his mouth to tell her not to worry about it.

"I was a very talented Shaper in my youth, considered a prodigy. I won a scholarship to the Academy from one of the Summer Court nobles, but was never told who. I was full of myself, knowing that I was going to be sought after by the elite for my Talent. My beauty was also well-known at the time, and I was courted by many lesser noble houses and rich merchant families who sought to tie me to them. I was very selective in who I gave my attentions to—I was a bitch, frankly," Fiona paused as Sean chuckled.

"Sorry," Sean said, "that is just so far from the Fiona I've come to know."

"I was humbled years before you met me," Fiona said, squeezing his hand. "When I graduated, after five years of schooling, I was the best wood Shaper in Southpoint. I made sure my mother was taken care of, as it was her blood that made it possible. A year after graduating, I had done piecework for many Lords, when one of them finally approached me with terms for a Bond. Lord Caligula, one of the Winter Queen's advisors—powerful, rich, and known for throwing exclusive parties that were spoken of in hushed whispers. It was while I considered his offer that I started to hear rumors of his other proclivities. The coin, and social boost it would have given me with the other higher nobles, was too much to pass up, which I'm sure he knew and counted on."

She paused in her story, and Sean slipped an arm around her waist. "Take your time. Don't feel like you have to tell me the whole thing right now."

"You deserve to know, after this morning," Fiona told him before taking a shuddering breath. "The Winter Queen knows the truth. She's the only one I've told the whole story to." Taking a few more deep breaths, she continued, "I Bonded with him for a year, thinking that a single year would be enough for my ego and ambitions. The conditions on my end were being able to quit, if I warned him a week beforehand, and never having to attend one of his parties. I should have known it wasn't a good idea when he so easily accepted my conditions. I was young, foolish, full of myself, and thinking that my conditions would shield me."

Sean gave her a reassuring squeeze, but kept silent and waited for her to continue. He had a pretty good idea of what was going to come next.

"He had me crafting simple, but ornately-made items at first. After a couple of months, he was having me craft things to be used at his parties. Some of them made my stomach clench to think about. The entire time, he kept inviting me to his parties, trying to wear me down." A look of revulsion crossed her features as she shivered. "The last straw was a set of stocks, evil in their design. A person locked into them would never have a moment of peace. I could barely force myself to do it, I kept thinking of how many other women he must have coerced into his parties. I told him it was over, and that I wouldn't be continuing past that week. His simple acknowledgement and seeming sadness at my leaving should have warned me, but I didn't see it."

"Sounds like I wouldn't have gotten along with this freak," Sean said.

"You two are very different people, for which I'm grateful," Fiona said, placing her hand on his arm around her waist. "A couple of days later, as I was finishing the project, he invited me to tea to discuss the ending of my Agreement. It was the morning of one of his parties, but that didn't register on me at the time. It turned out that the tea was drugged," her face went cold as she continued, "I should have known he wouldn't let me go so easily. When I woke up, I was chained to a bed, one that I had Shaped months before. The sounds of the party were oddly amplified, like they were being funneled into the room somehow."

"He made a room that he could indulge in, while still feeling like he was with his guests?" Sean asked, not quite understanding.

"The other rooms of the manor had decent soundproofing, so yes.

The sounds of women being pleasured and tortured filled the room, along with the music from the main hall, like the most perverted symphony ever played. The worst part was that he was nude and between my legs, his hands groping my body while his, *thing*," she spat the word, "rubbed against me, not penetrating, but teasing at the entrance." She stopped walking as a shudder overtook her.

Sean stopped with her, holding her as he chewed his lip. "Fiona..."

"No! No, I will say it. Don't stop me," Fiona said. Taking a deep breath, she started walking again. "He mocked me when I woke, telling me that he was willing to accept whatever punishment was meted out, but that it wouldn't change anything. He laughed at how easily I had fallen for his trap. The chains that held me to the bed were adamantine, and enchanted to make my limbs heavier than normal. He made an error, though; my hands could reach the posts that held the chains." Her voice was cold and full of hatred, "I Shaped the posts, freeing my chains from them and pulling a dagger to my hand. I can still see his eyes going wide as he realized what my intent was. I knew the Winter Queen wouldn't accept it, but I didn't care. I plunged my dagger into his chest over and over, screaming at him the entire time. I don't know how many times I stabbed him. I was only pulled from my rage when the Winter Queen's guards pulled me off him."

Sean stopped them and pulled her to him. Holding her, he could feel her crying into his chest as old memories engulfed her. Rubbing her back, he held her and wished he could have been there instead. Raping bastards had no right to life. He was upset she had to endure the trauma, but part of him was glad she had killed the fucker.

"I was brought before her, still nude, and forced to my knees in front of the Court while her guards explained what they had walked in on." Sobbing into his chest, she continued in a rush, determined to finish the story. "She had a Truthsayer come in, then she had me wait until the court was cleared before I told my tale. When I finished, and the Truthsayer verified my account, she told me that she had to Shame me. She would have trouble with her other nobles if a commoner, even a talented one, were to kill a noble and go unpunished. I can still recall her cold voice, like the heart of winter. But I would swear to this day that, for a moment, the ice was not as thick when she apologized to me for not acting sooner against him. That moment passed quickly, though, and her voice returned to its normal, imperious tone. It was then that she changed me. My Shame caused me to lose half my body to metal, which took half my Talent away with it. It hurt me, and also clearly marked me for my crime. The pain of having my body changed caused me to black out. When I came to again, I was in my mother's home, in my old room, being cared for by my mother. She looked like she had aged years in the few months since I'd last seen her."

Continuing to rub her back, Sean kissed the top of her bowed head. He didn't agree with the Winter Queen's decision. She'd known about Lord Caligula and done nothing about it, but still punished Fiona for doing what needed to be done.

"The Shame I bore was too much for my mother. All her friends stopped speaking to her and we were shunned by everyone we'd known. We fled Southpoint after a month and moved from town to town, trying to find a place where I could live. During the year we moved about, mother grew ill. I never found out what the sickness was, but she died within a week of catching it. Alone, I finally settled in a town about the same size as Oaklake and accepted my new life as an outcast. I had no friends, no love, and no happiness for decades. Then Darragh suddenly appeared on my doorstep to ask for my help. That is my story, Sean. Do you still think—"

Cutting her off, he tilted her head up and kissed her. It was a soft, reassuring kiss that made no demands. Pulling back after a moment, he met her tear-filled eyes. "I still feel the same, my beautiful friend. You did exactly what needed to be done."

More tears spilled from her eyes as she clung to him, falling into his love and acceptance and hoping she would never be free of it. The two stood in the middle of the road until Fiona was able to control herself again.

"We're going to be late," Fiona finally sniffled.

"I'll tell Darragh it was my fault. I did ask for your story, after all," Sean said, kissing her once more and putting an arm around her waist, starting them moving again.

"You're too good for me," Fiona sniffled.

"I was thinking the same of you," Sean smiled.

CHAPTER TWENTY-EIGHT

They walked along in silence for hours, each comfortable and happy with the other. Both of them were wondering if this kind of thing really happened in life, meeting a stranger and falling madly in love in less than a week—both of them would have considered it fantasy just a few weeks ago. Sean knew that, at least in theory, it was possible; James had met the love of his life via an online chatroom and loved her for ten years before she died of a blood clot in her brain. Shaking his head as he recalled how devastated James had been for well over a year, he wondered how he would feel if the same happened to Fiona.

Sean's hand tightened on her waist and Fiona looked at him with questioning eyes. "Something wrong?"

"Thinking of my one real friend, back on the other world. He told me how quickly he fell in love. I didn't believe him at the time, but if I ever see him again, I'm going to have to apologize."

Fiona's light laughter filled the air for a moment, "I'd have to, as well. I didn't think it was possible, either. I never thought I would get the chance, after…"

Giving her another squeeze as she trailed off, Sean kissed her cheek. "Yet here we are," the words were soft but filled with love.

"Today is the best day of my life," Fiona said as she returned his kiss.

"It's a damn good day," Sean agreed. A weight seemed to lift from him with those words and his smile grew broader.

The light was waning by the time they made it back to the village. In high spirits, they were laughing when they realized that something was amiss. No new logs were by Fiona's home, but the lumberjacks should have been back by now. The normal small sounds of people were absent, an eerie hush clinging to the small village.

Fiona stated the obvious a moment later, "Something is wrong."

Finally taking in the small clues that his brain had been trying to nudge him about, Sean froze. Bloodstains were soaking into the ground, a furry ear was pinned to a wall, and a single finger with a three-inch claw lay by Darragh's front door. "Moonbound?"

Fiona turned to look at him as five doors burst open. They spun back to back, both bringing their walking sticks up before them. Whelan and his hunters stood in the open doors, and they released held breaths. "Whelan, what happened here?" Fiona asked, as none of the five said anything or moved for a long moment.

"The Moonbound attacked the village earlier today," Whelan's voice was glacial. "It seems someone broke the Agreement with them, and they came to collect our heads. Myna is missing. We're about to go hunt her down. We thought she'd gone to town to join her blood cousins."

"Myna? No!" Fiona gasped, her eyes wide.

Sean frowned. Whelan's words, and the way he stood, didn't seem to add up with the scene in the village. All five hunters appeared to be unwounded. "Where is everyone else?"

Whelan's lip curled into a sneer. "Outsider, why does it matter to you? You're not part of this village."

"I have an Agreement with Darragh. Where is he?"

"Didn't you feel the Agreement dissolve?" Whelan chuckled darkly. "The weight of it should have left you feeling lighter. Darragh died to the claws of the beasts."

"No," Fiona's whisper was pained. "I didn't realize. That's why I felt so light earlier."

Sean Shaped the wood in his hand into a spear. "You all seem strangely uninjured," he finally gave voice to his issue with the scene before him.

Whelan's laughter was wild and full of madness. "That's what happens when you kill the unwary. I'm sure the Moonbound will be really upset when they find the one we killed to paint this picture. Myna tried to get back here to warn Darragh, but she didn't make it back before us. We'll be hunting her down shortly, but first, we'll deal with you. I promised her that I would leave no one alive behind us."

Fiona went still, her words freezing as they left her mouth, "You killed them all?"

"Of course. That was the deal with the Lord's servant. Darragh never suspected my blade, he just stared at me when I tore it from his body. The fool, he thought he actually had a chance to make this place grow," broken laughter came from Whelan, the other hunters all chuckling as well.

"And Misa?" Sean asked as his hands tightened on the haft of the spear.

"She got away, but we'll soon be tracking her down, as well. Not that we need to, with Darragh dead," Whelan replied, his laughter stopping. "Any last words before we end you?"

"Fiona, do you trust me?" Sean asked, puzzling the hunters.

"Yes," Fiona said without hesitation.

"Bond with me for a single day, with everything you can give me, and we'll get through this," Sean asked her, keeping his eyes on Whelan.

"Agreed," Fiona said. With that word, Sean felt a rush of energy from Fiona, along with a basic understanding of Shaping. In return, he gave her back everything she gave him, plus everything he knew he could do. "Goodness," Fiona gasped, as the power she had given him came flooding back threefold, along with the access to his Talents.

Whelan was laughing the entire time. Drawing the sword from

his waist, he asked, "Do you think a bit of Shaping will get you through what we're going to do to you?"

"No," Sean grinned like a wolf. "I think what I can do, given to her, will be enough."

Fiona Shaped her walking stick into a beautifully crafted scimitar, "I'll hold the others at bay, you deal with him?"

"Gladly," Sean said, stepping away from Fiona and toward Whelan, "Time to pay the piper for your crimes."

"That's enough of this idiocy," Whelan snarled as he came at Sean in a rush. "Kill her, I've got him."

Sean lunged forward with all the speed he had, but Whelan parried the spear away, his sword coming back to cut across Sean's chest. Going with the blow, Sean staggered. The cut wasn't deep, but blood steadily soaked his shirt from the wound. Sean felt at a loss. He wasn't faster than Whelan, as he had been against every other opponent. *No, that's not it. He's more skilled, so he read the attack*, Sean growled in his mind as Whelan smirked at him.

"Fool, your minor tricks can't stop me from gutting you like a fish," Whelan laughed, the madness creeping back into his tone.

"It's true—I'm not the fighter you are," Sean agreed, glancing quickly at the cut across his chest. "I might surprise you, though."

Whelan came forward in a rush, and Sean barely managed to push the slash away. Backing up, Sean found himself completely on the defensive, pushed back by Whelan's onslaught. Numerous small cuts began to accumulate on Sean's arms and legs. Whelan was content to continue taking the attacks he could land easily, slowly carving Sean into ribbons.

Backing up to give Sean a moment to realize how doomed he was, Whelan grinned evilly, "Like a child trying to stop his father from beating him. So sad. Goodbye, Outsider."

"Sean!" Fiona cried out. Looking over, he saw two of the hunters were down, but the other two held Fiona by the arms. "I'm sorry."

Feeling his heart clench as he saw the despair in her eyes, he tried to find a way to save her. Before he could even formulate a plan, Whelan spun and a dagger flew from his hand, sinking into Fiona's chest. Her cry of pain, along with Sean's shout of rage, mingled with Whelan's maniacal laugh.

"Your broken bitch is dead now," Whelan sneered back at Sean.

Blood becoming ice in his veins, Sean's expression reflected the rage he felt. "I'll make you pay for that."

Whelan began laughing again, but stopped when Sean rushed him, his sword coming around to parry the spear away again. He hadn't expected the spear to split and shift into two short blades. Using the left sword, Sean slashed Whelan's arm as he drove the right blade into Whelan's gut. He twisted the blade as he drew it out, Whelan's sword falling from his fingers as he dropped to his knees, using both hands to try to hold his intestines in. Stepping back, Sean drove his boot into Whelan's face. The sickening crunch of bone was clear as Whelan was flung ten feet away from Sean. He turned to the remaining hunters, who dropped Fiona to face him.

"You'll be joining him," Sean hissed as the blades transitioned into a single spear again.

"Sorry..." Fiona whimpered from the ground, her eyes closed.

That word only fueled Sean's rage, and before the hunters realized he was coming, he was on top of them. The spear punched right through Zaire's chest and back, a shower of gore painting the ground. Duggan's sword dug into Sean's hip, the strike a little lower than Duggan had aimed for. With a hiss of pain, the spear vanished from Zaire's body and Sean held two daggers, which he slammed into Duggan's neck hard enough to rip his throat out, showering Sean in blood.

As Duggan collapsed to the ground, Sean dropped the wooden daggers and went to his knees next to Fiona. Grabbing her gently, he cradled her in his arms, tears falling from his eyes as he looked down at her barely rising chest. Her shirt was soaked in blood from the dagger embedded just to the side of her mithril skin. "I'm sorry, Fiona," Sean whispered as he held her.

"I failed...," Fiona whispered, her eyes fluttering open as she looked up at him.

"I'm covered in cuts," Sean told her, "I won't be long behind you."

Fiona's hand grazed his arm, but there was no pain from her touch. Sean was surprised to see unblemished skin under her hand. "Wait, what?" His mind went back to the gifts the Tuatha Dé Danann had given him, recalling his fast healing.

Looking down at Fiona, he could see the wound in her chest was barely trickling blood, and her skin seemed to have closed around the dagger. "This is going to hurt," he told her softly, kissing her before pulling the blade from her chest.

Her gasp broke the kiss. Eyes wide, she looked up at him, not understanding why he'd removed the blade so quickly. "Why?"

Eyes full of happiness as he watched the wound closing, his tears fell faster. "You're not dying on me today, Fiona."

The pain from the hole in her chest was fading. Fiona couldn't understand why Sean seemed so happy until she looked at her chest and watched in awe as the muscle knitted together, the blood now only a thin trickle. "How?"

Taking her arm, he kissed her blood splattered fingers. "I gave you access to everything I can do, including the gift of fast healing from the Tuatha Dé Danann." Pushing as much of his energy into her as he could, he watched the wound close up exponentially faster. Fiona bucked in his arms, feeling like she was about to burst.

"Stop," she managed to gasp, and Sean quickly withdrew most of his energy from her. "How much energy do you have?" She recalled seeing him glowing with it when she'd worn the monocle. "You break all the rules I know of," she said as her hand cupped his cheek. "You are more than even you know."

Pulling her in tight, his lips found hers in a passionate kiss. Both of them reveled in the fact that they were still alive. Sean sent up a silent thanks to the Tuatha Dé Danann for their gifts, gifts which had saved Fiona's life. Fiona, for the first time in her life, offered a silent prayer to the Tuatha Dé Danann for sending Sean to her.

A broken laugh caught their attention. Their eyes opened wide when Whelan sat up, the broken pieces of his skull knitting together. "You're not the only one who can heal," Whelan said as he struggled to his feet, one hand still holding his gut, which was closing slowly.

"I'll kill you both this time." Whelan's skin began to take on a rocky texture and he grew in size, standing ten feet tall by the time he stopped. "I'll use all the Talents she gave me if I have to."

Sean got to his feet, pulling Fiona up with him. Fiona picked up the silver dagger that had pierced her earlier, and Sean drew his bronze dagger. "We can do this," Fiona said, grabbing her spear from the ground. As her hands came together, the dagger fused to the top of the spear, forming a metal point.

Sean picked up his wooden daggers, creating a spear. "He's much better than I am, but I'll try to buy you time," he told her as he split away from her to the right.

"Fools," Whelan's voice was deeper as he flexed watermelon sized hands into fists. "I'm going to tear your limbs off."

Fiona moved to Whelan's other side, "Even your troll's strength can't tear mithril apart."

"I'll break you in two," Whelan roared, lunging at Fiona.

Seeing the attack, Sean darted in to stab at Whelan, but the attack had been a feint as a long rocky arm came swinging back at Sean. Pulling away, Sean saved himself from being crushed, but was still thrown twenty feet through the side of a house. Sean gritted his teeth against the pain of several broken bones as he tried to pull himself back to his feet. Struggling, he made it upright and staggered towards the door. His eyes fell on Darragh's axe, leaning beside the door.

His hand tingled as he picked the axe up, as if it were trying to connect with him. Leaning against the wall, he struggled to breathe, his eyes focused on the adamantine weapon. A warm sensation tingled along his arm, not the same as when he'd used it before. This was more like a friend taking his hand. "You want me to accept you?" Sean murmured in a wheeze. The tingle intensified in apparent response. "Conditions?" The tingle vanished. "You want to be mine, with no conditions?" The tingle surged over his entire body, his bones shifting back into place as the sensation swept over him. Standing upright and taking a deep breath, Sean grinned ferally, "I accept." A lance of cold, piercing energy punched straight into his core, latching onto his soul. After a second it went from cold to warm and welcoming, like a dog getting comfortable in a bed. "Let's go kill the fucker who killed Darragh," Sean growled as he pulled the door open, the axe vibrating in his hand as if in agreement.

Fiona was backpedaling for all she was worth, her spear breaking bit by bit as she tried to parry Whelan's attacks. She paused for a heartbeat when she saw Sean, which was long enough for her to get caught by a massive fist and sent flying through the open doorway into Darragh's home. Whelan roared as he took two steps to follow, but pulled up short upon seeing Sean.

"The bug comes back. Why won't you just lay down and die?" Whelan growled as he turned to face Sean. "The axe is dead—only Darragh's chosen successor can wield it and I already killed Cian."

Those words hit Sean like a hammer. If what Whelan said was true, then Darragh had chosen him; but why would Darragh have done that? With a growl of his own, Sean started forward, wishing he still had the reach of a spear. As he ran at Whelan, the axe became a spear, the point gleaming with deadly intent, and Sean felt a burst of joy that he could Shape his newfound weapon.

Whelan slowed, seeing the axe transition, "No! No! That isn't possible!" Whelan screamed in rage and slammed both fists into the ground. "She promised it would be mine..." Eyes wild, Whelan charged at Sean. There was no finesse to the charge, just a wild animal trying to overrun an obstacle.

Sean tried to dodge to the side, but the spear urged him to charge in return. Following the seemingly suicidal plan, he charged at Whelan. As the distance between them closed, Sean dove to the ground and planted the shaft of the spear against the dirt, the gleaming point set to accept the charge of Whelan's troll body. Expecting the weapon to snap at the impact, Sean was surprised to see that the spear was holding Whelan's body completely off the ground.

"No... I was promised... She told me... Ve..." Whelan whispered, before finally falling silent.

Grabbing the spear just behind the blade where it jutted out from Whelan's body, Sean yanked it from the corpse. Shaping it back into an axe with a thought, he brought the blade around and hacked the head off Whelan's body, which had shrunk back to human proportions.

"Sean," Fiona hissed from the doorway, teeth gritted in pain, "you killed him?"

"I let him kill himself," Sean said as he went to her. "Are you okay?"

"My ribs are knitting back together," she winced.

Carefully, he fed her more energy so that she could recover faster, but not to the point it would overwhelm her. "I've got you," he said as he slipped her arm over his shoulder.

"Sssean," Misa's voice came from beside the home.

Turning, he saw Misa slowly slithering towards him, her vibrant scales now dull and her movements sluggish. "Misa, what happened?"

"Darragh sssent me away from him, forced me away from him," Misa hissed with fading strength. "Made me promissse to wait for you, ssso you could accept hisss gift and hisss lasst few wordsss." Coughing, she shuddered, rolling onto her back. Her eyes were white and sightless as she looked up at the sky. "You come from the Tuatha Dé Danann. Darragh guesssed thisss. Long ago he wasss visssited by a crone, who told him that he would meet the Emisssary of the Tuatha Dé Danann near the end of hisss life. Lasst night, he dreamt of hisss death at Whelan'sss handsss, ssso he made me leave ssso you could claim hisss legacy. Life Bind me. It wasss hisss lasst wisssh."

"I can't do that," Sean said, horrified at the idea of binding her on her deathbed.

"Fool," Misa hissed softly. "I will die anyway. I have all of Darragh'sss life in me; he wanted to give it to you. If you deny the Bond, it will all be losst. For the man I loved, pleassse, do thisss."

"Sean," Fiona said as she nudged him towards Misa. "Do as Darragh wanted."

Feeling as if he was being forced on a path he wasn't sure he wanted, he did as he was asked. Kneeling next to Misa, he touched her snout. "Do you wish to Bind your life to mine, Misa?"

"Yesss. On my death, everything I hold isss yoursss," Misa hissed, her voice fading. "Darragh sssaid you would hesssitate. Do not think of thisss asss a path you mussst walk, but an option to you for the yearsss ahead." With a last shuddering breath, her eyes closed. "I come to join you now, my warrior king, Darragh Axehand..." her last few words were barely audible as her body went limp.

Sean felt a surge of energy and knowledge fill him as tears welled in his eyes. Misa's last act, pledging her soul again to Darragh in death, moved him. The tears fell from his eyes as Fiona's tears fell on his neck and her hands touched his shoulders. They stayed that way until, as the sun fell below the horizon, a feral yowl went up from the forest.

"Moonbound," Fiona whispered. "Whelan must have been telling the truth about killing one of them."

"Fuck," Sean sighed as he got to his feet. "Grab what food and gear you can. We need to find Myna before the Moonbound do—they'll blame her for their loss."

"I'll make it quick," Fiona said as she darted for her house, her wounds now completely healed.

Sean picked Misa up as best he could, taking her inside Darragh's home. He found Darragh headless on the ground next to the table, his head placed on his chest by Whelan. Setting Misa next to Darragh, he silently whispered a prayer to Aed to keep their souls together and happy. Sticking his head into Darragh's room, he spotted a pack stuffed and waiting by the door. Grabbing it, Sean exited the home and found Fiona coming toward him.

"Which way do we go?" Fiona asked as she looked at the dark forest all around them.

CHAPTER TWENTY-NINE

Bringing his Mage Sight up, Sean scanned the area around the village. Off to one side, a shape was leaning heavily against a tree. "Myna?"

Myna appeared as she dropped her Camouflage. Blood stained her front, and bloody furrows crossed her chest, leaving her leather armor in tatters. "You should run," Myna managed with a wince, "they'll be here soon. Madness consumes them now—I had to kill another of them when I tried to tell them about Whelan breaking the Agreement." Slumping to the ground, Myna groaned, "All of our hard work, Darragh's vision and promises, all for nothing..."

Sean raced to her side, but by the time he got there she was dead. "No, gods dammit," Sean cursed as he touched Myna's face. "Fucking Whelan," Sean snarled, feeling a burning anger rise in his chest. "He was working for someone. That fucker is going to pay for all of this death."

Fiona touched his shoulder, "We should do as she said and flee."

His right hand clasped hers on his shoulder, a wild thought occurring to him. "Fiona, you still trust me, right?"

"Of course," Fiona said as she kept looking at the woods, "but there is nothing we can do here."

"There is," Sean said, brushing Myna's cat ears tenderly.

"She's dead. There is no healing that can fix death," Fiona said, thinking she knew what he wanted to do.

"You are probably right," Sean said as he gently pulled her down next to him. "Myna was kind to both of us. She wanted to learn more, she wanted to be accepted and live a happy life. I think I can still give her that chance. It will require everything, though, every last dreg of energy I can muster. If you share with me, we'll both be greatly reduced, but maybe not empty."

Biting her lip, Fiona wanted to deny his request, but she couldn't deny him. He had given her so much in the last few days, and what he was asking could, if he was right, bring back a friend. "Okay, but if it fails we need to run."

"Yes," Sean agreed. Focusing on Myna's body, he began pushing his energy into her where his hand rested on her head. He'd felt the energy he used for Shaping and water magic being drawn out of him, but this felt like his very core was being dissolved and rushing out of him, down his fingers and pouring into Myna.

The torrent of energy seemed to go on forever. Fiona gasped as she slumped against his side. Sean's lips pulled back into a snarl as he began to question what his gift from Aed was useful for, if he couldn't save a friend. "Come back, Myna, come back and we'll track the fucker down and kill him."

Thick black bands formed on Myna's wrists and neck a second before her body convulsed under Sean's hand. Sight wavering as he felt lightheaded, Sean didn't let up. Myna's eyes fluttered open, a dark light filling them.

"I agree," Myna's soft voice croaked.

The energy flowing from Sean into her snapped off like a broken rubber band, then reversed. Energy from Myna poured into him and he gave some back to Fiona, who started crying as she lunged at Myna.

"You brought me back," Myna whispered as she held Fiona. The blackness faded from her eyes, replaced by wonder, "Who are you, that you can bring back the dead?"

"A friend," Sean said, getting to his feet and wobbling for a moment. "We need to go." As if to punctuate his statement, another yowl went up, closer than before.

Myna got to her feet, pulling Fiona up as well. "I had to Bind my soul to yours, but you promised me retribution on the one behind all of this. That's one of my deepest wishes, now."

"We'll talk more later, but you need to lead us. You have the skills we need to disappear from here and escape them," Sean said, making sure that all three of them had the ability to use Mage Sight and Camouflage. "There—we're all equal. We're in your hands."

Pushing Fiona away, Myna locked eyes with her. "Later, we will mourn the dead. We need to flee now."

"Yes," Fiona said as she scrubbed at her eyes. "Lead us."

Myna spun and started away at a jog, carefully picking her way. "No talking until I say it's okay, got it?"

Sean and Fiona didn't say anything, but followed her as quietly as they could. She would be their only chance at getting out of the area without having to kill more people. As the group fled, Sean was surprised to notice that Myna's footprints seemed to linger on the ground for a few seconds before fading from his Mage Sight. He made a mental note to ask her about it later, if they had a later.

The next two hours were a blur for Sean as he doggedly focused on putting his feet where Myna and Fiona had. Myna led them up into the trees at least a half dozen times, down fallen logs a few times, and even into the stream and out the far side. When she finally called a halt, both Fiona and Sean were barely standing, exhausted.

"I haven't heard any hunting calls for a while, so we can rest for a bit," Myna whispered as she turned to find them both wavering on their feet. "Rest, I'll keep watch."

Slumping down next to Fiona, who dropped like a puppet, Sean nodded. "Wake me in a few hours and I'll give you a break."

"Sleep," Myna said as she drifted back down their trail. "I'll see about laying some false trails, just in case."

A hand gently caressing his face woke Sean, and he came to groggily. "Not what I imagined my life partner looking like, but you have many Talents, it seems," Myna whispered as she leaned over him. "Are you going to tell me what my place will be with you?"

Scrubbing at his face, Sean felt his mind start to kick into gear. Shifting backwards, he sat up, prompting Myna to sit a few feet from him. "What do you mean?"

"You have Life Bonded me. My soul is now tied to yours, much like Misa was to Darragh. I cannot deny you anything you want of me. Am I guard, hunter, sexual plaything, maid, servant, or some combination? What is it you will do with me?"

Jaw dropping, Sean finally had time to feel the Bond that connected him to Myna. "I didn't mean for this to happen," he finally said. "I feel like I've violated your soul."

"No," Myna said as she scooted towards him, "you called out to my soul and I came back of my own will. You promised me vengeance, and I accepted and bound my soul to your will. Like all Life Bonded, I must know my place. I know you and Fiona were close when you left, and from the way she defers to you, I would say closer still now. I will not harm you. I can't harm you, as my Holder, but I won't cause issues for you, either. I tried to show you that I was interested before you left, but I think I've lost the race, haven't I?"

Exhaling slowly, Sean's mind whirled with clashing thoughts. Eventually, he nodded. "Fiona and I are a couple."

"I see," Myna said, a melancholy tone filling her voice. "It won't be as I'd hoped, then." Laying down, she closed her eyes. "I'll get a quick nap in. Wake me in a few hours, or if anything happens. We should move further away, and I don't think Oaklake is the way we should go."

"Whelan said he was working with someone. We might need to go there to search for clues," Sean said, still trying to wrap his mind around the woman he had called back from the dead having feelings for him.

"It will be risky. His contact will know he died, and will either be waiting for us or have fled," her words slurred and dropped in volume as she slipped into sleep.

Sitting in the dark, Sean called his Mage Sight back up so he could actually see in the dark. His mind churned over the thought that the woman with cat ears, one of his fetishes, was so openly offering herself to him. Grimacing, he shook his head. *You're a one woman kind of man, Sean. Your father would have a fucking heart attack in his grave if you even considered it.*

He was still chasing his thoughts around in his head when Fiona woke. "Did we make it?" she asked softly, seeing Myna sleeping nearby, her eyes going to the black bands on Myna's wrists and throat.

"It seems like we might have," Sean whispered back. "How are you?"

Fiona looked to him, then to Myna. "She… is Life Bonded. You bonded her to you when you brought her back?"

"It seems that's what happened," Sean said, looking away from Fiona and wondering if she would hate what he had done.

"You're upset?" Fiona asked as she took a seat next to him.

"This kind of thing was never possible on my old world. I don't know how to feel about it. Magic, Binding, Dryads, Moonbound, all of it… it's all new to me. I haven't even been here a tenday yet, and everything I was starting to get familiar with was destroyed just hours ago."

"Not everything," Fiona said, covering his hand with hers. Her eyes met his when he looked at her. "I'm here, and Myna is here. She can never betray you, or hurt you, not with a Life Bond. I will never hurt or betray you either, because I love you. Thank you for saving her, even if it required a Life Bond. She was always nice to me. Even when she kissed you before we left, I wasn't upset with her, only worried you wouldn't look at me."

Putting his arm around her waist, he leaned over and kissed her softly. "You have a very large piece of my heart, Fiona. Silly that it happened after just a few days, but here we are. Myna… she has feelings for me, but I turned her down. I don't want to cause you pain or distress, so please, if you—"

Fiona placed a finger over his lips. "You still have things to learn about this world, Sean MacDougal. Don't utter words we might both regret later. Do you think Misa and Darragh were always lovers?" she asked suddenly, throwing Sean's thoughts off track.

"Huh?"

"Misa and Darragh. Do you think she was always his lover?"

"No?" Sean said, confused by the apparent change of subject.

"Any Bond other than a Life Bond can be betrayed. At a high cost, but it can be. A Life Bond can never be broken. Misa was Bound to Darragh for over thirty years. It was only when he went blind that Misa asked to Life Bond with him. He refused for months, before finally giving in." Fiona looked over at Myna. "You'll grow to love her. You won't be able to stop it. It happens with Life Bonds—your minds will start to sync, and in time, you'll even learn to speak without words. If you care for them at all, you will fall in love with one whose soul is tied to yours, unless they die before then. Like the tide, it is inevitable. The more you care or love them, the faster the bond grows."

Shaking his head, Sean felt an emptiness growing inside of him. "You're going to leave?"

Her lips bloomed into a smile. "No. I won't give up the man who gave me happiness that easily. I will be here with you, smothering you with my love. I will make her earn every second of your time. I'll try to not be mean, or petty, or angry with you, when she finally gets your attention."

Biting her lip she looked into his eyes, he could see hesitation but determination in them. "You know my past, Sean. I won't let that stop me from asking this of you. I ask that you Bond with me, for ten years. I will give you everything I have, and in return I ask that you teach me everything you can. I know you will never hurt me, and that is why I am even taking this step. So, please teach me everything you can, and I will be yours."

His mind reeled, stunned by her offer. She was all but offering her life to him, and not asking for anything he wouldn't give her already. *Why? Why is this happening? This isn't how life is supposed to work! Am I really dead, and all of this some twisted afterlife?*

"Sean," Fiona touched his cheek, "please?"

His chest warmed at her entreaty. He remembered the image of himself standing on a bluff that Morrigan had showed him. Two of the followers were now Fiona and Myna, both smiling brilliantly at him. Identical tattooed bands around the third finger stood out on their left hands as they held their hands out to him.

The image vanished, replaced with Fiona's nervous smile, "Sean?"

"I agree," Sean said, feeling the Bond connect him and Fiona again. This time, both of her wrists grew black bands as he watched.

"Thank you," the words were barely audible. Without warning, she lunged into him, knocking him to the ground as her lips found his with feverish passion, "Thank you."

As they kissed, Myna's eyes opened and she watched them for a moment, a pang of jealousy echoing through her before fading. She knew that, in time, he would grow to love her as much as he did Fiona, if not more. "I'll wait for you," the words were the barest whisper, but the two kissing heard them all the same.

Fiona silently acknowledged the challenge that had just been made. Sean worried about what he might have just stepped into. Their kiss lingered, though, as neither wanted to break the moment.

"We should get moving again," Myna said as she got to her feet. "Or I can go check the trail, if you need a few minutes alone."

"We'll get going," Sean said. "If not to Oaklake, where should we head?"

"Pinebough," Fiona suggested as she got to her feet.

"Agreed," Myna nodded. "It's a tenday or more of overland travel from here, but it will help us lose any pursuers, and also disconnect us from the tragedy we left behind."

"You don't want to go back and bury them?" Sean asked.

"No need," Myna said as she looked back the way they had come, daybreak brightening the sky. A plume of thick black smoke rose from the direction where the village had been. "The Moonbound have erased the village from the map."

"May their spirits find rest," Fiona said softly, her head bowed.

"May their spirits find rest," Myna echoed.

"May Aed give them solace and welcome them home," Sean said.

"We don't need to be as stealthy today, but we should still practice the new skills that Master has given us," Myna said as she began to walk away.

"No," Sean said, bringing both girls to a stop. "I'm not anyone's master."

"If I call you anything else in public, it will bring shame to us both," Myna said levelly. "Besides, you *are* my Master, and my soul belongs to you." Myna's tone was possessive, softening as she went on, "I know you have some issues with this new world, Sean MacDougal, and if it pleases you, I will call you Sean when we are alone, or with those that know. But publicly, you must *be* my Master."

Scrubbing at his face, Sean sighed as he mumbled, "James would have had a field day here." Dropping his hands, he nodded. "Public only, understood?"

"Yes, Sean," Myna said, her lips twitching into a smile as she turned and walked off. "I will always do what you tell me to."

"Well played," Fiona muttered as she took Sean's hand. "Shall we follow our guide?"

"Oh gods," Sean muttered as they followed Myna, "it's already begun."

Sean Aragorn MacDougal
Human
Age: 33

Gifts:
Metal Bones, Viney Muscles, Mithril Blood, Magic Bond, Mending Body, Death Ward, Linguist, Hunter's Blood, Infinite Possibilities

Spells:
Summon Water

Talents:
Shaper- (Wood and Metal)

Mage Sight
Camouflage

Bonded:
Fiona Mithrilsoul- Ten year Bond
Myna Mooncaller- Life Bonded

AUTHOR'S NOTE

Please consider leaving a review for the book, feedback is imperative for an indie author. If you don't want to review it then think about leaving a comment or even just a quick message. Remember positive feedback is always welcome.

The places you can keep up to date on me and my works:
   http://schinhofenbooks.com/
   https://www.patreon.com/DJSchinhofen
   https://twitter.com/DJSchinhofen

 A big thank you to my editors, Jennifer York, Samantha Bishop, and Daniel Stetson. Also props to Geno Ferrarini, and Sean Hickinbotham for being my Alpha Readers. I'd be remiss if I didn't include my beta readers, in no particular order: Zee, Ian McAdams, Arthur Cuelho, Scott Brown, Buddy Brown, A. J. Bishop, Tarcha Saleeba, Alec Young, Jay Taylor, Justin Johanson, Josh Holmes, Rob Bunting, Isidore Fitch, Christina Norton, Luke Reynolds, Sawyer Aubrey, Nigel Hollingworth, Aoife Megami, Robert Peterson, Sullivan Grimm, Shane Bird, Steve Robles, William Reid, and Nick Kuhns.

The cover for Morrigan's Bidding is brought to you by Anthony Bishop, a very talented artist. You can find him at https://grimmworks.tumblr.com/

Full wrap cover for the paper back done by Bonnie Price https://bonnielprice.com

A big thanks to my Patreon supporters who have gone above and beyond in their support:

Kyle J. Smith, Cody Carter, Godofcookie, Kevin McKinney, James Patton, Sean Emanuel, Sawyer Aubrey, Christopher B., Jack Ling, Bradley White, Stephen Wise, Markdsm, Zach Hicks, Evan Cloud, Joseph Keyes, Kyle Gravelle, Robert Shofner, Travis Cox, Jarred Medlock , Charles Groark, Aaron Nirider, MrNyxt, Joey Dawson, Viking, J. Patrick Walker, Ian McAdams, Timothy Eskew, Michael Jones, Avery Doxtater, Michael Moneymaker, Alexander Rodriguez

The last big thanks goes out to Nick Kuhns, who helped get this book formatted for physical copies. You would literally not be holding this book if not for him.

Printed in Great Britain
by Amazon